ALYC HELMS

The Conclave of Shadow

ANGRY
ROBOT

ANGRY ROBOT
An imprint of Watkins Media Ltd

Lace Market House,
54-56 High Pavement,
Nottingham,
NG1 1HW
UK

www.angryrobotbooks.com
twitter.com/angryrobotbooks
By the toe

An Angry Robot paperback original 2016

Cover by Amazing15
Set in Meridien by Epub Services

Distributed in the United States by Penguin Random House, Inc.,
New York.

ISBN 978 0 85766 518 8
Ebook ISBN 978 0 85766 519 5

Printed in the United States of America

9 8 7 6 5 4 3 2 1

For my mom, Conna.
Thank you for always telling me to take a chance.

The darkness drops again; but now I know
That twenty centuries of stony sleep
Were vexed to nightmare by a rocking cradle,
And what rough beast, its hour come round at last,
Slouches towards Bethlehem to be born?

W B YEATS, "The Second Coming"

ONE
Mystic in the City

"I've come for Mr Mystic."

I stopped halfway up the steps of the old Russian Hill Victorian, canvas bags filled with farmers' market produce slung over my shoulders, sunflowers cradled in one arm, the other arm thrust through the frame of my collapsible shopping cart. All of it because I was too lazy to make a second trip up the stairs. Humans are funny creatures. The lengths we'll go to just to avoid retreading old ground.

My cart banged against my knee when I stopped. I squinted, peering into the shadows of the landing. The late spring day was San Francisco cool, but the sun still shone bright enough to be unforgiving, even for me, and I have a knack for seeing into shadow.

I forced some of that brightness into my tone. "He doesn't live here. Hasn't for years." We got visitors sometimes – fans, tourists, the occasional low-powered creep with delusions of grandeur, looking to throw down with San Francisco's resident Ace. Westboro had picketed us once. That had been a treat. We kept police non-emergency on speed-dial and chalked it up to the price you had to pay for affordable city digs.

Even so, I leaned my cart against the railing, let my bags slide to the steps, and prepared to dish sunflower death. "Mystic Manor is a non-profit service co-op now. Nobody here but us social justice types."

"That line really work on people?" The figure stepped toward me, into the sunlight, revealing a woman about my age with a cloud of witchy hair half-contained by a plait and the sort of loose-limbed confidence of an Eleanor Roosevelt or Kat Hepburn – the *African Queen* years.

"Abby." I sagged out of my defensive stance. The sunflower heads banged against the steps. They could hack it. They were sturdy, like the woman on the stoop. "Jesus, did you have to be so dramatic about that?"

"I wanted to see what you'd do. Interesting that you went with the flowers as your weapon of choice. I'd have gone with the cart."

"Stems. Long and fibrous. Make an effective garrote." I struggled to collect all my bags and the cart. Abby's appearance had unbalanced me. In more ways than one.

"Need a hand?"

I hesitated. I hated mixing lives, but if Abby was here, it was too late to prevent that. Better to move this inside where there'd be fewer witnesses. "Yeah, thanks."

I let her take the cart and a few of the bags and led the way through the house into the communal kitchen.

Mystic Manor – don't blame me, I didn't name it – seemed like a fairytale castle to me when I was growing up, albeit in the Gothic vein. It had all the eccentric charm you'd expect from an original structure – pokey hallways, creaky stairways, wood moldings and crannies for collecting dust, and high ceilings for the cobwebs. The rooms were small and dark, with the exception of the huge solarium at the back of the house and the illegal bottom floor in-law I shared with my best friend, Shimizu. And the kitchen, where I'd sunk all the renovation funds not earmarked for upkeep.

"Anyone home?" I called up the center stairwell, and held my breath until I could be fairly sure the lack of answer was deliberate. It was Sunday. The Maker Fair was going on down on the Peninsula, and anyone who wasn't there would be doing a drunk-run across the city with Bay-to-Breakers. Shimizu knew about my double identity as Mr Mystic, so I didn't have to worry about her wondering why an Argent Ace was standing in our kitchen, and Patrick kept grad student hours. Even if he was home, he wouldn't be stumbling downstairs until early afternoon.

"You want these anywhere specific?" Abby asked, opening the fridge with a bag of Japanese eggplant in hand.

"Hold off. I have to log them first." I pulled down the communal grocery sheet and started marking down what I'd bought and spent. Abby put away the perishables as I noted them. I could feel her gaze on me, her growing smirk. I ignored them in favor of collecting myself via mundanity.

"You weren't kidding about the co-op thing," she muttered when the silence had stretched on too long.

"Mitchell Masters left his house in trust. I'd have had to come forward to claim it. Didn't want to expose myself like that. But the executor was able make it available for non-profit use. I had him set up the residency fellowship, and then I applied. This way I get to live in the house I grew up in without anyone knowing it's the house I grew up in."

"Nice digs if you can afford them," Abby said, knocking on the well-oiled walnut of the vintage cabinetry.

"The eight other fellows think so. Lets them do their work without worrying about rent. And I figured it was better than leaving a huge place like this empty." And it meant I didn't have to live alone. I'd walked away from my life and family in China. Having people around was better for my

mental health. I set the pen down across the food
ledger and folded my hands.

"Why are you here, Professor Trent?" I asked, a
bit of Mitchell's distant cool slipping into my tone.

Abby leaned against the counter, crossing one
ankle over the other. Her loose khakis and worn
blue work shirt were the closest she'd ever come
to a costume, but her swagger was pure Argent
Ace. "Ah. There's the limey bastard everyone's
scrambling for a piece of. Would you really have
choked me out with sunflowers?"

"I use the weapons at hand," I murmured.

"Sunflowers." She rubbed her brow, chuckling,
and tucked away a few frazzled curls. "And what
would you have done if someone had come looking
for me after you dumped the body?"

"Are you saying that anyone else knows I'm
here?" I couldn't share her amusement.

"Oh, don't worry, Old Man. All I told Dame
Chillybritches was that I knew how to get in touch
with you. If you'd answered her calls, it wouldn't
have been necessary."

Dame Chillybritches. I bit my cheek to contain
a smile. Sylvia Dunbarton, Lady Basingstoke, had
been using every method in her not-insignificant
arsenal to try to contact me – or rather, Mr Mystic
– since his disappearance after taking down the
New Wall in China. Apparently, it wasn't enough
to stop World War III. People wanted you to stick
around so they could thank you for it. And Lady

Basingstoke, grande dame of the Argent Aces, wanted to make sure she was standing next to you so that the Argent Corporation could claim credit.

So far, my lawyer and the lack of connection between Mr Mystic and his secret granddaughter had been enough to keep Argent off my back. But Abby knew me from my early heroing days, back when I ran around in cobbled-together ninja garb as Mistra, fighting petty street crime with my inherited shadow powers. Back before I hid myself under my grandfather's mantle of Mr Mystic. And while I trusted Abby not to blab my secret to just anyone, Professor Abigail Trent was an Argent Ace – The Antiquarian – and who could say what she might tell her bosses, the very people I most wanted to stay hidden from.

Twitchy from her continued scrutiny, I snatched up the food log and poked through the cupboards. "If I wanted to speak with her, I'd have answered her calls. You could have told her to piss off."

"You're the only person with enough balls to tell Sylvia Dunbarton to piss off."

"And yet, it seems to have little effect." I opened a cabinet to assess our grains and nearly got beaned by a bottle of zaatar. Several of the other spices had toppled. I scowled and righted them. We were going to have to have another house meeting about keeping the kitchen neat after cooking.

Abby must have misinterpreted my glare. She stopped laughing at me. "Look. She did you a solid.

Argent did you a solid. We got you to China. We got you out of China. All she wants from you is a report and a photo-op. You can't give her that?"

"Skyrocket was there. His report covers everything I'd share." And probably a bit more than I'd want shared. "And I can't seem to turn on the telly without seeing him smiling at me from all the morning shows. He looks better in photos than Mr Mystic ever would."

"Tom is doing what he can, but everyone knows Mystic was at the center of what went down with the New Wall." Abby grabbed a chair and turned it around to sit, resting her arms across the back. "I don't know if you've been following the news, but relations with China are still a mess. The People's Heroes got a broad mandate to deal with the New Wall crisis, and they're riding that along with a new wave of nationalism. That kid in charge of them – sorry, don't mean to be ageist, but he looks younger than my undergrads – everyone there is hailing him as the hero of the day. And it would be really helpful if Argent could produce Mr Mystic to counter that narrative."

"Lung Mian Zi Mien is his name." I abandoned my diversionary puttering and sat, swallowing to contain the churning in my gut that rose up every time I heard mention of China's new hero. Mian Zi. My son. We hadn't spoken since he raced off to fight his sister in the skies above Shanghai. Since I'd freed the Guardians of China from their prisons by swearing myself in service to the asshole who'd imprisoned them. Which had been Lung Di's plan from the start.

"Right. Well, this Lung Mian Zi Mien is coming to New York next week to meet with some members of the UN Security Council–"

I grabbed her arm. "I hadn't heard that." True, I'd been avoiding the news, but I would have heard if Mian Zi was coming to the States. Somebody who knew how much he mattered to me would have told me.

Abby looked down at my hand. I released her and tucked it under my butt. "It's not official, so they're keeping it quiet. He's going to be stopping in San Francisco to attend the opening of the Argent Age installation at the California Academy of Sciences. All Dunbarton wants is for you – Mr Mystic – to be in attendance as Argent's guest. Doesn't have to be official. But Mitchell Masters was involved in Argent's early days. This is his city. Hell, he's got a display in the exhibit. It'll be weird if he's not there."

Bait, bait, and more bait. I'd heard about the exhibit. My lawyer, Jack, had forwarded me several increasingly pleading invitations from the event coordinator and increasingly insistent ones from Sylvia. But none of the invitations had mentioned that Mian Zi would be there.

Missy Masters didn't have any way of getting a call through to China's new political darling. Mr Mystic wasn't in much better a position. Sylvia couldn't know how effective this bait was. Did Abby? "What do you think?"

Her smile curved. She knew she'd hooked me, even if she didn't know why. She stood, flipping the chair back into place at the table. "I think some sort of new status quo has been unavoidable since you came out of retirement, Old Man. I don't know what happened to your grandfather. Maybe he's hiding. Maybe he's dead. But you're Mr Mystic now, and the longer you try to pretend that Argent isn't an issue you have to deal with, the more harm you do to all of us. You can force a confrontation or you can accept a reconciliation. And I don't think you like confrontation."

"I do try to avoid it," I murmured, following her out.

She paused in the doorway. "So, I'll see you Thursday night?"

"You'll be there?"

"You're kidding, right? I helped curate the damned thing. Besides, I'm an archaeologist. We never turn down free museum booze."

I don't know what devil made me do it, save that I didn't want to walk into Sylvia's clutches without at least one ally, even if that ally was one of her own Aces. "Need a date?"

In San Francisco, the fog is a living thing. His name is Karl. He has a Twitter feed.

Saturday night must have been a hard one for

old Karl. Sunday morning found him slumped across the Pacific like a hungover tech bro, leading edge rolling away from the bright, late-morning sun streaming from the East Bay.

I squinted against it and wished I'd thought to bring sunglasses.

"Did you know your brother was coming into town this week?" I asked Mei Shen as we strolled along the eastern walk of the Golden Gate Bridge. My daughter had moved to the city in the aftermath of the New Wall debacle, though she'd ignored my offer to come live with me at the house on Russian Hill. She refused most of my overtures these days, claiming to be "busy" with "things". I wished I could chalk it up to being the mother to an eternally seventeen year-old girl, but Mei Shen and I had barely spoken more than Mian Zi and I had. Her excitement at being reunited in Shanghai had curdled into fake smiles and a quick change of topic any time we got too close to anything serious. She blamed me for usurping her plan in Shanghai. If she'd had her way, David Tsung would have been Lung Di's new champion instead of me. My kids wouldn't have to take me out to take their uncle down.

I countered Mei Shen's forced cheer by being deliberately obtuse, and I finally roped her into giving me Sunday afternoons. We spent them doing all the touristy things natives never do: Fisherman's Wharf, Sutro Baths, the zoo. It made talking about anything serious impossible, which might have been why Mei Shen caved so easily.

Today was ice cream and walking the bridge to the Marin Headlands, except there was no ice cream to be had on the far side of the bridge, and the wind had us both eating our hair instead.

"Pah!" Mei Shen made a face and dragged a few strands of her bob from her mouth, carefully cleaning off the cherry-red lipstick so she wouldn't end up with a streaked face. "Yes... his fault... Argent Corporation... to me or... I don't... he told them–"

"Wait." The wind had also whipped away half her words. We were coming up on one of the towers. I pulled her into the half-moon observation bay skirting the tower, letting the red-painted steel cut the wind. Faster-paced walkers – mostly old Chinese couples with matching visors and Fitbits – glared at us as they diverted around us. "What's this about you and Argent?"

Mei Shen leaned over the railing, watching a freighter pass under us, cutting the sun's glare with her hand. The bay waters sparkled blue rather than the sullen steel color they sported when it was foggy. The Marin headlands were California gold. Even Alcatraz was a pale, picturesque accent in a sailboat-filled bay.

"You know I've been consolidating the Shadow Dragon Triad, yes? Retiring some of the old guard to honored advisory positions, putting a stop to the human and drug trade."

I took a moment to gather up my hair to cover my surprise that she was talking to me about something of substance. "I'm surprised your uncle is letting you, now that he's back on the scene," I said. Mei Shen had usurped her uncle's place while he was caught in the New Wall trap. In order to free the other Guardians – Lao Hu the Tiger, Gui Dai the Tortoise, and Feng Huang the Phoenix – I'd had to swear myself as Lung Di's champion. And I'd had to free Lung Di in the bargain. He was aeons older and more manipulative than my daughter, so why did he let her continue to run things now that he was free?

Because power corrupts. And because it puts her at odds with Mian Zi.

"My uncle has bigger worries right now, what with Lao Hu hunting him. If Lao Hu can't find him, he can't challenge him, and you don't have to act as his champion, which keeps you alive." She flicked a seagull feather off the railing and watched it catch the wind. "Yay, everyone wins."

It could have just been the effort of talking over the wind that gave her words that sharp, overly bright intonation, but no. I heard my voice echoed in my daughter's, the sort of thing I might say when I was pissed off and didn't care who knew it.

"Mei Shen…" I touched her shoulder.

She shrugged me off. "You know what, it's fine. You didn't trust me or David, and you ended up playing right into my uncle's plan."

I winced. She was playing dirty. "Can we just enjoy the day without fighting?"

Mei Shen laughed. "Certainly, mother. You want to dance while Rome burns. Let us dance."

"I think that's fiddle," I muttered, but Mei Shen was already striding away. I hurried to catch up. "What's burning?"

"Perhaps I should say shaking instead of burning. Did you feel the earthquake yesterday?"

I thought back to the fallen spice bottles in the kitchen. Felt the surge of smug condescension that marked me as a native Californian. I was only surprised that I hadn't had to talk Shimizu down from fleeing back to Iowa. She must not have felt the tremor. "Barely a three-pointer. Earthquakes happen. Doesn't mean–"

"Do you have any idea what's going on in my uncle's absence?" Mei Shen snapped. "The things that he maintained that are now falling apart?"

I hadn't the foggiest, nor did I have any clue how best to answer her. I nearly collided with her when she stopped again and pressed back against the rail, looking across several lanes of traffic to the fogged-over expanse of the Pacific Ocean. "Do you even know what's out there? Do you ever look?"

I looked. The fog had crept inland during our walk without my noticing. Little cat feet, indeed. It brushed against the red cables of the bridge, which seemed to shred it like so many layers of tulle. And yet it was completely opaque. I couldn't see anything beyond that shredded divide. And even if I could, I had no idea what she wanted me to see. "Is it such a bad thing that your uncle's Triads are falling apart?" I asked softly, looking for a way to the heart of what lay between us. Tsung. Mei Shen's relationship with him. He was the one who'd gotten her involved in her uncle's sordid dealings in the first place. "Maybe you should let them–"

"The Triads are a tool. A useful one. Like Mian Zi and his People's Heroes. But my uncle had other tools, more important tools, that I can't..." She glared out at the fog like she was angry at it, then turned her back on it and hung over the rail, peering down at the choppy bay waters beneath us. The press of the fog had chilled the cobalt blue to a dull grey marked by white flecks, some seagulls, some foam. "David has been hearing things. Rumors. Things Argent needs to know, but Mian Zi has them convinced that if they speak to me, he won't speak to them."

The amassing fog had finally managed to press past the bridge cables. It blotted out the sun and beaded the hair on my arms like cobwebs. I unknotted the hoodie sleeves tied around my waist and tugged it on, shivering. That had been fast, even for Karl. "I'm going to this exhibit opening at the Academy of Sciences. Or Mr Mystic is. If you tell me–"

"So you can decide if it's important? If you approve?"

"That's not–"

"No. Y'know what? It's fine. Forget it. I'll figure it out on my own. It's what I've been doing since you left." Her accusation froze me in place. She wasn't talking about Shanghai. She was talking about... before.

Mei Shen climbed up on the rail. The walkway was empty coming and going. Even the traffic traveling across the bridge seemed misty and distant, the fog buffering us from the rest of the world.

"Mei Shen, get down."

"Why? I'm not like you, mother. I'm in no danger of falling." She jumped off the railing. I lunged for her as if that could stop her, but too late. She fell into the fog passing under the bridge. It flashed red and gold, as though a rogue firework had gone off below the span, and then a long, slender shape shot up past me. The dragon twined between the cables like a red-and-gold streamer before streaking off in the direction of the city.

I sagged against the rail and buried my face in my hands until the chill of the fog bit through my layers and forced me to flee.

TWO
Argent for the Ages

I parked my new Triumph near the Panhandle and walked the rest of the way to the California Academy of Sciences. The night was a bit on the chilly side, but I was warm enough. I'd forgone a tuxedo, opting for my usual attire: black trench coat, tailored suit with faint pinstriping, crisp white shirt and black tie. My only nod to the occasion was the opera scarf draped over the shoulders of my coat – cobalt blue silk, the ends fluttering in the light breeze coming in from the Outer Sunset. And then there was my felted wool fedora. Always the fedora. The short wig of dark hair I wore underneath it helped hold it firmly in place. It was easy enough for me to deepen the shadows cast by the brim to obscure my face. And thus my disguise was complete.

I swept past the long line of luxury automobiles and Priuses winding around the circle between the Academy and the de Young Museum. Valets drove the automobiles off to who knew where, and I was doubly glad to have left my motorcycle elsewhere. We were only just getting acquainted; I didn't trust her in Argent's hands.

I managed to make it most of the way up the entry plaza before the gathered press noticed me, and even then it was only because they were following the progress of my date as she came down the steps to greet me.

As well they should. Gone were the khakis and the worn work shirt. The Antiquarian wore a coppery colored frock with a tight bodice that fell somewhere between a corset and a vest, and a bias-cut skirt that swished around her very fine calves. Her hair was pulled back, the witchy curls sculpted into waves. The park lights caught the red tones, giving her the look of a desert-setting sun.

"My word, Professor Trent. You do clean up nicely." I lifted her hand and bowed correctly over it.

She smirked, a laugh caught in her throat. "Careful, Old Man. You're in danger of becoming effusive."

I straightened my tie and pocket square. "To be fair, I wouldn't have been surprised to see you in a safari coat and pith helmet." I offered her my arm. She took it and led me through the gamut of fans, photographers, and security clogging the steps up to the Academy of Sciences. "Dare I ask, have you decided to expand your fan base into the realms of steampunk?"

She gave in to the laughter. A full, rich belly laugh. The flashes of cameras blinded me for a moment. I deepened the shadows around my face until they were nearly opaque. It helped to cut the glare.

"No. They're all a little too 'Yay, colonialism' for my taste. Anthropologists have enough to answer for on that front," she said. The smile she gave the photographers was close-lipped. Impatient. The Antiquarian wasn't one of the faces Sylvia trotted out for these occasions. Abby was likely as happy to be dragged into this show as I was. "Speaking of fandoms, you know that you're disappointing your entire base right now."

"I'm happy to let them think you're my beard."

"At least I'm older than the usual arm candy."

"And yet still quite fetching." Abby shot me a narrow-eyed glare. I smiled, though she wouldn't be able to see it for the shadows I'd brought forth to hide my face. "I confess, I did expect the khakis."

"For a formal event?"

"Rhinestone studded?"

Another too-loud, too-honest laugh. More photo flashes. I wondered that they thought they could catch that rich deep timbre in visual form. "I usually wear a suit to these things," she said. "But I was afraid we'd be mistaken for the Blues Brothers. I'm resigned to being gender conforming for a night."

"Yes, that's what we're doing now. Being gender

conforming," I murmured, and earned another laugh.

A young man at the door was handing out programs, while a young woman passed out little silver *Kestrel* pins. I waved off a program but took the pin, attaching it to my lapel. It was a charming bit of nonsense. Say what you will about Argent, but they know how to pay attention to details.

The press parted as we entered the Academy of Sciences. I thought it was because they were barred entry until I saw the silver-clad sentinel awaiting us at the door.

"Mitchell. I'm so pleased Professor Trent convinced you to join us this evening."

Sylvia Dunbarton, Lady Basingstoke, held out her hands in welcome. She wore evening-length gloves and a 40s inspired silver gown with a blouson top, high waist, and long skirt patterned in chevrons of pewter and chrome.

"Sylvia." The last time we'd met, she'd tetched at me for using her title. In her eyes we were closer than that, and who was I to gainsay the grande dame of the Argent Aces? "How could I refuse such a persuasive request?"

I took her hands. She gave me cheek kisses. Flashes went off like silent fireworks. I wondered if they would catch the sharpness in Sylvia's crescent-moon smile.

"Hm. Persuasive, was it? I wonder which part managed to persuade you. Professor Trent?" Sylvia turned her smile on Abby. "I know it is terribly gauche, but would you mind overmuch if I hied off with your escort? Mitchell and I have so much catching up to do."

"I expected nothing less," Abby said, waving for Sylvia to take me. I shot her a glare that nobody could see for the shadows obscuring my face, but I couldn't make a scene without it being forever captured in digital form. Abby had been correct. I hated unnecessary confrontation.

Thus did I enter the gala launch of *Argent for the Ages: A history of looking forward* on the arm of the most powerful woman in the world.

We passed through the crowded entry and into the central atrium between the butterfly-filled rainforest dome and the planetarium. The roof high above rose and fell in a series of iron bubbles that supported the Academy's living rooftop. A full-sized model of the *Kestrel* hung from the domed ceiling on thick silver cables. It had to be a model. Argent's signature aircraft was now a scatter of charcoal parts across some nameless Shadow Realms plain, thanks to a rough crossing into China.

The model *Kestrel*'s sleek design, all flowing lines and riveted panels in Argent's patented titanium alloy, complemented the rest of the Academy's style, making it look like a permanent installation. In the shadow beneath her fuselage, a fountain of silvery pins of the same alloy rippled with a soft clacking echo, rising and falling in an imitation of water. A woman leaning over the display laughed, and the pins rose and fell in a rush of metallic clicks in response to the sound.

The other displays set up around the atrium were more museum-typical: artfully spaced boards with black-and-white photos and blocks of text. Faceless mannequins with paper hair wearing iconic costumes from bygone days. I caught a glimpse of a familiar hat and trench coat and tensed against an unexpected chill.

"Relax, Mitchell," Sylvia murmured. "Nobody here is your enemy."

I plucked her hand from my arm so that I might remove my trench coat. The scarf and hat, I kept. The perky coat-check girl didn't even bother to ask for them.

"I don't take kindly to being manipulated, Sylvia. If you insist on perpetuating this farce that we are friends, pray remember that."

"What choice do you leave me?" She hooked us two wine glasses off a passing tray – kept the white for herself and handed me the red. She sipped. I didn't. My stomach wasn't nearly settled enough for drinking. "I need to know what you did in China."

"You want to do this here?" I nodded at the atrium filled with mingling people in their evening best. Some were probably harmless. Many were Argent. But that still left an unaccounted-for third contingent.

"Here?" Sylvia chuckled. "Look again, Mitchell."
She swept the room in a gesture. Skyrocket and La
Reina were involved in an animated argument near
the metallic pin fountain. It involved quite a few
swooping hand gestures, fountain rods rising and
falling in time with their words. The tawny-tipped
feathers of La Reina's wings puffed and resettled as
though she wished to give an aerial demonstration
of her argument. Beyond the fountain, Abby
already had a plate of hors d'oeuvres and a tumbler
filled with two fingers of amber. She lounged
against the butterfly dome, idly watching the crowd
as she sipped. Around the room, other Aces stood
out from the crowd – some marked by their iconic
costumes, others by their watchful, ready air.

And, easily overlooked, blank-faced men and
women in suits much like mine stood at the exits,
moved along the edges of the crowd, spoke into
their cuffs.

I glanced aside at Sylvia, watching me notice
them. "Not everyone here tonight is one of yours,"
I said.

"And everyone who isn't has been thoroughly
vetted and has an agent tasked to keep an eye
on them. There are few places as protected as the
Academy tonight."

"Why do you need anything from me? Tom's
report–"

"Tom's a fine boy, but he can't explain the
players to me, or what their motivations were, or

how they became players. And do not forget, he was incapacitated for much of his time in Shanghai. He would have missed important details. Details I need to know if I'm to keep the world in check. Who is David Tsung? For that matter, who is this young Mr Long who has risen so high so recently? I assume he's no relation to the Mr Long who Tom indicated was responsible for the New Wall. I need to know how wary I should be in our dealings. I know there's magic involved, and you know that Argent has always been weak in that department."

"Yes, well. Most practitioners are iconoclasts. Hard to keep one of those on the payroll."

"Tell me about it. Professor Trent, La Reina, Sadakat... they're the best we've got when it comes to the mystical. And you. Until you abandoned us."

So much I wanted to say to that, to question, to refute, that I dared not say. But she'd given me much with that admission. Information, yes. But also, power.

"Tsung is..." *not to be trusted*, I wanted to say, but he had been trying to stop his grandfather in his own secretive and duplicitous way. I just didn't like him for the influence he held over Mei Shen. "Something of a whistleblower. He found out about Mr Long-the-elder's plans for the New Wall and brought them to my attention. Too late to stop it from happening, but quickly enough to end it before it became any worse."

"And Mr Long-the-younger?" She kept her tone

light, disinterested, but her knuckles were white around the stem of her wineglass. I took it from her before it could snap, which left me foolishly holding two wine glasses. The staff, the guests, and the other Aces were respecting the bubble of empty space around Sylvia and myself.

"Not the same man as the one who created the Wall. I'd say Lung Mian Zi Mien is our best hope for putting an end to Lung Di."

"So he got away. This Lung Di?"

"In a manner of speaking."

Sylvia pursed her lips, annoyed.

"Lung Mian Zi is well intentioned. Quite brilliant, and could be a formidable ally. Deal with him as you would with me, and you should manage quite well."

Sylvia arched a brow. "You mean, pester, prod, manipulate, and generally annoy until you do what I want?"

I snorted. "Very well, deal with him as I would have you deal with me. Expect exponentially worse recalcitrance if you do not. Understood?"

"Very much not, but the advice is appreciated." She took back her wineglass, studied me over the rim as though calculating how much more she could tease out of me. "I don't suppose you'd tell me who this Lung Di is and how he managed to cut China off from the rest of the world? And why?"

I didn't dare tell her the how. Argent might focus on science rather than magic, but I didn't want Sylvia – or more likely one of her underlings – deciding they could capture China's Guardians and attempt to recreate Lung Di's wards. As to the why? No, I was not ready to admit to anyone that I had been the reason for so much chaos, that Lung Di had done it to force me into a compact I might never have agreed to otherwise. That to keep my promise, I was sworn to defend him against his enemies – including my children. And that if I broke the compact, the stain on my honor would render my children illegitimate, nullifying any possibility that they might someday be able to permanently remove their uncle from creation. Some days, I barely believed it myself.

But who? I took a careful sip of my wine, a dry cabernet that tasted of Napa evenings and reminded me of the dinner where Lung Di admitted that he feared my children and what they might do to him. "Would you believe, a dragon?"

Ever a gentleman, I was ready with my pocket square when she choked on her wine.

Not even Sylvia Dunbarton could keep the world at bay for long. By the time her coughing fit subsided, several of the more socially oblivious guests had circled us, most of them intent on catching *her* attention. I was a curiosity. Sylvia was where the true power lay. I abandoned her with my pocket square and made my way around the exhibits. Hardly anyone was paying them any mind, so they were my best hope to avoid the mob.

I'd clearly chosen the backwards route, starting at a display featuring Argent's technological advances in agriculture, medicine, and sustainable energy. A slowly spinning globe flashed with pinpricks of light across its surface, demonstrating how much of the world might be powered by Argent's proprietary energy conversion process in a year, five years, a decade.

Past the globe, a hands-on exhibit invited guests to touch some of the parts made from the titanium alloy that gave Argent its name, from cooling coils for spaceships to sections of crush-resistant deep water pipes. And of course, a riveted panel from the *Kestrel*. I ran my fingers over the rivets and moved on to a multimedia installation on the Death Valley sinkhole crisis from a few years back. The display featured the work Argent engineers had done to save the people of the small town that had fallen into the earth. Newsreel-style footage played on a loop, showing La Reina landing on the lip of the depression carrying two small, dusty mooplings. That shot had been on the cover of every periodical that month.

My inexplicable discomfort grew, an impending twitch between my shoulder blades that refused to shake loose. I had no desire to be a part of this. I skirted the crowd around the "Be a Skyrocket!" interactive exhibit, which looked more like a full-body video game than something belonging in a museum. Moving further around the edges of the atrium, I traced the history and accomplishments of Argent back to her origins, until I came to the exhibit I was most curious about and least wanted to visit.

"Shoulda figured I'd find you over here," said a voice behind me in a soft, Midwest drawl.

"Tom." I didn't look at him, didn't look away from the blank paper face of the figure in the familiar suit, trench coat, and fedora. They'd done my mannequin in a dark grey instead of creamy white, and the lighting in the installation was purposely dim, a corner of darkness in the bright, space-age atrium. I'd braced my hands on the railing to counter a strange sense of vertigo, looking up at self-not-self.

"It's good, though. The exhibit, I mean. And also, this display. Good to remember where we come from." Tom Carter came up beside me and thumped the little placard explaining that Mr Mystic's association with Argent had always been complicated. I suspected Abigail Trent's snark behind the carefully worded text.

I sighed and released my grip on the railing, forced my flirtation with the uncanny back to manageable levels. There was no deeper truth hidden in the display's shadows, nothing to learn here that I didn't already know from news clippings and my grandfather's rarely updated journals. "In this case, it's hardly memory that draws me. It's narcissism." I paused, tilted my head since he wouldn't be able to see my smile. "And of course, avoiding the crowds. Professor Trent was to have been my buffer, but it seems she prefers the canapes to my company."

"Heh, that woman and free food." Tom's smile charmed, even in the dim light. That was Skyrocket. He brought his own light and energy with him wherever he went. He'd even managed to banish my dour musings. "You know, I could take you around. Introduce you. There's folk who'd like to meet you but don't want to impose. And there's others who wouldn't mind a catch-up. La Reina says you still owe her for a dust-up you two got into way back in the day."

"Do I? Fascinating. She has a better memory than I do, it seems." I glanced around the room, recataloguing the attendees. Yes, it was a minefield of relationships I didn't fully trust or comprehend, but it was also as Tom said – a chance to unearth old stories that might help put the rest in context.

And also, I realized as I noticed several staff photographers eying Tom and myself with cameras poised, a chance to make my fans incandescently happy with a bit of inadvisable gay-baiting.

"Why yes, Tom." I placed my hand on his arm. "As my official escort seems to have abandoned me, why don't you lead me through the rounds?"

"… So there I am, flying across the Huangpu River with the Old Man dangling by his armpits and the biggest damned firefight I ever did see going off in the smog above our heads, and me only minutes out of recovery."

"By the armpits? Really?" asked a young Canadian Ace with the too-on-the-nose sobriquet of The Mountie, who'd been gazing at me like an eager puppy since Skyrocket took me up to the living roof and into the orbit of a group of younger Aces. Beyond the group rose the rooftop's grass-covered model of the seven hills of San Francisco. Plexiglas bubbles inset into the domes allowed light to stream up from the atrium, limning a scatter of whalebone – vertebrae, ribs, baleen – set out to dry on the grass. In the street below, streams of sedans – and the occasional Uber – continued to drop off passengers. On the other side of the concourse, ground lighting illuminated the de Young Museum's strange, inverted pyramid.

I cleared my throat, as discomfited by the young Ace's admiration as by the story of my exploits as rendered by another. "Hardly my most graceful entry, I'll admit. And you," I nodded at Skyrocket, "were rather spry for a man recently emerged from his deathbed."

"Don't recall much in the way of spryness."

"Jiu Wei?"

Tom smiled in happy memory. "Ah, yeah. She was quite a lady. Kissing her'd give any fellow a kick in the seat."

"Who is Jiu Wei?" asked a pretty young woman with the sort of soft curves and features that marked her as one of the hordes of support staff that made the Aces possible in a modern world.

I suspected she had a bit of a crush on Skyrocket. "His nurse–"

"Oh, but she's far more than that." The interruption came from behind us. I turned. David Tsung stood at the top of the stairs. Handsome, urbane, and far too like his grandfather for my comfort.

And at his side, wearing an exceedingly short crimson cocktail dress that made me want to wrap her in my coat and drag her home, was Mei Shen.

We hadn't spoken since her dramatic departure on the bridge, and we could hardly speak now, not with an audience. Not when I wasn't… myself.

"Yes, far more than that." I cleared my throat of the frog that had set up residence. "But for the purposes of this story, nurse is enough. One doesn't wish to weigh down with unnecessary details."

"Ah, but the details are where the devil lives, isn't that the saying?" Tsung glanced at Mei Shen, as though she'd know more about English colloquialisms than he did. "Paying attention to details can save one from much grief."

"Mr Tsung. It's good to see you again," Tom said, interrupting the extended silence that followed Tsung's pointed observation.

Tsung eyed the hand Tom thrust out in greeting before taking it. "It is?"

"Well, yeah. I know things got complicated at the

end, but I still owe you my life." Tom pulled Tsung – and by proxy, Mei Shen – into our little circle of gaping Argent employees. "Mr Tsung is the fellow who pulled me from the wreckage of the *Kestrel* and got me out of the Shadow Realms. Wouldn't be here today if not for him."

Saving the poster boy for the Argent Corporation won Tsung enough approbation that attention shifted to him with demands for details. I slipped out of the group, took Mei Shen's arm, and firmly escorted her down the stairs and back into the Academy proper.

The bridge above the atrium was shadowed and empty of people. Good enough. We settled at the railing, the model of the *Kestrel* at eye level. Below it, the pool of pins rose and fell in time with the chatter of the crowd.

"I hope this time you have no plans of jumping over?" I murmured, gripping the rail and pretending to watch the crowd from above. I kept Mitchell's voice, his accent, his posture, but the irritation was one hundred percent my own.

"That might upset the guests."

"How did you get in here?"

"David secured us invitations through a back channel. I suppose Mian Zi doesn't entirely have his claws in Sylvia Dunbarton."

So it seemed. This wasn't a Beyoncé concert. Even back channel tickets wouldn't be available unless someone in charge had authorized it. I rubbed my face. "Mei Shen, just... promise me you won't do anything rash. I don't think anyone at Argent knows of your involvement in this. Tom never knew, and I'm not telling. I don't think Mian Zi is, either."

"My role?" she snarled. "My role would have been to sacrifice David to stop my uncle, if you had trusted me to play it. Instead, you are the sacrifice. How are Mian Zi and I supposed to put an end to Lung Di when we must go through you to do it?"

"We'll work out a way." I shot a worried glance around the room. So far, nobody seemed to have noticed our presence on the bridge. Even so, uneasiness tightened the muscles between my shoulder blades, and no amount of rolling or twitching them would dislodge it. Hello paranoia, my old friend. "We can discuss this later–"

"Because you are so afraid to be yourself. So afraid David or I will give you up."

She turned away. I pulled her back and stepped in close. "No, because I'm afraid you'll give yourself away. I said before, nobody knows your role, but if they did... do you want to be marked as the terrorist behind the New Wall? They're looking for someone to blame, and you're a likely target because of your association with Tsung and the Shadow Dragons." And now I was worried that I had made it worse with my flip comment to Sylvia.

Mei Shen's gaze flicked away. She hugged herself. "Now you sound like David. You're not this protective of Mian Zi."

I sighed. I wanted to pull her close, rest my chin on her head, but even if I dared here and now, she'd grown too tall for me to do that. "That's because he has the support of the Chinese government and her people. You have… Tsung. And the Shadow Dragon Triad. Of course I'm more worried for you."

Still hugging herself, she studied the suspended *Kestrel* and then lowered her gaze to the atrium's windowed entrance. "Mian Zi was always better at wei-qi. It is no surprise he had the better opening move. But this isn't a game of wei-qi. Don't discount me yet."

"Never. You're my daughter. If you don't like the rules of the game, you'll find a way to change them."

"Perhaps I will. Tonight is only the beginning." She stepped back from the railing. "Mian Zi has arrived."

I turned to see where she was looking. Sylvia Dunbarton greeted my son at the entry of the atrium, both of them obscured by a cloud of flunkies. For what was supposed to be a private corporate function, it bore a troubling resemblance to a State visit.

"Shall we see who takes the *ko*?" Mei Shen asked and headed downstairs. I followed, unable to think of a plan to avert disaster.

Lord save us all.

•••

Abby waylaid me at the base of the stairs, preventing me from following Mei Shen. "There you are, Old Man. I'm fine with my date ditching me for my boss and Mr Apple Pie, but I draw the line at hot young things half my age." She latched onto my arm and hauled me into the atrium. We stopped at a display on Disco Dana and Java Joe, two of Argent's more embarrassing Aces. The disco ball cast us both in moving spots of light. What about the 1970s hadn't been embarrassing? Argent had gotten off light.

Abby gave the display a rueful nod. "I know. I begged Sylvia to let me skip the entire decade, but she refused. Said the progress of the feminist movement and the EPA was too important, and it would cheer folks up before they hit Reagan and AIDS."

"And yet you decided to downplay Argent's role in the oil crisis, I see." Back in the entry hall, Mei Shen had reached Mian Zi. It looked like my kids were having a civil conversation, but I didn't believe it. They had the knack of speaking on levels that only twins could understand.

"That tar's on your name too, Masters. Now uncross your arms like we're having a nice conversation." Abby scanned the room rather than looking at me. Her smile stopped at gritted teeth and tight lips. Most of her lipstick had been eaten off with the canapes. I glanced around the room, noticed several of the nondescript suits drift into clusters and back out.

I uncrossed my arms. Whatever was going on might just be more important than stopping my kids from creating an international incident. "What's wrong?" I asked, keeping my voice low. The shadows around my face meant I didn't have to fake a smile.

"Not sure. Mr Long's people had information about a suspected security breach. Passed it along as a gesture of goodwill. Our people are looking into it, but Dunbarton wants our Aces mobilized in case something goes down."

Information? I wondered if it was the same warning Mei Shen had been trying to deliver. If so, Mian Zi had outplayed her again. "What sort of breach?" I scanned the room again, assessing.

"Electrical grid. Primary. Doesn't make sense. There's nothing of value in the Academy displays, unless someone really has it in for that albino alligator, and all the tech in Argent's displays is disabled or removed. And the alarms are on secondary backup even if there was something here worth stealing."

"Quite a few civilians. Perhaps theft isn't the point." The collateral costs of Ace battles were always a hot button issue, good for taking up a month of news cycles. It was the PR reason for exhibits like this one, and Argent's close ties with the NRA, and some would say Skyrocket's entire existence. His reassuring smile and plain-spoken Midwest charm seemed designed to comfort such fears. "What's on the primary grid? Only the primary grid?" In other words, what would fail if an attack on the grid succeeded?

"Only primary?" Abby shrugged. "HVAC, PA System, non-emergency lights, some of the–"

"Get everyone out. Now." I was already moving, searching the crowd. Tsung. Where had Tsung got off to? Was he still on the roof with Tom?

"Masters?" Abby swiped for my arm. I shook her off and made for the stairs. The itch at the back of my spine finally gave way to a full body shiver. Lights. And Mei Shen had said her information came via David Tsung. I knew what was coming.

"Evacuate the civilians. Now. Before they attack." I paused at the base of the stairs and tentatively reached out with my senses to prod at the veil between worlds. It was in shreds. Practically non-existent. I searched for my kids in the crowd. They were nowhere in sight, nor was Sylvia Dunbarton and her personal protection unit. All I saw were civilians.

"They who?"

The lights flicked out. Emergency lighting kicked in, sullen red and useless against this foe. The first screams started.

"The Shadow Realms."

THREE
Science!

Abby shrieked as something from the depths of the disco display whipped out and wrapped around her waist. She chopped a deflecting hand through the tendril, but two more shot through the dissipating cloud, going for her arms.

She ducked, rolled, and came up with a gun.

"Don't shoot!" I caught the two tendrils – solid for me as they had not been for her – and tore the tangle of darkness out of its nest. Whipping it over my head once, twice, I cast it back into the Realms from whence it came.

"No shit, Masters. I'm not going to fire around panicked civilians."

I hadn't even considered that aspect. "It wouldn't be effective. You're better off shooting at smoke." Another shadow hurled itself at us, this one vaguely beast-shaped, with spiky fur and claws that reflected the dull red emergency lights. I struck it at sternum level, followed up with a front thrust kick, and opened up another conduit to the Shadow Realms for the beast to fall back into.

Except it was a temporary fix. With the lights out and the veil between realms torn open, anything I sent back could easily come through again. And, as Abby had said, there were too many confused civilians for one person to protect.

She stood by, holding the gun down at thigh level. "What's the plan?"

"Clear the Academy. Get people out into the light. Get the lights in here back on."

"Right. Outside! Everybody outside!" Abby dug deep into her diaphragm to be heard over the confused 'what's going on?'s and the growing cries of distress.

Evacuation wouldn't entirely protect the civilians, but at least there was light outside – headlights, street lamps, the de Young. I released my hold on my unsettled senses, usually clutched close as a church-lady's pearls for fear I'd brush up against something on the other side that I didn't wish to wake. Now, I flung them as broadly as I could.

Shadow couldn't just cross over in any old dark place, which was a blessing, or the world would be filled with every manner of terrifying folktale monster. Shadow didn't have the spark necessary to cross into our world. It required power on the Shadow Realms side, or else a bridge made by someone like me.

A bridge that had been laid at the Academy, now that I'd opened my senses enough to recognize it.

In the pockets of darkest dark – the Planetarium, the butterfly dome, the sunken pool that housed Claude the albino alligator – the darkness broke open, and shadows poured out. Someone had deliberately created the bridge. Someone not me.

"The roof," I yelled at Abby. "I need to find Tsung!"

Abby shoved a terrified young couple in the direction of the front exit. She looked over at my shout. "I don't know who that–"

"Did you do this? Are these your devils?" My arm was near wrenched from its socket when someone grabbed it and yanked me about. I blinked up at the woman, not recognizing her for a moment. She was taller than me, broad shouldered, dark skin, and darker hair scraped back in a severe braid. Liquid black eyes and a nose and brow as proud as Heaven's host.

La Reina de Los Angeles.

"Not mine," I spat, yanking my sleeve from her grip.

"Then I have your leave to dispatch them to the Hell from whence they came?"

I snorted and gestured to the room. There were more than I'd ever been called on to exile at once. "If you think you can..."

She pushed past me, her wing nearly knocking me into the tide pool exhibit. "You may wish to seek shelter, little shadow," she said over her shoulder. "I've no wish to sear you."

Her wings lifted, spread. How could anyone seeing that graceful display think it was the product of a healthy special-effects budget? The vane of each feather glowed softly like the filament of an old light bulb just turned off. Except these filaments were growing brighter. Slowly. They burned my eyes, yet I couldn't look away. Deep in my bones, beyond the place that crawled and ached and itched whenever I touched the Shadow Realms, a deeper hunger rose up. A hunger for that light. I *had* to have it.

Something hit me in the gut, bowled me away from the light I was reaching for. I struggled, but my arms were pinned to my sides until the light snuffed out and sanity returned.

"Hey, Old Man. Snap out of it!"

Abby. Abby was shaking me, and none too gently. We were in the stairwell, the emergency doors shut against the searing light of La Reina's wings. From beyond the door came the screams of shadow creatures as they fizzled out of existence. They sounded disturbingly like screams of ecstasy.

"Wha–" My voice cracked somewhere between Missy and Mystic. The shadows around my face had been burned away. My cheeks and nose felt stretched like I'd spent the day on the Playa with no SPF protection. I cleared my throat and used the stairway banister to steady myself, gathering shreds of shadow and identity back around me. The renewed shadows about my face cooled my heated skin. Somewhat. "What happened?"

"Dunbarton gave me access to your dossier for the display, at least the parts that weren't redacted. La Reina's light hurts you almost as much as it hurts shadow demons." Abby brushed my lapels, settled the little pin, straightened my tie, comforting by putting me back to rights. "You didn't know?"

I shook my head. The pain hadn't been half so unsettling as the deep yearning that went with it. I'd *wanted* to be incinerated by La Reina's light. "Now I understand how moths feel," I muttered.

"You good to keep moving?"

"Do I have an option that isn't yes?" Depending rather too much on the railing, I hoisted myself up the stairs and headed for the roof.

The fighting was worse up top, and no surprise as to why. "Conclave knights," I muttered. The shadows that served the Conclave weren't wild and chaotic like other shadow creatures. They were disciplined. Organized. The same sort of organization that would be required to stage an attack like this.

But the Conclave had never taken much interest in the real world that I knew of. Why would they start now?

The Mountie's scarlet coat and gold buttons were a colorful beacon, drawing the knights as surely as La Reina's flame had drawn me. He'd planted himself between the knights and the support staff that had been on the roof, using a thick, curved beam of pale wood to hold the armored shadow knights at bay. Skyrocket mowed down the back line with a comet-like flyby.

Of Tsung there was no sign.

"Worse trouble?" Abby asked.

"Yes, but at least this trouble is tangible," I said. The Mountie took Skyrocket's pass as an opportunity to shove the knights back with his... what was that? A club? Tree?

Whalebone, I realized, recalling the scattering of ribs and vertebrae from before.

Abby drew her gun. "Good."

We waded into the disoriented rear of the dozen or so knights pressing down on the civilians. I caught one from behind in a choke hold. Living shadow didn't need to breathe, but the closer it got to life, the more it took on the semblance of it. I'd seen Conclave knights bleed. I'd made Conclave knights bleed.

This one seemed desperate as any living foe to keep breathing. He flailed a gauntleted fist at me. I ducked my head against his back to avoid it, pressed harder until he sagged in my hold, and then forced him into the long shadows covering the grassy rooftop.

Abby had taken out two more knights to my one. I hadn't heard gunfire, so I assumed cold-cocking them had been her weapon of choice. I'd never met a woman who liked a good brawl more than Abigail Trent.

I sent her downed opponents to join mine across the veil and rose from my knees to face the knights

who'd turned to meet us. Abby was locked in a
tussle with two of them, which left far too many
for me.

A streak of copper and silver landed at my side.
"Hey, Old Man. These friends of yours?"

First La Reina and now Tom, assuming I had
anything to do with this attack. "My friends have
better manners," I muttered. Nothing about this
made sense. If this was Tsung's doing, then how did
he manage to weaken the veil in both the atrium
and the rooftop? And if it wasn't his doing, then
where was he?

And either way, what interest did the Conclave
have in an exhibition of Argent memorabilia?

"Then I guess we better teach them some," Tom
said, cheerful as always, and waded into the fray.

Between the four of us, we were able to rout the
knights handily – for the most part. While I was
subduing the last few, shunting them back into
Shadow, two of the remaining knights broke free.
They dropped off the far side of the rooftop and
escaped into the wilds of Golden Gate Park.

"I got 'em. The rest of you get to safety."
Skyrocket spared a wink for the accountant who'd
been swooning over him and launched off the
rooftop in pursuit.

I sighed and faced The Mountie, now using his
whalebone to usher the civilians down the stairs.
"Do you know where Mr Tsung went?"

"The fellow who helped Skyrocket? He was by the railing over there, then he hared out of here. We figured he was going after you and his date."

"Do you think he had something to do with this?" asked the girl from legal-or-accounting.

I tugged my fedora brim lower. "Get them to the concourse," I told The Mountie and headed for the rail separating the cement patio from the grassy hills.

Abby followed. "You think they did this."

They. Not he. Abby had seen my argument with Mei Shen. *Damn* David Tsung for dragging her into this. The last thing I wanted was for Argent to target my daughter.

"I don't know." I searched the railing and information placard with eyes and fingertips, looking for... I wasn't certain what. My fingers brushed something existentially unsettling on the backside of the placard. It reminded me of reaching blind under a paving stone to find a spare key and instead finding only slime and skittering. I recoiled, cursed, and hopped the rail to better examine the backside of the placard. A line of sigils was painted onto the brushed metal base. The last one smeared. I checked my fingers, and they were smeared as well with the same black paint. Fresh. That last mark had been fresh, as though someone had painted the others beforehand and then returned to complete it just before the attack.

"No. I don't think he did this," I lied. I didn't want to think he'd done this, or that Mei Shen had been a part of it, but who else could have? I cleaned my fingers on the grass and stood. "We need to get someone up here with paint thinner. Have them check the displays in the atrium for similar markings. I need to find…"

I broke off, heading for the stairwell. I'd discovered the *how* of the attack, but I still didn't know the *who* or the *why*. It couldn't have been Tsung. Or at least, he couldn't have been working alone. Whoever had done this had access to the Academy in the days leading up to the exhibit. They had to have set up the sigils beforehand throughout the building, had to have known which grid to target to take out the lights, allowing the shadows free rein. It screamed inside job.

I stopped at the second-level exit, recalling the paranoia that had overcome me when I spoke with Mei Shen. I'd been sensing the rending of the veil somewhere close by, and I hadn't recognized it for what it was.

At least I could alibi my daughter. That still left Tsung. Or… several other someones?

"Masters?" Abby lowered her phone – she'd been relaying my instructions to the people who could actually do something – and paused a step above me. "What is it?"

I pulled out my own phone, cupping it in my palm. "Who besides you was involved in making the exhibit?" I asked. I quietly pushed open the access door and peered out. Down one direction was the bridge that crossed above the atrium. La Reina's light had been replaced by more conventional floodlights.

The other direction led through a darkened gallery. I spied movement in the shadows.

I held my finger to my lips to silence Abby's response and cocked my head in the direction of the movement. She nodded, darkened her cell phone, and drew her gun.

We slipped out of the stairwell, each taking one wall of the corridor. Soft sounds came from the other end of the gallery – the scrape of metal on metal and the creak of hinges. I reached out with my senses, but aside from the lingering unease that came with a thinned veil, I sensed nothing of living shadow. Whatever moved in the darkened gallery wasn't a shadow creature.

I nodded at Abby and we both came round the door frame, cell phones blazing light. I tossed mine on the floor in case I needed my hands free. Abby held hers atop the stock of her gun as a police officer might hold gun-and-flashlight in a film.

The double glow of phone screens illuminated a woman standing before an open case. No, a line of open cases with scattered pottery and display cards knocked askew. The woman's left hip swelled with the misshapen bulge of a duffel bag. The contents shifted with the hollow sound of pottery knocking into pottery as she turned to face us. She held her hands high, her braid swinging just above her ass.

I gaped. I knew her.

"Hello, Abby," she said.

My companion cursed. "Asha. I should have fucking known."

"Should you have? Because large-scale coordinated attacks are *so* my style." Except for the incongruous duffel bag, Asha was dressed as one might expect of a cat burglar – black, form-fitting, many pockets, right down to the tailored gloves, save that these gloves were fingerless. She'd worn something similar the night we first met. I recalled that even after so many years. As well I should recall. That was the night I met Abby. That was the night Abby shot me. That was the night I decided to go to China.

"Hands where I can see them, bag on the ground," Abby said when Asha reached over to close the display case that hung half-open between us. Asha sighed, rolled her eyes like a bored teenager, and let the duffel strap slide off her shoulder. It hit the floor with another grating shift of fired clay against clay. She lifted her hands again.

Abby nodded. "Masters, you have anything you could use to bind her hands?"

I began unbuckling my belt. "You mean her wrists?"

"No. Hands. What's that buckle made of? Forget it, use your scarf. I want as little of her skin exposed as possible."

"*So* dramatic."

"You shut up. The only thing I want to hear from you is where you put those sigil things so that we can stop the shadow creatures from coming in."

I slid my scarf from my neck and approached Asha from the side so as not to obscure Abby's line of fire. I'd gotten between these two once before, and I'd come away bleeding and self-doubting. The past two decades of my life had been shaped by that night. Be damned sure I was going to be more careful this time.

"I told you, I've nothing to do with the rest of this. I'm merely taking advantage of the distraction to do some window shopping." She let me take one hand and wrap it in silk. I knotted it in place with the end of the opera scarf.

"So you knew there was going to be an attack."

"Darling, I make it my business to know about things like this. And then I take advantage of them. Free agent, remember? Doesn't mean I had a hand in planning it. This has the stink of the Conclave all over it. But I will tell you what I did have a hand in." She proffered her other hand for me to wrap and bind. Flinched when I grasped her wrist a little too roughly at the mention of the Conclave.

"What?" Abby asked.

"The party favors." Asha twisted her wrist neatly out of my grip. I lifted my arm to block a strike, but she came under my guard and brushed my lapel with her bare fingers.

"Fuck!" The light swung as Abby rushed forward.

"Masters, I am going to kill you!"

I stumbled as the woman I was holding collapsed into a shapeless column of smoke. The smoke hit my chest and seemed to be flooding into me. I fell back against a display case, batting at it, trying to shove it back into the Shadow Realms as I would a creature of shadow. But though it pulsed with magic, it was like no shadow creature I'd ever encountered.

Abby grabbed a handful of my suit and ripped something away. "This! You approached her wearing *this*!" She shoved something pale and flashing right before my nose. The silver *Kestrel* pin I'd received on entry, along with every other guest.

"I..." I choked on nothing to say. How had Asha done that? Why hadn't Abby warned me she might do that? "What... how did she–"

"Oh my fucking god." Abby shoved away from me, pacing back and forth as though looking for something to hit. "I really am going to shoot you again and have Argent cover it up."

"Professor Trent?" A squad of four Argent suits clustered at the end of the gallery, likely drawn by Abby's shouting and the bouncing light from her phone screen. "Is... is the situation contained up here?"

"No. It's not. Agent Fuller, take Mr Mystic into custody." She shoved past the startled agents. "The mastermind behind all this? He just helped her escape."

FOUR
The Morning After

I didn't fight the agents Abby set on me, but after several interminable hours of Argent custody, I was beginning to wish I had. They'd escorted me out of the Academy via a back way and bustled me into a black Lexus with smoke-tinted windows. That didn't keep me from tracking our progress through the city, past the stadium, and down into China Basin. Inside one of the newly constructed office buildings that were springing up like high-tech mushrooms, another agent not among my original escort moved to search me.

I stopped him with a hand. "I have been pleasant up to this point. Please do not give me reason to become unpleasant."

Ah, the wonders of a British accent and a well-cultivated reputation. The agents led me, unmolested, to a windowless room with painted cinderblock walls. I was left with a table, cot, chair, and adjoining bath, and little else to do but wait.

And wait.

I contemplated leaving via shadow, but that would negate any goodwill I'd won by being cooperative. And besides, the Shadow Realms were invariably dangerous. Best to leave them as an option of last resort.

Instead, I fumed over Abby's accusation. She had to know I wasn't involved. I'd only attended the exhibit opening because she'd cozened me into it. And I understood she was furious that for the second time I'd unwittingly let her nemesis get away, but how was I to know the woman could escape via a damned lapel pin? I'd only vague recollections of my first encounter with Asha and Abby – most of them dominated by the remembered pain of being *shot* – but that time, hadn't Asha smoked herself into a banister?

What the hell was she, besides Abby's nemesis? What had she been doing at the Academy, assuming she really was an opportunist taking advantage of someone else's attack? And what connection, if any, did she have with the Conclave?

And what was I going to say when – if – someone came for me?

By the time the door opened, I had an answer to the last question, at least. I stood, covering my anger with icy civility. "What time is it, how long do you intend to keep me, and should I be asking for my lawyer?" I studied the young woman in front of me: dark tailored suit, bundle tucked under one arm, and neatly draped hijab. "And who are you?"

"Mr Masters. Thank you for your patience while we sorted matters out. I am operative Sadakat. I specialize in advising Argent Corporation on matters of the arcane." Her accent was soft, sitting mostly in the w's and th's. German, likely of Turkish descent, given her coloring and the hijab. Argent prided itself on being a global corporation.

She shook out the bundle – my trench coat – and handed it to me. "Your phone is in the pocket." She flipped open a tablet, speaking as she tabbed through screens. "You are welcome to contact your lawyer if you would like, but the confusion about your involvement in last night's attack has been resolved."

Last night's attack? I checked the time on my phone. Sure enough, morning had come and gone while I waited in my windowless room. I dropped my phone back in the pocket and bundled my trench coat under my arm. I wouldn't keep either, not when Argent had had their way with them for several hours. I could dump them after Argent let me go.

"I am glad your confusion is cleared up, Ms Sadakat," I said. Clipped. Bordering on rude. "Mine is still in full force."

"Then perhaps we can be of assistance to each other. Do you recognize these?" She showed me the tablet screen, swiping through a series of close-ups of the same sigils I'd seen on the underside of the placard the night before. These came from a half dozen different locations. I recognized a seat bottom in the planetarium, one of the ribs framing the rainforest dome, the lip leading down into Claude the albino alligator's exhibit. All places easily accessed, just as easily overlooked.

"They're the same sigils as those on the rooftop placard." The ones that David Tsung had discovered, that had set him rushing off to who knew where. "I believe they're meant to weaken the veil between the Shadow Realms and the real world. Professor Trent should be able to corroborate that I had nothing to do with putting any of them in place."

Sadakat lowered her eyes, tilted her head as though in apology. "I should have been more clear. We are aware of what they do, and that you had nothing to do with them. My question is whether you've seen such like this before. I am schooled in several traditions, but these match none of those. La Reina and Professor Trent are equally puzzled as to their origin."

"Let me see those again." I took the tablet, swiped through the pictures. The markings were hard to focus on, as though they were trying to twist away from being captured in pixelated light. Not bothering to hide what I was about, I forwarded them to Jack with instructions to forward them to me for further study. "The traditions you've been trained in, they're all human traditions from the real world?"

She nodded. "Mostly Abrahamic mysticisms, yes."

I handed her the tablet. "That explains it, then. Whatever that writing is, it isn't from around here. It originated in the Shadow Realms."

She held the tablet at arm's length. "Ah. That explains… La Reina said they…" Sadakat pursed her lips and shut the tablet down.

"What?"

"She… said the writing had an infernal look to it." She held up a hand in apology. "You must understand, the creatures you deal with to her seem very like–"

"Demons. I know." It wasn't the first time I'd heard them referred to as such. "So whoever – whatever – was behind this has an even deeper knowledge of the Shadow Realms than I do. Does Argent have any notion as to whom it might be, or what they might have wanted?"

"Our investigation is still preliminary." She fought a smile at my snort. "We are very eager to speak with your friend Mr Tsung. I understand from Skyrocket's China report that he might also have some experience with these Shadow Realms. And of course, the young woman who accompanied him. She was last seen in the company of Mr Long's delegation."

My gut clenched at the mention of Mei Shen, and I was grateful for the perpetual shadows dragged across my face. "Then surely she can't be a suspect.

I understand Mr Long was the one to warn you of the impending attack."

"So he was. And we are understandably grateful."

Grateful. Sylvia Dunbarton didn't do grateful, and I suspected she looked on favors with suspicion. So now I got to worry about both of my children falling under Argent's scrutiny. Lovely.

I draped my trench coat over my arm. I'd wasted enough of the day sitting around. "I will do what I can to assist in tracking down Mr Tsung."

"You have our thanks for that. We took the liberty of retrieving your motorcycle. It is awaiting you outside." She stepped out of the doorway, leading me through an open plan office with thick cement columns, vaulted ceilings with exposed ductwork, and a general feel that important innovation was being accomplished, this despite the fact that everyone we passed seemed to be staring at me rather than working. I focused on the drape of Sadakat's hijab and ignored the stares until we achieved the lift.

The office building lobby was equally cold and self-important, dominated by a twisted glass chandelier that resembled some sort of strange, tropical sea life. The wall of windows let in fog-grey light from outside, two glass doors opening onto a half-circle parkway curving around a plaza with a dry fountain surrounding a metallic blob of public art. Fog ghosted through the plaza, heading towards the piers and the bay just on the other side of the street. It reminded me of the shadows the night before. I shivered and pulled on my trench coat.

My motorcycle waited in the turnabout. So much for keeping it out of Argent's hands. "You never answered my other question," I murmured to Sadakat.

"What question was that, Mr Masters?"

"What was their purpose?"

She gave a little head bobble and a sad, close-lipped smile. "Who can say what is the purpose of such acts? To sow chaos, confusion, fear? Last night's attack was an act of hate against all the good Argent does in the world. But we mustn't let their hate stop us. We must stand united to show we are unbroken."

I didn't believe her for a moment, but she spoke the words so smoothly that for a moment I almost believed she believed them, save for the twist at the corner of her mouth. "But we both know it's never as simple as the rhetoric would like us to believe, is it Ms Sadakat?"

She tilted her head. One brow lifted, and she nodded. "No, Mr Masters. We both know it rarely is."

I ditched my trench coat with a confused-if-grateful homeless kid at Fort Mason Park and headed for my lawyer's place in North Beach. Jack would have a better idea how to safely rid myself of the motorcycle and the phone. Perhaps I'd seen a few too many spy movies, but I didn't feel comfortable keeping anything that had been in the hands of Argent's techs for any length of time. Jack would also have a better idea of what the hell sort of trouble I'd gotten myself into now.

Jack – or Jonathan Q. Wentworth, III, Esq., but seriously? – had an office in the Financial District that I'd visited all of twice. Once as Missy when Jack first found me after years of searching for Mitchell Masters's heir, and once as Mitchell when one of the senior partners questioned Mr Mystic's return. I preferred dealing with Jack in his cozy North Beach townhouse. Half the time I could horn in on whatever cooking-show quality dish he was making when I arrived. Even if I missed out, there were always baked goods left over from the day before.

Sadly, there were only leftover baked goods to greet me today. I took the basket of cheesy muffins down to his office, waiting until the door was locked and the blinds drawn before ditching Mr Mystic.

"You didn't wait long to stir things up, did you? I thought the plan was to lay low until the New Wall stuff blew over?" Jack set the electric kettle on and puttered with tea things, keeping his back to me while I changed into a loaner t-shirt covered in sparkly Disney princesses and plaid pajama pants in Giants colors. My scalp itched from being crammed under a cap and wig all night. I loosened the braids and massaged blood into my scalp, not caring that it turned my hair into a frizzed-out red fright wig.

"What can I say? I'm a sucker for a dame in a pith helmet." I took my tea and curled up in one of the leather wingbacks, breathing deeply the steam and woodsmoke in my mug. Lapsang Souchong. Jack had upped his tea game in the past few years. Probably got tired of me bitching about being served Constant Comment.

"Shady dame if she turns on you like that." Jack sat behind his desk and flipped open his laptop.

"I know. I'm such a cliché."

"You sure you don't want me to pursue any sort of unlawful detainment charges?"

"Against Argent?" I shook my head. "I'm feeling pretty grateful they let me go. Don't want to push my luck."

"But you still want me to get rid of your bike."

"And phone." I'd already handed it over to him. Mystic's phone was a burner. I don't keep any of Missy's information on it, but better safe than... "Shit. I need to let Shimizu know I'm okay." I looked around as though a phone would magically present itself.

"Already texted her while you were complaining about my taste in nerd chic."

I relaxed, plucking at my borrowed t-shirt. "It's Disney *and* sportsball. I feel like I need a third identity to hide that I ever wore this."

"Let it go, Missy. More important fires to put

out." He turned his laptop so I could see the screen. A muted YouTube video showed dark, blurry images wrestling with other dark, blurry images. "I'm not sure if this was deliberately leaked by Argent or if they don't have as much media control as they want folks to believe, but someone posted cell footage of the rooftop fight. You fighting what look like Nazgûl alongside a few of Argent's best. Whether you like it or not, public consensus is that Mr Mystic has rejoined the fold."

I sipped my tea in the hope that it would settle my churning gut. No such luck. "I've never much cared for what public consensus said. Me or Mr Mystic."

"There's more," he said, and underlying those ominous words, *it's worse*.

"What?"

"Photos of Mr Mystic having a quiet tête-à-tête with a young Chinese woman. Photos of the woman departing with Mr Long's delegation just before the attack. The story being put about is that last night's attack was some sort of retaliation for the New Wall. Even split as to whether it's a Chinese group with radical leanings or one with covert state sponsorship. Either way–"

"My kids are being blamed."

Jack shut the laptop. After Shanghai, when I'd told him that the fifteen years I'd gained during my first trip to China also included two kids, he'd been completely thrown. Now he barely flinched. He'd come a long way in a few months. "Nobody's being blamed yet. Argent still has control of the story."

That wasn't as much of a comfort as it might have been. I rubbed my face. "What about the Shadow angle?"

"The usual spread. A few people believe. Most think it was staged effects and fear tactics. In this case, folks think that the attackers threw in some Shadow-type special effects because you were involved."

I sat forward. "Have you had any luck finding out where Tsung lives? Where Mei Shen is staying?"

Jack spread his hands. "My property search-fu is not that good. They have all of the Shadow Dragon Triad holdings and subsidiaries to hide behind. We had a hard enough time tracking those when the San Francisco branch was being run by Lao Chan, and your daughter is a lot smarter than he ever was."

And even if I could find where they had been staying, there was no guarantee Mei Shen would be there anymore. She'd been taken by – or left willingly with – Mian Zi. I had no doubt she'd be safe with her brother, whatever their philosophical differences, but only so long as he was safe.

If Jack didn't have the chops to find Mei Shen, then he definitely wouldn't be able to find out where the Chinese delegation was staying or put me in contact with them. And I didn't think Argent would be forthcoming. However, they weren't the only ones Mian Zi would have had to work with to make this visit possible. "Right. I think I've got my next step, then." I downed the rest of my tea, even though it was still a fair way to scalding.

"Okay. You going to share with the rest of the class?"

"Nope. I'm going to find me the teacher."

I borrowed a hoodie and left Jack's the way I usually did – by rooftop, under the cover of darkness. Since it wasn't yet noon, I had to make the darkness myself. The gloom imparted by the fog made it easier. I crossed rooftops to the end of the row of houses and slipped down a drainpipe, sauntering toward Russian Hill as easy as you please.

Two local news vans were parked in front of Mystic Manor when I got home. They usually came out whenever Mr Mystic hit the news, trawling for B-roll. I diverted down the back alley to avoid being caught in my borrowed jammies.

Shimizu was out, our bottom floor in-law empty. I scrawled her a quick note and didn't bother poking upstairs to check in with the other housemates. With the possible exception of Patrick, our resident grad student and pothead, none of them knew about my secret double life. They had no reason to be concerned that I was involved in last night's attack. The only thing I'd find upstairs was the usual grumbling about the media surveillance.

It was a relief to be back in my own clothes –

oxblood docs, leggings, an overlong button-down that *wasn't* covered in glittery Disney princesses. I ran my head under the tap and brushed out the worst of the kinks. Wet, it just about matched my docs. I've trailed so far behind on fashion that I practically set it again. I retrieved my cell phone – Missy's cell phone – and sent a cryptic text to Abby: *You owe me*. Then I grabbed a coat and scarf, and headed for Chinatown.

San Francisco's an odd conglomeration of twenty cities mashed into one seven square-mile area. The fog curling around the northern shore of the peninsula nudged up against Russian Hill, but it didn't follow me into Chinatown. By the time I hit Broadway, the afternoon was clear and warm enough to make me question the need for my coat. I wasn't fooled. Another half mile or half hour and I could be in soup again. Gotta love microclimates.

The Chinatown streets were relatively empty of tourist traffic. Tourism had nosedived in the wake of the New Wall crisis, everyone afraid that another set of barriers might go up and trap them in Chinatown, but it had been slowly recovering. I suspected last night's attack had squelched that small resurgence. You could taste it in the air, the renewed tension, more enervating than any fog. A few shopkeepers made a halfhearted attempt to lure me into their emporiums, but they backed off in what I suspected was relief when I waved them off in Cantonese.

If I needed any more indication that all was not right with the world, I got it in the form of the CLOSED sign on the door of the Dragon's Pearl.

I slipped round back and was relieved to see that the kitchen-side door was still open. The scents of five-spice and sesame oil wafted out, chasing away the rank alleyway smells of sweet rotting garbage and sour urine. I nodded at a few regulars on their way out. So, the Pearl wasn't open for tourists, but Doris was still feeding the locals. And more likely providing a safe center for them to come and share news, comfort, and concerns.

I bypassed the kitchen and headed up the narrow back stairway to the second floor.

Johnny Cho was in the middle of his open class. Students of all ages and a variety of backgrounds – mostly Chinese, but also Korean and a few *laowai* like me – faced off in sparring pairs. With his bleached-and-dyed hair – fire red and purple these days – he might look like an escapee from FanimeCon, but there wasn't a better sifu in Chinatown. Johnny had to have noticed me coming in, but he paid me no mind. He passed between the rows of students offering correction and encouragement.

I frowned at Johnny's back as I pulled off my boots and stuffed them in one of the few open shoe cubbies. He was never this nice to me in our training sessions. My corrections usually came with my cheek pressed to the mat and his knee pressed into my spine. Encouragement was provided by not wanting to end up with a mat burn permanently reddening my cheeks.

I knelt by the mat as the class progressed, watching. Learning. If Johnny was feeling ornery, he'd test me on one of the forms he was reviewing.

I cultivated patience as the class ended and the students dove in to their various cleanup duties, sweeping the mat, cleaning the mirror and the windows looking out onto the street. In pairs and threes they finished up their chores and drifted out. It seemed like every damn one of them needed to talk to Johnny, and Johnny seemed in no hurry to move them along. Finally, the last student – a teen boy with more bone than muscle – bowed at the edge of the mat before shoving on his shoes and *kwoon* jacket and pounding down the stairs to catch up with his friends.

Johnny snapped his towel at me to get my attention. "Took you long enough to come by."

Whatever patience I'd cultivated fled. I hadn't slept enough to put up with this nonsense. "Excuse me for being in Argent custody all night."

Johnny wiped his face, stepped off the mat, bowed, and tossed the damp towel in the laundry bin. "And you came here looking to take it out on someone?"

"I came here looking for my kids."

Johnny sat in lotus, knees nearly touching mine. Like Jack, he'd only learned about Mei Shen and Mian Zi after my return – my second return – from

China, but we hadn't talked about them. I was pretty sure he was pissed at me for keeping certain details of my first trip a secret. If having it out now with Johnny was the price I had to pay to make sure my kids were safe… sure. I'd pay that. This silent staring contest, on the other hand…

"I know you must know where Mian Zi is, at least. He would have had to pay his respects to you when he arrived. If not for himself, then for his people." Mian Zi had taken over the People's Heroes, China's state-sponsored version of Argent. With a population of over a billion and a culture not as steeped in rationalist dogma, China had a respectable pool of gifted individuals to draw on. Only the best made it into the People's Heroes, but even the best owed respect to the Masters who predated China's Mao-induced surge into modernity. Like the City Guardians. Like Johnny.

"He did. Two days ago. He was supposed to move on to New York today."

I groaned and ran my nails over my scalp. It still ached from a night in braids and wig. "Do you know where they were staying?" I couldn't believe that Mian Zi had moved on already. Not after last night's attack. Not when all the action was here.

Johnny looked down at the floor, then back at me, mouth twisted in an odd smile. "You really can be dense sometimes, Masters."

I opened my mouth to protest, but shut it at his next question: "Why didn't you tell me about them? Three years you've been back, and I know something gutted you in China, but… kids? With one of the Nine?"

"Surprise," I muttered. I hadn't said anything because I'd wanted to avoid this very conversation. Even after three years, the pain of walking away from Jian Huo and my kids…

I couldn't look at Johnny. I dreaded the question I knew was coming.

"And you left them?"

I sagged in on myself, folded my knees up so I could hug my legs and rest my chin on them. Johnny didn't say *after Mitchell left you*? He didn't have to. That thought had dogged me for three years. Part of the reason I'd taken on my grandfather's mantle was to escape the realization that when shit got too hard for me to cope, I'd done the same.

Or maybe I just thought that if I could understand my grandfather and why he'd left me, then it would make leaving my kids not so bad.

"It… wasn't the same. They had their father." I studied my twisting fingers as though they were the most interesting thing in the world. "And it wasn't like it was easy for me. But I couldn't stay. Not after…"

"Mei Shen says you left without saying goodbye."

I lifted my chin. "When?"

Johnny lifted one shoulder. "We hang out sometimes to play Kingdom Hearts. Don't change the subject."

"Well, when you learn that the man you loved used you as a walking baby incubator, let's see you make good life choices," I snapped.

"When you have kids, you can't afford to make bad life choices."

"Thanks for the free advice."

"And you didn't tell me. I thought we were... and you didn't tell me. I could have helped. I could have reached out to them and made it easier. For all of you."

I hated Johnny the most when he was right. I hugged myself and let out a shaky breath. "So what do I do now?"

Johnny rose to his feet and held out a hand to help me up. "Accept that you messed up and that your kids have every right to be pissed at you. And go downstairs."

I took his hand. "Downstairs?"

"Like I said. You can be dense. Can you imagine Doris Han closing her restaurant for anything less than a State visit?"

FIVE
Light and Shadow

I would have dashed downstairs with bootlaces trailing, but Johnny made me take the time to do them up proper. He said his insurance didn't cover broken necks in the stairwell.

The kitchen staff – half of them part of the extended Han clan – barely looked up from their steamers and fryers when I hurried through. However, the two agents at the door to the dining room stopped me cold.

"Private function," one of them said, holding me firmly by the shoulder in a grip that could easily dislocate with the proper application of weight and leverage. I tensed, ready to down him, but Johnny came up behind me and tapped the back of the fellow's hand like we were sparring students.

"It's okay, Franz. She's with me."

The agent released me and let Johnny lead me past. I looked back at the two men – both definitely Chinese.

"Franz?" I asked Johnny.

"One of them got uppity about me being Korean, so I've been calling all of them that. Annoys the hell out of them."

I stifled a chuckle. "Johnny, don't ever change."

The dining room of the Dragon's Pearl was an open space that hadn't been redecorated since some time in the mid twentieth century. Red dominated – carpet, drapes, upholstery. The chairs were flocked gold, the table cloths a startlingly crisp white, and all the wood was dark and heavily carved. And none of it mattered. Folks didn't come to the Pearl for its decor.

The tables in the main room were placed together as closely as Doris could get them and still allow the dim sum carts to pass. She refused to get rid of the carts and go to table service the way so many places did these days. But today, all those tables were empty. Crisp. Set. Waiting. Empty.

I headed for the private banquet room that Doris only opened for New Year's and family birthdays. Two more agents stood at the doorway, but I didn't need Johnny's help getting past them. Doris was personally setting out dishes in front of a lone figure. He spotted me and sent the agents and Doris away with a softly spoken command.

Johnny waylaid a confused Doris and led her back toward the kitchen, closing the doors to give my son and me some privacy.

Mian Zi stood at the far side of a large, round

banquet table, the sort that usually got crammed with people at weddings. He'd eschewed the Mao suit he'd worn in Shanghai in favor of a more Western style, like his uncle, but his hair was still long like his father's. I'd grown used to Mei Shen's blunt-cut bob and skinny jeans. The juxtaposition of inhumanly long hair and a western tailored suit sat oddly on Mian Zi.

"Where's Mei Shen?" I blurted.

"She is safe." My question had been in English, but Mian Zi answered me in Mandarin. I couldn't tell if he meant it as a reprimand or if it was simply a product of his ethnic bias. Whatever the case, the reassurance chased away the worst of my fears. No matter their ideological differences, Mian Zi wouldn't be taking time out for dim sum if his sister was in danger. I relaxed and sank into one of the empty chairs, sparing him my urge to hug him close. Mian Zi hated PDA even when he wasn't upset with me.

"What happened? Last night, I mean."

Mian Zi sat. Neither of us touched the food, even though he'd presumably ordered it and my stomach was rumbling. "I delivered a warning to Lady Basingstoke. Too late, as it turned out. I convinced Mei Shen to leave with me before either of us could be implicated, but she wasn't inclined to stay beyond this morning. I do not know where she went. I presume Tsung is with her."

"Why didn't you deliver your warning to me?" I

leaned forward, placing my hand on the edge of the table – the closest I dared come to touching him.

Mian Zi leaned away, ostensibly to serve us both pork buns. "What happened in Shanghai is my fault. I didn't see my uncle's distraction for what it was. If I had allowed David Tsung to enter Lung Di's sanctum, you would not have had to dishonor yourself." He pushed the pork bun around his plate with his chopsticks, but he didn't eat. I don't think either of us was in the mood for eating. "I didn't want to make the mistake of involving you again."

I strangled my napkin to keep from strangling my son. "So your solution is to leave me in the dark? Literally?" I'd been ready to follow Johnny's advice to let Mian Zi be pissed at me, but I hadn't expected him to blame himself. And I wasn't ready to touch the queasiness that washed through me at the words *dishonored yourself*. It made me feel unclean. "If your uncle is up to some new evil plan, maybe it might be a good idea for us to, oh, I don't know, work together to stop him? I mean, who needs a nemesis when we've got each other? That's the lesson I took away from Shanghai."

"But now you're his champion," Mian Zi said. "You can't risk working against him."

"Just watch me…"

He touched the back of my hand, much like Johnny had tapped out the agent, and drew my strangled napkin from my lap. "I can't risk letting you," he said.

It didn't quite sound like a threat, but that was because Mian Zi didn't threaten. He played the game without investing in the pieces. I might be his mother, but I was also a piece. Mei Shen might not be willing to sacrifice me to get at Lung Di. I wondered if Mian Zi was.

I pushed away from the table. Stood. I'd changed his nappies. I wasn't as easily intimidated by him as the rest of the people around him. "Are you going to stop me?"

"From involving yourself in this? No. I don't think my uncle is behind it. It was inelegant. The sigils used were rudimentary. The shadows have been dispersed or fled back to their masters. Let Mei Shen and Tsung chase what they're chasing. I need to make sure that China is not blamed, but that is as far as my interest goes."

He stood. He was taller than me now, almost as tall as his father and uncle, and yet he still carried the beanpole thinness of youth. So young-looking. I wondered if he'd look this young for eternity. I wondered if all parents thought their kids stopped aging at seventeen.

Mian Zi hesitated, and then pulled me into a stiff hug. I made it doubly awkward by clinging to him a little too hard and burying my nose into his lapel. There might have been a tear or two.

"Stay safe, mother. And try not to make more

enemies than you already have."

I sniffled something like a laugh. "Well, where's the fun in that?"

I didn't have Mian Zi's aura of importance to protect me from Doris Han's curiosity. He managed to make his escape without delay, but it took me a good hour to answer her questions about how I merited a private audience with Mr Long. At least I got a good meal with my mouthful of lies. And a show, because the expressions of disbelief Johnny kept shooting my way were comedy gold.

After extracting a promise from Johnny that he'd let me know if he heard from Mei Shen, I headed out. Abby hadn't responded to my text. I sent another, this one with a little more detail. *You owe me an explanation.*

With Mian Zi exhausted as a lead and Mei Shen and David Tsung AWOL, I was fast running out of ways to find out what the hell was going on. I considered heading back to the Academy, but I suspected it would be cordoned off as a crime scene, and I wanted to keep Missy Masters as far away from that mess as I could manage.

I spent the walk home scanning useless news articles and Twitter debates on the subject and deleting the social awareness spam that was already piling up in my junk account. I switched over to my Mr Mystic account as I was letting myself in through the back of the house.

And only then remembered that I'd asked Jack to forward Sadakat's pictures.

"Shimizu?" I called as I entered our bottom floor in-law. Echoes answered. I sent a quick text and got an almost immediate *Date=Late* followed by a string of emojis: scissors, a thumbs up, and a winky face.

"Kids today," I muttered and fired up my laptop.

The afternoon light faded and darkness shrouded the apartment, only broken by the light of my computer screen as I paged through the pictures, taking notes on placement, figure patterns, sigil repetition, variation. A few of the sigils looked familiar, and it was only when I got up to pull down my grandfather's journals for comparison that I realized how dark it had gotten. Shimizu was always after me to turn on lights. That Midwest accent of hers made her sound like a crotchety grandma, warning me I'd lose my eyesight if I kept reading in the dark.

But Shimizu wasn't home to tut at me. I made tea by the light of the Google homepage and went back to trying to decipher the sigils that had been used at the Academy.

My grandfather's journal provided one key. The symbols were ideographic, modified by diacriticals to indicate function and relation. I supposed that made sense. I'd picked up the rudiments of Shadow speech growing up with Mitchell – not that I knew that's what he was teaching me – and I'd improved my grasp of it during my years with Jian Huo. It was a language almost entirely composed of proper noun-verbs. No pronouns. No adverbs. It had confused the hell out of me until Jian Huo hauled out Plato and had me read up on the Realm of Forms.

I suppose it followed that the written language, such as it was, would be comprised of sigils that could be marked as actor, action, or object: Dancer, Dancing, Dance.

I came up for air when my phone dinged with a reply from Abby. Just a time and an address on Berkeley's campus, but that was fine. I could sort out the rest with her tomorrow. I rubbed my eyes. The sigils were starting to dance as well from a combination of exhaustion and bad lighting. I couldn't do anything more with them, not in this format.

"Time to William S. Burroughs this shit," I told the empty apartment. I fired up the printer, checked paper and ink levels, and set the pictures to print while I hunted down a pair of scissors.

I found a pair in Shimizu's side of the bathroom. I suppose I should have looked there first – she was obsessive about split ends. By the time I returned to the living room, the printer was quiet and my laptop had gone into sleep mode, leaving the apartment dark enough that even I had trouble making out shapes. My gut rolled, and a shiver crawled up to kiss the back of my neck. I tightened my grip on the scissors. Sometimes being afraid of the dark is silly.

Sometimes, it makes absolute sense.

I hesitated in the hallway. There was no light there, and I'd shut off the bathroom light after I'd finished my rummaging. The living room switch for the lamps was all the way across the room next to the entry alcove. My bedroom door yawned open behind me, another potential danger unless I could reach my bedside lamp. That was the problem with century-old Victorians and questionably legal in-laws. Neither were known for their robust overhead lighting.

So, retreat, forge ahead, or accept that I was being paranoid? A sound like a whisper of silk dragged across wood decided me. A footstep. I wasn't alone. Flipping Shimizu's scissors underhand – better for slashing that way – I darted around the corner, going for the table we used as desk, eating surface, and occasional craft workspace. I didn't need much light. Just enough to give me an edge over whatever shadow monster had invaded my home. All I had to do was hit a key, knock my mouse an inch.

My stocking foot hit something not-wood and slipped out from under me. I fell fully prone, with only enough wits to fling my scissors aside so I didn't end up a cliché. I could just see my gravestone: *Missy Masters. She ran with scissors.*

My chin smacked hard against the wood floor, and it was only luck that I didn't bite my tongue in half. And then something descended on me, heavier than shadow, thick as a waterlogged wetsuit. It pinned my arms to my sides, and I feared if I rolled over, it would wrap around me and cover my face. I'd seen people suffocated by living shadow before. I didn't want to be among that number.

I crossed my arms and brought my knees up underneath me, trying to peel the shadow over my head like a latex prom dress. It got stuck halfway off, binding one arm against my head, but at least my other arm was free. And my legs. I rose to my knees, flailing with my free hand while I used my forearm to keep the shadow veil from closing over my face. Didn't need much light... just enough to...

My hand caught the curved wood edge of the table. I grabbed it and dropped back to the floor, using my weight as counterbalance to pull the table down with me. My elbow banged hard into the floor, jamming my nails into my forehead, but my hiss of pain was lost in the louder crash of the table toppling over onto me and my attacker. Light danced crazily across the walls, my view of it half-obscured by the thing wrapped around my head. I twisted again, and this time the creature slackened enough to let me pry it off and fling it aside. I caught sight of something flapping across the room, fleeing the laptop screen's light.

It disappeared into the darkest corner of the ceiling, right above the entry, blocking my escape route out of the apartment.

I scuttled back on my ass, fumbling for the

laptop. It had fallen on its face, and the clamshell bend was the only reason it was casting any light at all. I grabbed it and turned it screen-out to the room.

Dark shapes with thick, smooth wings like manta rays cringed in every corner of the ceiling. There were so many that the black edges of their wings overlapped, creating that silken whisper as they shuffled over one another to escape the light of my laptop. It looked like something had hatched and was spreading out from the dark alcove near the front door.

"Fuck."

Something crinkled under my hip. I flailed at it to cast it away, but it was only paper, not shadow. Paper with a clear photo print of one of the sets of sigils from the Academy.

"Fuck!" Several other sheets scattered across the floor where the printer had spit them out. I was a goddamned idiot. And now I had to get rid of the portals I'd accidentally created before something worse than creepy, cringing manta rays blundered through. But first I had to flush my flock of shadow mantas before they stopped cringing from my meager light and decided to attack. I rose to one knee, still wielding my laptop like a shield, and sidestepped to the kitchenette. The mantas shifted with my movement, shuffling across the ceiling to stay as far from my light as their overlapping mass would allow. Good. I opened the fridge door, inciting a wave of flapping and hissing. The mantas clustered in the entry alcove fled to the corner above the TV.

Even better. I darted to the entry and flipped on the main switch, illuminating the room with lamps and Christmas lights. The new illumination sparked a mad, flappy exodus into the dark hallway and through my open bedroom door.

I was never going to be able to sleep in my bedroom again. I set aside my laptop and gathered up the fallen printouts, tearing them into quarters, eighths. I put the pieces next to the laptop for burning later.

The shadow mantas didn't like the light, but it didn't seem to hurt them the way it did some of the weaker Shadow Realms denizens. That meant I couldn't just turn on every light in the apartment and wait for them to sizzle out of existence. I'd have to open a portal back to the Shadow Realms and herd them through it.

Right. I grabbed a flashlight from the utility drawer. Bypassing my room, I turned on the bathroom light to make sure that room was clean and then closed the door. The door to Shimizu's room was already closed, but I reached in, flicked on the light, and closed the door again, just in case.

With the rest of the apartment as brightly lit as it had ever been, I set the Maglite on the floor in the hallway and ventured down the beam into my room.

My walls and ceiling seemed to be made of shifting sheets, and the rustling sounded loud as trees in a windstorm. But close. Close enough to stir the hair on my arms. Something brushed past the top of my head. I grabbed it, twisting it like taffy, and swung it down to one side of my beam of light. Instead of hitting ground, it hit the space I'd created between darkness and light, hurtling back into its proper realm with the force of my throw.

After that first brush, every shadow in the room descended on me. Only my Maglite beam kept me from being overwhelmed. I couldn't keep my portals open long for fear that the mantas would fly right back through them – or that something worse would follow. In my experience, most of the denizens of the Shadow Realms make up in mindless hunger what they lack in basic sense.

Each manta I slammed into floor, wall, and bed was another portal opened and closed. I was flagging, fingers slipping, grip slackening, as the effort sapped my energy. I felt a little of myself bleed away each time I connected to the Shadow Realms.

I thought maybe the crowd was thinning when three of the mantas attacked at once. I stumbled back from their combined force, my heel hitting the Maglite. It spun crazily, beam shining back down the hallway and casting my room into gloom once more.

The three on me became legion, all flapping

and hissing and bearing me to the floor with their weight. I think I managed to shunt one or two back into the Shadow Realms, but I didn't dare fling them *en masse* for fear I'd fall through with them and never make my way back. What was left was too much for me to beat off. A wing folded around my face. I choked for breath, but it was like trying to breathe through wet neoprene.

And then the weight was gone. The flapping ceased. I lay on my bedroom floor in the darkness, cheek pressed to cool wood. The light shifted. Someone had moved in the hallway, had picked up my Maglite and was shining it across me.

"What a fascinating device," said a voice, a woman's voice, except that it also echoed with howling winds and the ticking of spider legs and the rustle of bat wings high above. Every creepy sound I'd ever associated with the Shadow Realms was contained in that voice. I shivered and wished for the protection of a covering of shadow mantas.

No such luck. The mantas were gone. I lifted my cheek from the floor. The Maglite shifted to one side before the beam could catch my eyes. A woman stood in the doorway, backlit by the indirect light from the living room, or so I thought at first. I reached behind me to turn on my bedside lamp, which lit up my room but did nothing to illuminate the woman. Everything about her was made of shadow. Her hair was the same as her skin was the same as the gown that swirled around her like an oil slick. Her fingers cradling the Maglite were just a bit too long, as though they had an extra joint. She held the light up, shining it into the dark blank where a face should be. Nothing reflected. Her form sucked up the light.

"May I keep it?"

"Buh…" I blinked up at the woman, trying to make sense of this new invasion. Was she threat or ally? Had she been the one commanding the mantas, or the one who sent them away? There was something else about her voice beyond the creep factor, something that reminded me of another shadow denizen I knew. Her tone held the same delight and wonder as Templeton's, my old shadow rat friend, whenever I called him into this world. "Who are you?"

"I am the Lady. I hope you don't mind that I sent the kraben away. They can be such a nuisance when they're confused."

The Lady. A lady who thought murderous shadow mantas were a "nuisance". And one who, despite being made of nothing but shadow, did not cringe from the light as the mantas had. I rose to my feet, still wary. She was blocking the doorway. "You don't have a name?"

"Not one that I give out so freely." I couldn't read any sort of expression, but enough scorn dripped from her tone that it was easy enough to read the unspoken "duh".

"Do you mind if I…" I gestured past her to the

well-lit living room. She stepped aside.

I scuttled out into the light, feeling better, safer, just for standing in its glow.

The Lady followed, which put a damper on that feeling of safety.

"How did you get here?" Stupid question. "You came through the portals?" I uprighted the table.

The Lady moved past me, touching everything with her spider-leg fingers – a poster for Madoka, the back of the couch, the colorful quilt that Shimizu's mother had made her last Christmas, a picture of mini-me, missing a tooth and wearing a crisp white gi, from the days before my grandfather had left.

"I was exploring the Gumshan and I noticed the kraben amassing. May I keep this?" Without waiting for my assent, she tucked the picture under her arm alongside the Maglite.

"The Gumshan?" I asked, surprised to hear the Chinese nickname for San Francisco on the lips of a creature from the Shadow Realms. I closed the refrigerator door. The Lady's curious meandering and capricious hoarding had the odd effect of putting me at ease. She did remind me of Templeton.

"It is the name we give places like this where the Lung Di holds sway. Held sway. Until recently, nobody dared venture into such locations, but the Lung Di is gone, and his protections fade without his presence to sustain them. I am not the only one curious to see what lies on the other side of the forbidden."

So the sigils thinning the veil might have allowed the Conclave knights to cross over, but until recently they'd been leery of intruding on Shadow Dragon territories. Was that how Mei Shen and David Tsung had learned about the attack? Was that what Mei Shen had been talking about that day on the bridge, her uncle's protections unraveling?

But that raised the question – protections against what? "Are you with the Conclave, then?"

The lady paused in the act of sniffing a Nightmare Moon figurine. She carefully set it back among the other ponies. "No."

Ah. Okay then. Definitely a mis-step, if that icy curtness was any indication. I picked up fallen junk – mail, pens, a coffee mug that had survived the impact with the floor. I'd need a brush and pan to catch all of Shimizu's rhinestones. I swept them aside with my foot for later. "Do you know why they were here last night? In the Gumshan?"

"That is what I came to investigate. Whenever the Conclave amasses its forces, that bodes ill for the rest of us." She stopped again at a listing, life-sized figure stashed in the corner behind the TV. Blue-white Christmas lights wound through an old lace bridal gown that Shimizu and I had rescued from Goodwill. We'd draped it on a headless frame of chicken wire and papier-mâché and bundled a cluster of red lights at the breast, blasting Florence + the Machine and giggling all the while over how utterly goff we were.

"May I keep this?"

Shimizu was going to kill me. "Uh. Sure." I'd get her a replacement. "What did you find out?"

"The Conclave gathers power – artifacts like this manikin – so they might shape the Voidlands to their purpose." The glass lights clinked and rattled against each other, and the papier-mâché creaked as the Lady struggled to pull the goff bride out of the corner. "Last night they acquired such an object."

I went over to help her. She made a little noise of disappointment when the Christmas lights winked out.

"It needs a power source," I said, holding up the plug I'd just pulled from the wall.

"Ah. Yes. I've encountered such before." She tucked the bride under one arm and retrieved the Maglite and framed picture from where she'd dropped them on the couch.

"The Conclave, you said they succeeded?" I trailed her back toward my room.

"They usually do."

"Should I be concerned about what they want this object for? The thing they stole?"

The Lady juggled her treasures to turn off my bedside lamp. The room sank into shadow except for the Maglite beam. Even that seemed dimmer than it had been a few minutes ago, as though it had run through its batteries even though they were fresh. "Lung Di was the power that held both the Voidlands and the Conclave in check. The Conclave feared him. Now they fear nothing. They are gathering power. That is cause enough for concern." Christmas lights rattled as she hitched the sagging bride higher on her hip and flicked off the Maglite.

"Wait!" I held out a hand to stop her. I could feel the veil between this world and the Shadow Realms thinning, but it was none of my doing. Whatever this Lady was, she was more powerful than any Shadow Realms denizen I'd ever met. Not even the Conclave knights or Templeton had her kind of power. And yet even she seemed to fear the Conclave. "Maybe we can help each other. I don't want the Conclave to go unchecked any more than you do. Is there some way I could call you if I wanted to talk?"

"You think I would give a shadow mage my name? You wish to summon me to a circle and bind me to obedience?"

I took a step back. I couldn't see her at all now. The darkness that had crept into my bedroom was complete. But her voice shook with anger, and I felt that anger and darkness pressing down on me like the fins of the kraben. "No. I don't know the first thing about summoning anything. I just want to keep the Conclave out of my world. Out of my home would be a nice start."

"Ah. Then." Something squealed like nails on chalkboard, loud enough that I covered my ears. Goosebumps washed over my skin. "That should serve."

The darkness receded, leaving my room in a soft dimness that seemed as bright as a foggy day compared to the absolute blackness of before. I uncovered my ears and nervously stepped into that dimness so that I could reach the bedside lamp to turn it on.

On the wall above my headboard, the plaster had been scratched away in jagged clumps. Left behind were rough sigils oozing black in the center. They looked like the sort of thing a horror movie killer would leave over the bed of a dead roommate.

I nudged against the veil between realms, and it shoved back against me hard enough to make me stumble off-balance.

"Well, great." The Lady had made my room safer from the Shadow Realms than just about any place in the city. I studied the oozing sigils. Shame I was never going to sleep in it again.

SIX
The Road to Hell

I had the place mostly set to rights by the time Shimizu got home, which didn't get me off the hook for explaining what had happened.

"How'd the date go?" I asked. Classic delaying tactic.

"And a swing and a miss. She spent the entire night talking about her primary and their agreements and how he's totally cool with her dating women. I peaced out at the third mention of 'clearing conversations'. I have no interest in your bi-curious bullshit." Shimizu left her boots at the door and flopped on the couch, hugging her Totoro quilt close. "How hard can it be to find one good, old-fashioned femme in this city? No butches, no Asian fetishists. Just a nice, monogamy-minded princess. Is that too much to ask?"

"You're too vanilla."

She poked her head out from under the quilt. "I guess so. What's with the redrum on the walls?

And where'd Estelle go?"

I explained about the shadow attack and the Lady's sigils, which I'd painted on the walls of every room, including Shimizu's. Tomorrow I'd hit Home Depot and do the rest of the house.

My explanation of the sigils and Estelle the Goff Bride's fate led to longer explanations about the attack on the Academy and the ongoing threat that lurked in our closets and cupboards, under our beds – any place that held shadows – now that fear of Lung Di wasn't holding everyone back. We decided that, sigils aside, we both felt safer that night sleeping on the couch with our feet in each other's faces and Totoro shielding us from danger.

We were woken in the early morning hours by an earthquake. Just a baby tremblor, barely cracked a 4.0 and only toppled a few of the figurines. Even Shimizu had trouble mustering her usual diatribes about how the ground wasn't supposed to be a thing that moved and how she was heading back to Iowa before the Big One hit. But the quake reminded me of one thing I hadn't told her: Mei Shen and her nebulous warnings about some greater threat that I was being deliberately oblivious to. I decided to refrain from sending Shimizu into a Big One panic until I had more evidence that there was something to panic about.

Which explained the depths of my foul mood that afternoon when I strode up the central staircase of Berkeley's Anthropology building. I had a crick in my neck, my back ached, and not even a double shot of concentrated matcha had been enough to chase away the stripped raw feeling of being overtired. I'd only had a few hours' sleep after a day and a half of being up. Such adventures tended to leave me grumpy these days.

Saturday at the start of the summer term meant the halls were mostly empty, but what traffic there was cleared as I strode through. Whispers followed in my wake: *Is that…?* and *Oh my god, it is!* and *You know, his whole thing with China is deeply problematic…* and *Jesus, he's hot for an old guy…*

The walk-by commentary only increased my irritation. I deepened the shadows around my face and loomed, a little blot of peeved darkness, in the doorway of the office of Abigail Trent. The Antiquarian.

Abby.

"I didn't know you taught here," I said when she didn't immediately notice my looming.

Abby looked up from the legal pad she was scrawling notes on. Her braid was fighting a futile battle to contain her hair. She had a set of half-moon reading spectacles perched on her nose and let them drop to the end of a chain around her neck as she stood. Her blue work shirt was rumpled and her khakis had creases from sitting in an un-airconditioned office all day.

"Visiting lecturer. Year-long appointment. I'm still moving in." She gestured at the bookshelves lining the walls, dusty but mostly empty, and the stacks of boxes forming a wall behind her and blotting out most of the light from the windows. She shifted her weight to one hip and back to the other, and it took me a moment to realize she was fidgeting. Abby, one of the most rock-solid women I knew. "About the other night…"

I waited for her to continue, but Abby seemed determined to run through every way to begin to say something before she arrived at the actual saying of the thing.

"Might I sit down?" I asked, because my hip flexors were starting to twinge again.

"Oh. Yeah. Just move that junk to the floor."

I relocated the pile of papers as she'd suggested and sat in a slat-backed chair I was fair certain had been designed as a torture device for students. Perhaps I should have remained standing. "Why don't we start with an explanation of how Asha escaped, and we can work from there?"

Abby's shoulders sagged on a sigh. "Right." She dug in the top drawer of her desk and pulled out a lump of folded fabric. Tossing it to me, she crossed to the door to close it.

I unwrapped the lump and lifted the silver lapel pin that was inside. "This isn't an explanation."

"The explanation is coming." Abby returned to the front of her desk, half-leaning, half-sitting. I had to crane my neck to watch her face, which improved my mood not one whit. "That's how

Asha escaped. She reverted to her true form and fled through that."

"Her true form." I recalled the smoke. "Which would make her...?"

"She's one of the Djinn. A djinni."

"As in 'I Dream of...?'" I asked.

Abby snorted and picked at a nick on the edge of the desk. "Not even remotely. Except for the smoke thing."

I took several careful breaths, giving myself time to process. It wasn't that difficult. Some of my best friends weren't exactly human. "How did she get away?"

"Djinni are similar to your shadow creatures. They're from a realm of elements – Alam al-Jinn – but everything's out of whack there. It's all fire these days, and the Djinn can't remain there long. Most of them have moved into small enclaves in the Shadow Realms. It's more bearable than Alam al-Jinn and easier to shape than this world."

"Asha doesn't seem to have much difficulty navigating this world," I said, turning the silver pin over in my hand. She'd made sure that everyone had one. Why? I held up the pin. "And that still doesn't explain how she got away."

"Not even the Djinn can handle the fires of Alam al-Jinn for long, but they can still travel through it, like you do with shadows." She nodded at the pin. "They get there through unalloyed metal."

"Unalloyed metal?" I tapped the pin.

"Silver, gold, platinum, copper, iron, tin. Those are the most common."

"No metal content is entirely pure."

"No, but the higher the alloy content, the harder it is for a djinni to use it for travel. There used to be entire branches of alchemical study backed by the Djinn, pursued by the Djinn, to try to determine the exact cutoff and figure out ways to create purer metals for safer travel."

I set the pin down on the edge of the desk. "Why does that matter?"

Abby went to the stack of boxes and pulled the top one onto her desk. She began unloading its contents. I recognized a polished copper knob the size of a baseball with a cylindrical hole bored through it – the banister fixture that had gotten me shot. The other objects – all metal – could have been from anywhere.

"The impurities in a metal build up a resonance when a djinni passes through it. Like an afterimage. If a djinni uses the same object too often, or if the impurity content is too high, a djinni can get trapped."

"And from there we get the legends of the slave of the lamp?"

"Exactly. At least some of that alchemical research was dedicated to looking into how to free a djinni from that sort of imprisonment." She set aside the empty box and surveyed the jumbled array of artifacts. "There's no record of anyone succeeding. Most of the Djinn tend to limit travel between realms to avoid becoming trapped. Asha is different."

I picked up a gold bathroom faucet that looked like it had been ripped from its mooring. "These are all things she's traveled through?"

"She's careful." Abby nodded at the silver *Kestrel* pin. "She sets up escape routes beforehand. Never carries anything on her. Never uses the same object more than once."

The faucet clunked when I set it back on the desk. All of Abby's attention was on the artifacts she'd collected. "What's your connection to her? What was she doing at the Academy? And why did you blame me for her escape?" I waved a hand at the scattered artifacts. "How could I possibly have known any of this?"

"I was pissed. And I'm sorry." Abby rubbed her face, ran her fingers through her hair, which caused a few more witch curls to spring free. "I'm not exactly rational where Asha is concerned. But I think – Argent thinks – she was telling the truth for once. She's a lone operator. A... liberator of antiquities, is how she puts it."

"A thief?"

Abby fell back into her chair, arms crossed, lips twisted into something between a grimace and a grin. "And when she isn't stealing for private collectors or sorcery consortiums, she does pro-bono work for indigenous groups. She succeeds where repatriation fails just often enough to be really annoying."

"So the other night was...?"

"Not a part of her pro-bono work. Just a failed theft."

I thought back to the Lady's words. "Asha may have failed. The Conclave didn't."

The chair creaked as Abby leaned forward, hands braced on the desk. "You know about that? How do you know about that?"

"I have my sources."

"Do you know what they took?"

Pretending knowledge would gain me nothing. "No. Does Argent?"

Abby stood and started packing her collection back in its box. "It's why I asked you to meet me. They did manage to take... something. Highly experimental. Potentially dangerous."

"What did they take?"

Abby chewed her lip and toyed with the little *Kestrel* pin. "I really can't say. It's proprietary information that–"

"The Conclave doesn't much care about the real world, which means if they took something, it's to do with problems in the Shadow Realms. That concerns me more than Argent's loss." I stood as if to leave, mostly so I could meet her eyes without craning my neck, but it had the added benefit of an implied threat. "If you want my help, you'll tell me what they took."

"Wait!" Abby reached to halt me, even though I hadn't made a move towards the door. "Argent was working on a more efficient titanium extraction process using thorium, and we ended up stumbling onto a more efficient thorium fuel cycle instead. One that could be safely miniaturized and…" She sighed at what was probably my expression of utter bafflement. "Basically, we made a mini nuclear reactor. A power source of immense potential energy."

Power. Energy. Yes, given my meeting with the Lady and my experiences that anything with a battery died a quick death in the Shadow Realms, I could begin to see why the Conclave might want something like that. Just as I could see why I might not want them to have a nuclear reactor, miniature or not. "I thought you said everything on display was dismantled."

"I was wrong. Argent wants your assistance in retrieving our stolen tech from the Conclave."

"And how do they suggest we do that?"

Abby held up the pin. "We recruit a thief."

"I have spent half my life hunting this woman. You are insane if you think a summoning ritual is going to work." Abby slammed her fists on the conference room table and stood to loom over the rest of us. She turned to Sadakat, who'd stopped tapping away at her tablet to look up in surprise at Abby's outburst. "There's a substantial Djinn enclave in the Shadow Realms near Pakistan. We need to go there."

"You know why we can't go there," Sadakat said softly. They glared at each other for several moments, neither woman looking as though she intended to back down.

"Pardon me," I said into the sullen silence that followed. "But *I* do not know why we can't go there."

Sadakat's brows furrowed. She seemed to frown at me rather a lot. "Where do I start, Mr Masters? We have no permission from the government and are not likely to get it. The entire region is unstable. Not even Argent has the pull necessary to get you there in a timely manner or to support you on the ground. And let me not even bring up Professor Trent's insistence on traveling with firearms."

After the past few days of discussion, plans proposed and discarded by Abby, Sadakat, myself, and whichever experts Sadakat dragged in to consult with us, I was a mite relieved to learn there were places where even Argent's power didn't extend.

"India," Abby said. "We'll go over the border–"

"All diplomatic incidents should be both intentional and necessary. To entertain one as a byproduct of the current operation is a failure of imagination."

I choked on a laugh. "Abigail. Sit down. These theatrics are getting tedious."

She shot me a glare. "Don't you fucking tone police me, Old Man." But she sat.

Due to Sadakat's presence and the string of Argent operatives parading through the conference room we'd commandeered in Argent's China Basin facility, I'd stayed in full Mr Mystic mode. I had a permanent headache from the wig. Today, one pin in particular kept poking into the bone above my temple, and no amount of surreptitious nudging relieved the pressure. I'd zoned out from half this morning's discussion because all my attention was focused on hating that stupid hairpin. Still, that was no excuse for me to dismiss Abby's frustration as I had. I tilted my head in her direction.

"My apologies. You are very right to take me to task. I understand how frustrating this is for you." I turned to the consultant who'd suggested the summoning ritual while I'd been wishing rusty death on my hairpin. "La Reina, could you explain in more detail? Why would such a ritual work now if it hasn't before?" I glanced at Abby. "Assuming it has been tried."

"It has not been tried." La Reina's wings rustled as she leaned forward. I had to force myself to meet her gaze. The wings remained as fascinating as they'd been to me at the Academy. Whenever they caught the light coming through the wall of windows facing the bay, I forgot my suicidal trance of the previous night, forgot the pin gouging into my head, and had to struggle not to stare in slack-jawed wonder. "How could it be? Even with the nodes collected by Professor Trent, you are the only sorcerer I know of who might construct such a ritual."

"Am I?" I murmured, shooting a glance at Abby. Her tight-jawed glare was fairly easy to decipher. We both knew I wasn't the Ace my grandfather had been.

"The pattern of the sigils you identified the other day bear similarities to other known rituals," Sadakat said, pulling up the pictures on her tablet. I tensed, but they had no effect on the veil between the real world and the Shadow Realms. I'd surmised after considering the invasion of my home that it was due to the medium. Any power the sigils might contain seemed to be diminished when they were etched out in pixelated light. "La Reina and I believe we can modify a ritual used to summon and contain demons, replacing the Enochian speech and scripts with your Shadow dialect."

I wiped a cold sweat from my upper lip under the guise of pondering the problem. "That still doesn't explain how it might work. As I understand it, Asha is from Alam al-Jinn. She isn't of the Shadow Realms."

La Reina and Sadakat exchanged a puzzled look. I suspected they assumed I should have known the answer to my own question.

"We already have Asha's name. Professor Trent's nodes will help us target her through any

misdirections she might have set up," Sadakat
explained slowly, like a student answering a
professor's question when she expected a trap.
"Your translations will open the path to the proper
realm."

"We realize that it may take a few tries, if that's
what you're getting at, Mystic," La Reina said, far
less patient with my obtuseness. Her lips twisted in
a sardonic sneer. "Only the Lord is perfect."

I raised both brows at the level of cynicism
in those words, but I didn't dare ask any more
questions. Every word out of my mouth was
another potential break in my already precarious
disguise. I resisted the urge to deepen the shadows
around my face even further. "I'll need some time
to look over your ritual and make the translations,"
I said slowly.

"I'll send it to you." Sadakat shut down her tablet
as though the matter were decided. "And I'll secure
the Academy's rooftop. In the wake of the attack,
the location has resonance with both the Shadow
Realms and Ms Asha."

She left with La Reina. Abby's glare kept me
from leaving with them.

"I am truly sorry about the tone policing," I said.

"Oh, we've got bigger issues than that." She shut
the door, pulling me close. Even then, her whisper
was little more than a tickle of lips near my ear.
"You have no idea how to do that translation, do
you?"

I took a breath. Let it out with puffed cheeks. "No."

"Masters–"

I forestalled the inevitable – and possibly deserved – dressing down with a raised hand. "I am perfectly equipped to address the verbal. Less so the written, but I would not have agreed if I didn't have a possible solution."

"Possible?"

"Two. If the first does not succeed..." I swallowed down a swell of anxiety and prayed that my first solution would work.

Abby's drumming fingers on the door frame indicated a disheartening lack of faith. She blew out a breath, much as I had. "Fine. Is there anything I can do to help?"

I considered Sadakat's comment about resonant spaces. I'd never considered such things before, but if I was going to pretend like I could do real magic, perhaps it was time to start considering the structures and practices of same. "Actually, yes. Do you recall the Pagoda Palace?"

Abby snorted. "Kind of hard to forget it."

For both of us. "Might you be able to get us in after hours?"

The restoration of the Pagoda Palace had jump-started a wave of gentrification in the slice of the city between North Beach and Cow Hollow – the last run-down area this side of Soma. The vintage theater was now the center of a growing hub of niche eateries, eclectic shops, and trendy bars. Only the bars were still open when I arrived to meet Abby. I'd shed Mr Mystic and twisted that damned hair pin straight with vengeful glee. My shoulder twinged as I approached the dark ticket booth – phantom pain, born of nostalgia. That wound was three years – or eighteen years – healed, depending on which timeline of my life I calculated by.

Either way, I'd come a long way from those early Mistra days. Now to see if I could prove that to Abby.

She opened the frosted glass front doors as I approached.

"No lock picks this time?"

She held up a fist. Opened it. A ring of keys jangled, catching the orange light from the street. "Argent might not be able to get us into Pakistan, but they can still swing a privately owned local business. I only need picks when I'm trying to be low profile."

I twisted my hair, glancing nervously around the darkened lobby. The concessions stand had been retrofitted – new popcorn machine, tablets instead of registers, and the soda fountain had a digital display. The rest of the darkened lobby had gotten a decor refresh. Nile-green carpets climbed up a central stairway that split into two wings up to the mezzanine lobby. The walls were painted cream and the same pale green, with copper trim and moldings branching out in the delicate, dragonfly curves of the Art Nouveau movement.

"I didn't think I needed to specify that I'd rather Argent wasn't involved."

"I'm an Ace, Masters. We're involved. But don't worry. Dunbarton's so giddy that Mr Mystic is helping us that she's being extra careful not to scare him off with looming. Your secret's safe."

I mounted the stairs. The banisters had been replaced, their brass fittings jarringly out of place compared to the copper that shone everywhere else. "Speaking of looming, I'd rather do this alone."

Abby ignored me, following me up to the mezzanine. "That's nice. Not gonna happen. What are you planning on doing?"

When Abby and I had met the first time, the mezzanine had been home to a loaned exhibit from the Asian Art Museum. The display cases were long gone, replaced by swoop-backed fainting couches in a slightly darker green than the carpet. I sat cross-legged in the middle of the space and pulled out a stack of Post-Its with sigils scrawled on them in thick black Sharpie. "Something like the summoning La Reina wants us to do, but it's—" I broke off in exasperation when Abby sat cross-legged in front of me. "Fine. Don't blame me if you end up feeling like you drank curdled milk."

I took a few deep, meditative breaths and began laying out the Post-Its in the order of the sigils at the Academy. With each successive sigil in the chain, the veil between realms trembled, stretched. I focused on Shadow, on a particular shadow, shaping it with my thoughts into a familiar form.

As I set down the last Post-Its, I channeled that sense of familiarity and connection into a whisper. A name. "Templeton."

The whisper fell from my lips and into my lap. Abby shrieked and scuttled back until she was pressed against one of the green divans.

I leaned over the bulky form now squirming in my lap, snatching up the Post-Its before something else could take advantage of the thinned veil to slip through.

"What. The hell. Is *that*?" Abby snapped, voice trembling from either anger or fear. Possibly both.

The furry form tumbled out of my lap and righted himself. I couldn't help myself. I smiled. "This is Templeton. You've met before. Heya, Templeton."

"Hello, Missy!" Templeton nuzzled my wrist, so of course I had to yield to his request for scritches. He squirmed under my hand, lifting his muzzle so I could reach under his ears and behind his jaw. His crooked little rat claws flexed in the carpet. Someone had fastened a leather gauntlet around his front leg, and three jewels glistened in the molded leather setting – a knob of coral, a cracked opal, and a water-smoothed chunk of green glass. They were the only spots of color on a pitbull-sized rat made of pure shadow.

Abby had recovered herself enough to get to her

feet so she could press against the wall. "I remember
a rat-thing. I don't remember it being so... so..."

"Big?" I asked before she could hurt Templeton's
feelings. Her hand was pressed against her side
– where she usually wore her gun, I realized.
I frowned at her. I tried to sympathize – I did! –
but the presence of shadow just didn't affect me
the way it affected most people. Especially not
with Templeton. He was mine in ways I was only
beginning to realize the extent of.

"Yeah. Sure. We'll go with 'big'."

Well, I'd warned her. I focused on Templeton,
still gazing up at me with all the adoration of an
abandoned puppy. "It has been so long. Where
have you been?"

I resisted the urge to hug him again. "Here. Well,
San Francisco." I recalled the name the Lady had
given. "The Gumshan? I tried calling you–"

"Oh. I haven't dared come near the Gumshan.
Not with the Shadow Dragon so upset with me."
He tugged on his gauntlet and glanced around
nervously, as though he feared lurking dragons.

"You don't have to worry about him anymore.
He's gone to ground."

Abby cleared her throat and gave me a pointed
look. I made a face at her and got down to business.
"Templeton, I need your help. Do you know how
to write the Shadow speech? Like this?" I showed
him a few of the Post-It notes. I'd deliberately used
the neon orange, pink, and green sheets – anything

to encourage him to focus.

He sniffed the sheets, turned one eye then the other on them. His claws scratched across the surface of one orange sheet, sending tingles up my spine at the sound of claws across paper. His whiskers drooped when he looked up at me. "No. I'm sorry, Missy. I don't know what you mean."

Well, it was too much to hope that the easy solution was the right one. I scratched his head to let him know I wasn't upset with him. A thought struck... "What about... do you know of someone called the Lady? She's–"

"No." Templeton cowered back from my touch. He snatched up his tail and began gnawing on it. "No," he said around his tail. "I don't know anything about the Lady. Can I go now?"

I was so surprised by his reaction that I nodded. "Of course. You never have to ask. Do you need me to–"

He scurried into the darkness underneath Abby's divan before I could finish my offer. Abby squealed like a cartoon damsel and hopped on top of the seat. I pressed my cheek to the carpet and peered into the darkness, but Templeton was gone back to the Shadow Realms.

"Well, that was unnerving. And pointless." I stood, frowning at the shadows where he'd fled. "He lied to me."

"About the language?" Abby asked.

"About the Lady," I murmured, wondering

why. Wondering what it meant. Templeton had only ever been that afraid of one person. Lung Di. Which didn't give me confidence for my next plan. "I think you should go now."

Abby climbed down from the divan. "Hey. I'm sorry if I insulted your friend."

"That's not why you should leave." I sat down again and shuffled my Post-Its back into order. "Templeton was my kinder, gentler option. I'm about to try something much worse."

"W-worse?" Abby hesitated for all of two seconds. "I'll… wait outside."

I considered my options as her footsteps receded down the stairs. I'd entertained the possibility of calling the Lady, hoping that name alone was enough to get her attention without offending her. But after Templeton's reaction…

The front door opening and closing shook me from my musings. Better the devil I knew than the one I didn't. I began laying out the Post-Its.

"Well now. Isn't this an unexpected meeting? Hello, *Lung Bao Hu Zhe*, my stalwart champion."

The voice came from behind me. I didn't need to see the speaker to feel the effects of his presence. I wondered if this was how Abby and other people felt in the presence of shadow, a moment of falling, like stepping off a curb they didn't know was there. I scrambled to my feet and turned. I wasn't about to leave my back exposed to this threat. I managed to resist backing against the wall as Abby had. What have I got that she hasn't got? Courage?

That or a dearth of brains, I thought as I watched my nemesis pace the room, examining the decor, the windows facing out on the street, the posters for a mix of vintage and B-movies. "Lung Di. I wasn't sure you'd come." I had no illusions that I'd summoned him. Not in the usual sense of forcing his presence. I'd done the Shadow equivalent of knocking politely, not even sure that he'd hear.

"Curiosity compels us all to be unwise at times." He finished his circuit. He wore his usual – dark business suit, dark shirt, dark tie. He looked like a mobster. Or, given how long he'd been around, maybe mobsters looked like him. He wore one glove covering the hand that he'd injured during our first confrontation. The hand I'd injured for him nearly four years ago. I was surprised that it hadn't yet healed.

He sat – no, lounged – on the divan opposite me, one leg crossed over the other. The leather of his shoes gleamed in the light from the street. "No traps. Given how assiduously Lao Hu hunts the both of us, I half expected you to have sold me out to him. Now I'm even more curious. What could have led you to invite my presence of your own accord?"

I opened my mouth to answer. Slowly closed it, eyes narrowing. Templeton's lie had surprised me, but Lung Di lied like breathing. If he'd really suspected a trap, he wouldn't have come. He knew why I'd called him here. "You know. About the Conclave attack on the Academy of Sciences last week."

"And the one in Lahore two days later. Melbourne yesterday." He grinned at my gasp and leaned back, arms spreading across the back of the divan. "You didn't? Well, I suppose the latter two are secret facilities rather than publicly hosted events. I understand the respective governments are none too happy to discover the Argent Corporation had quasi-military holdings on their soil."

Who could blame them? I was pretty fucking displeased myself. Lahore. No wonder Sadakat had shot Abby down on Pakistan. And Abby had conceded. Because she knew.

"You didn't have anything to do with these attacks?"

"My dear champion. I'm lying low. For your safety, I might add. Lao Hu in particular seems very eager to exact vengeance against me for his imprisonment. Unless you fancy being batted around by an immortal tiger?" He grinned, and I considered that it couldn't be any worse than being smarmed at by an immortal dragon. "However, I suppose the removal of my protections in certain cities around the world did create opportunities for the Conclave to exploit. Would you sit? I'm getting a crick in my neck."

"Somehow, I doubt that." But I sat. "Why did

you even bother with protections?"

"Not for Argent's sake. Everything I did was done to protect my people. The sorts of activities the Shadow Dragon Triad was involved in tended to attract otherworldly attention."

"And now?"

"They're no longer my people. Tell me, how is Mei Shen faring?"

Protectiveness surged. I swallowed my reflexive *get bent* response. Somewhere along the way, I'd gained a bit of sense. "None of your business." Only a bit. "You said back in Shanghai that you might be willing to help me on occasion."

He snorted. Then laughed. Kept laughing so hard he doubled over with it. When he collected himself enough to raise his head, there were honest-to-god tears in his eyes. I'd missed my calling as a stand-up comedian.

He wiped the tears away with a gloved finger. "I meant in situations of your imminent demise. You're asking for my help?"

I gave a half-shrug. I'd come this far. Might as well eat the whole bowl of stupid. "I need help with the Shadow writing system. The... sigils. These things." I help up my handful of Post-Its. "At least enough to translate an Enochian summoning ritual."

The mirth drained away. "And just who do you aim to summon?"

I wondered if La Reina's ritual might be strong

enough to summon and bind Lung Di properly. I doubted it. If he could create wards strong enough to dissuade the Conclave from his territory and keep them from crossing over the veil with impunity, he'd have protections in place against being at the beck and call of every sorcerer with a bit of chalk and charcoal.

Or Sharpie and Post-Its.

"Nobody you know." At his raised brow, I sighed and relented. "A thief. She's a djinni–"

"Ah. I think I know the one of which you speak." He waved a hand before I could speak. "She has no claim on any protection of mine. I'll help."

"J-just like that?" I knew better than to trust the surge of relief. Finally, I was getting somewhere. But I mistrusted that there was no associated cost.

"Of course." His grin was too sharp, all teeth and narrowed eyes. "You had fifteen years under my brother's tutelage. I would say that it is about time I picked up the slack, wouldn't you?"

SEVEN
To Catch a Thief

The first thing I did after Lung Di left – with a promise to send me what I needed to translate La Reina's ritual – was confirm that Abby was still waiting for me and that no unusual amount of time had passed. My experience with Jian Huo had left me just a bit paranoid about losing time where dragons were concerned.

My second thing was to ream Abby a new one. "You don't keep shit like this from me."

"It wasn't my intel to share," she hissed, keeping her voice low as we argued at the top of the stairs leading down to the BART. "You're not Argent. You're not even who Argent thinks you are. And apparently you have sources that are better informed than most of our agents, so maybe I should be turning you over to those agents for questioning." She held up a hand at my growl. "I won't, but I hope you appreciate the tightrope I'm walking for you, Masters. I hate this divided loyalty bullshit."

I waited for a couple of young bar-trawling types to pass. They barely paid us any mind. "And I hate being lied to."

Abby sighed and kicked the stairwell railing. I was coming to learn that she kind of sucked at apologies. "Did your friend happen to mention what the Conclave is after?"

"No." And I was kicking myself for not asking. I'd caught Lung Di in a helpful mood, and I'd let my own paranoia squander it. Sure, maybe everything he told me was a monkey's paw in disguise. It was still useful information. "But you can bet there will be more attacks."

I fiddled with my Post-It notes. Something had been bothering me since I laid them down to summon Templeton. I considered laying them out again in the hopes it would nudge the discomfort into a full-fledged thought, but out here on the street, that would be courting stupidity. I'd already pushed my luck twice tonight. I ripped up the Post-Its before I could be tempted to a third. I'd burn them once I was home.

"I need to report back to Sadakat. Any idea how long you'll need?"

"A few days. I'll let you know when I have a better idea." Like when Lung Di's promised help arrived.

"Fine. Okay. I'll wait for your call." Abby shoved her hands in the pocket of her coat and headed down the stairs. I stared at the confetti in my hands.

What would keep the Conclave from attacking after the sigils were in place? What would keep other Shadow denizens from wandering through the thinned veil like the kraben had in my apartment?

"Hey, kid!" Abby's call chased away the thought before I could catch it.

"What?" I snapped. Granted, I'd been a kid when we first met, but thanks to my lost years in China, we were now roughly the same age. I hated the way "kid" made me Luke Skywalker to her Han Solo.

She gave me a lopsided grin worthy of Harrison Ford. "Don't look so glum. At least you're not bleeding out. I'd say we're one up from the last time we were here."

"Yeah. Thanks." I thought about Templeton's lie and Lung Di's helpfulness. "I've got a bad feeling about this," I muttered, and headed home.

My bad feeling only increased as the days passed. Lung Di's help arrived in the form of a leatherbound book, a pair of cotton gloves, and a terse note that just said "Use them." Little wonder why. The book's pages were brittle animal hide, the inks faded in some places and a little too animated for my comfort in others.

Shimizu decamped for an ex-girlfriend's. "I'd rather deal with Sheila's particular brand of crazy than the Necronomicon over there," she said, giving me a buss on the temple.

"It'll only be for a few days," I said. If it weren't for the free rent, I'd be the crappiest roommate alive.

"Uh-huh. Just remember: Klaatu Barada Nikto."

I grimaced at her as she departed for safer couches.

The quiet helped the translation go more quickly, as it should. Turning off all the lights and working by the glow of my laptop also helped, which shouldn't have been the case, but thoughts and connections just seemed to flow better in the dark.

It had been the same when I'd learned the Shadow speech. My grandfather had spoken it to me growing up the way other people spoke Spanish or Chinese to their kids to help with language acquisition. And I had never thought it strange because to me it was just another language. Albeit one that was best spoken at night, in dark places.

There were many things about my upbringing that were only strange in retrospect.

I texted Abby when the ritual was translated and got the almost immediate response to bring it and Mr Mystic to her office the following day. Which was how I found myself spending my Saturday in a cramped classroom on Berkeley's campus with an avenging angel, an even-more-avenging archaeologist, and a soft-spoken theurge who was probably a lot scarier than she let on, but knew how to make a damned fine cuppa.

"Very kind of you," I murmured to Sadakat as

she filled up my cup from the pot before returning to our task. According to La Reina, the translation I'd done wasn't enough. We needed the nodes. And not just any nodes, but the ones with the greatest impurity in the metal and therefore the strongest resonance with our quarry. We'd broken into work pairs – myself with Abby and Sadakat with La Reina. Abby and Sadakat would hold one of Abby's collected pieces of junk, and La Reina or myself would focus power into it. Shadow, in my case, which amounted to little more than pulling the shadows over it as I did with my face to disguise my features. La Reina held her hands above each piece like she was placing a blessing on it, until the piece seemed to glow with an internal light. Whatever she channeled, it made my shoulders itch and my mouth run dry, hence my need for copious amounts of tea.

The next part was even more arcane to me. Abby would hold her piece with her eyes closed, finger pads running lightly over the metal. Then she would scowl, set it aside, and give it a ranking on the whiteboard we were using to track the process. The scowl, I suspected, was not necessary to her analysis. However, I couldn't begin to fathom how she was determining her rankings.

Abby's approach was less baffling than Sadakat's. She would raise each blessed piece to her mouth and press her tongue to it.

"It is rather like testing a battery for power,"

she explained early on in the process after I'd cast several curious glances her way. "I do not have Professor Trent's sensitivity. This one is a five." She set aside the candle snuffer, smacked her lips together, and made a face. "I believe I will make tea."

We worked mostly in silence. There were nearly a hundred artifacts to go through, and after the first pass, we had to begin the winnowing process.

"We'll need seven. One for each of San Francisco's hills," La Reina said when we'd settled on twenty.

"We're using the hills?" I asked, thinking of the diagrams and sigils I'd translated. The scale was... daunting, to say the least. "Isn't that rather spread out?"

La Reina blessed another artifact, a copper kettle that had Sadakat making more of a face than usual after she'd licked it. "We will use the model on the rooftop of the Academy. It has sympathetic resonance with both the city and with our thief."

"And that will draw her and contain her there?" Abby asked, setting aside a rusty iron horseshoe. She'd opted for the pieces that looked generally unlickable.

"There or Rome." La Reina smiled. Sadakat giggled. Abby and I exchanged a confused look. La Reina sighed and shrugged, her wings rustling and resettling over the back of her chair. "Sorry. Religious humor."

"How do you propose to convince Ms Asha to

assist once she has been caught?" I asked.

Abby's fists tightened around the lead plumb-bob I was drawing shadow around. "Oh, I've got a few ideas."

"I will be drawing up a contract with fair terms," La Reina said, giving Abby a quelling look.

"A contract." I let doubt color those words.

"It will be binding. As contracts with my kind are."

Her kind. I couldn't keep from looking at the wings. It was all I could do to keep from reaching out and touching them. I wondered if they would burn me.

The soft music of Sadakat's smartphone saved me from making a fool of myself. La Reina's echoed it a moment later.

"There has been another attack. São Paolo," Sadakat said. For Abby's and my benefit, I assumed. La Reina was already rising, pulling on the backless leather duster that made her look like a character from a Tarantino film.

"We'll finish here," Abby said, rising and following the women to the doorway. "Be safe."

"That has not been a concern to this point. They attack with speed, not violence," La Reina snapped. I flinched at how dismissive she sounded at Abby's concern. "If past experience holds, they will have already left with what they came for."

Sadakat's response fell into the silence following the *snap-whump* of La Reina's wings as she stalked away. "We will take care, Professor Trent. We should be back in a day or two."

"We'll be ready," Abby said.

We re-tested several more pieces before I dared give in to curiosity. "La Reina does not seem to like you very much."

"Well. I am an atheist."

Cognizant of the symbolic irony, I handed her a tin can – worms not included. "Does that imply that she really is… what she appears to be? Or that she merely believes she is."

Abby's laugh echoed in the empty classroom. "Masters, you do *not* want to fall down that theological rabbit hole. Believe me. If only for what it implies about you and me." She studied the closed door as though she could still see the two women standing there. "Sadakat believes she's the real deal."

"And yet they seem friendly with each other."

Abby's searching look focused on me. "Why shouldn't they?"

"Because… well…" I mimed the flow of Sadakat's hijab, already feeling rather stupid in my assumptions.

A stupidity Abby confirmed. "Abrahamic religions. They believe in the same god. Sadakat's more likely to get in trouble for her magical practice than her association with an angel, though there are interpretations of the Qur'an that allow for it as long as it is used to fight evil. I think working with

La Reina helps her justify herself."

"Of course. My mistake." I poked through the collection of our top twenty, pulling out the ones Sadakat had evaluated. Something about the conversation, about Abby's irritation and curt responses, failed to sit easily with me. There was something more. Something I was missing. I took a shot in the dark.

"Were you and La Reina–?"

"Complicated," Abby snapped, then just as quickly leaned back in her chair, groaning and rubbing her eyes. "We were... complicated. You wouldn't understand."

Bullseye. I clutched the copper kettle in my lap. "Actually, I think I might have some familiarity with that particular flavor of complicated." Congressing with perhaps-gods from a tradition you weren't a part of... Abby and I could form a support group of two.

She shook her head and took the kettle from me. "I don't think that's likely."

"Mm. Ask me about my ex sometime. At least you don't have kids."

"No," Abby murmured, closing her eyes to feel out the resonance. "I just have Asha."

I waited until she was done feeling over the kettle. I suspected she took longer than necessary because she knew I was waiting. When she finally put the kettle in the "yes" pile, I said, "It strikes me that I've asked you several times about your history with Asha, and you have avoided answering."

Abby's hand hovered over an iron spearhead and a lumpy gold cup with what looked like bee-women on it. She opted for neither. "And I'm not answering now. Not when you're being like this."

It took me several moments to comprehend her meaning. Most times, I didn't think of myself as an act anymore. "Ah," I said. I rose and locked the door before removing my hat. I left my wig in place, but I banished the shadows around my face and relaxed from my formal posture into something far more casual. My neck popped when I swiveled my head in an indulgent circle, which helped. Mitchell wasn't really the neck-popping sort. "Better?" I asked, accent somewhere between before and after.

Abby chuckled and leaned back in her chair. "Yeah."

"So?"

"She's my sister."

That, I hadn't expected. "What?"

"Half."

It only took a moment for the math to catch up with my surprise. "So does that mean you're a–"

"Yeah. On my father's side. Mom's a research librarian at Bryn Mawr."

I sank back into my chair, smoothing non-existent bumps from my fedora. "How'd that happen?"

Abby traced an old doodle on the edge of the desk. "The usual. Back in her undergrad days,

Mom had a fling with a hot international student. He went home. She raised me alone. When I graduated from high school, I decided to try to get in touch with him. Found Asha instead."

I peered at her. "And instantly hated her guts?"

Abby gave me a startled look. "Huh? No. She was the cool older sister I never had. I deferred admittance to go stay with her in Bangalore. We traveled all through India. That's how I fell into archaeology. All those sites. All that history. And it was mine."

"And your father?"

"We met. I thought he didn't like me. What he actually didn't like was me traveling with Asha. Or rather, Asha using the stupid American college student as cover for a year-long thieving spree." Abby rolled her head back, studied the ceiling. "Asha pissed off a lot of people that year. And so did I, though I had no idea at the time." She grimaced. "Americans, you know? Fucking tourists. Anyways, trouble caught up with us. Our father intervened. Asha and I got away. He… didn't."

"How do you mean?" I asked, though I suspected I knew.

"He got himself carried in to where we were being held hostage, rolled in this old carpet that had metal threads through it. Silver and gold. Asha dragged me through. He got trapped when he tried to follow. Resonance built up after too much prolonged contact. Helluva way to find out you're half-Djinn, huh?" She shrugged and went back to shuffling artifacts around when my appalled expression refused to give way to anything approaching humor. "Well, it was for me."

"Abby, I–"

"What about you?"

I wasn't surprised by the subject change. That sort of confidence required a bit of time to process. But I wasn't sure why she'd decided to change the topic to me. "What about me?"

"Oh come *on*, Masters. You are the poster child for fucked up family relations. Or you would be, if anyone knew who you were. What about your family? I assume you didn't spring fully grown from your grandfather's head. What happened to your mother? Your father?"

When had this become share time? I straightened the band on my hat and wished Sadakat and La Reina hadn't left. Fucking São Paolo. "My grandfather never knew who my father was, and my mother died when I was born. My grandfather raised me. He's the only one I talk about because he's the only one I had."

Which was both true and not true. Johnny was my family. Doris Han and her brood. Jian Huo had become my family. And there were my kids. I jammed my hat back on my head and then had to fix the resulting dent. "Satisfied?"

"Not really. You never wondered? What your mom was like, what happened to your dad. He could still be out there, you know."

I suspected a bit of transference on Abby's part – absent fathers and all that – which was the only reason I didn't shut the conversation down. I sat a little straighter, let the shadows creep back over my face. "No, I never wondered. Of the two who might still be out there, I'm more inclined to be concerned about Mitchell."

Abby wouldn't let me retreat. She snatched the hat from my head and held it out of reach. "That's weird. You know that's weird, right."

I scowled at her, but I refused to play keep-away. "Look, it was always my grandfather and me. He talked about my Grandma Anne more than he talked about my mother or father. It never… it just wasn't important. By the time I realized it was something that mattered to other people, my grandfather was gone and I had bigger shit to worry about."

"No. No, that is not how this works." Abby threw my hat back at me. "I grew up without a parent. Everything reminds you of that lack. The stories you read, the stuff in movies and on TV. Star Wars and Harry Potter and every Disney movie ever fucking made about kids with lost parents. The other kids at school and parent-teacher night and Daddy-and-me dances. I'm not saying a two-parent home is necessary or better in any way. I'm just saying that when you grow up without one, the world makes sure you know you're missing something. And you care."

My jaw had tightened during her rant to the point where my teeth ached with clenching. Deep breathing kept me from trembling, but the unsteadiness escaped with every breath. I couldn't find the words to answer her around the rush of blood to my face and ears. I stood, and that seemed to help as much as the deep breathing had.

"I know what happened to my mother. She died. I couldn't care less what happened to my father or my grandfather. They left. I think we're done here."

Abby left off glaring at me to look at the final collection. "Yeah. Fine. I can finish up on my own."

"Then I will meet you at the Academy whenever Sadakat and La Reina return." Donning my hat and pulling the shadows back around my face, I quit the room. The loud clacking of my heels on the hallway formica was an unsatisfying vent to my anger.

Several days passed before I got a text from Abby letting me know that everything was ready. The California Academy of Sciences was dark when I arrived on the appointed night of our ritual, no yellow crime scene tape to be seen, but a pall lingered. The veil still felt thin here, the darkness thick as velvet. I wriggled my fingers and could almost feel it against my pads like the softness of cat fur.

Abby and two agents waited for me by the front entry. "Old Man," she said. We hadn't spoken since our conversation about families, and it seemed we weren't going to speak of it now. "This is Agent Fuller. Agent Byrd. They're in charge of security. They're having a field day up there. Take us up, Fuller."

The more baby-faced of the two agents – Byrd – frowned. "We'll need some sort of identification."

"Gimme your flashlight." Abby took it from the agent and shone it in my face. I refrained from flinching away. The shadows around my face were more than enough to withstand the glare of a flashlight. Fuller also managed not to flinch, though Byrd didn't exhibit such self-control. Abby handed the flashlight back to him. "Proof enough?"

"Yes, ma'am." Fuller led us through the atrium and up the main stairwell. The displays from the Argent exhibit had been cleared out, even the model of the *Kestrel* and the fountain of clacking pins. The only light came from the rainforest dome, a soft blue glow that fluttered occasionally with the passing of birds and butterflies.

After the quiet of the building below, the activity on the rooftop was jarring. Floodlights lit the observation platform and the faces of the seven model hills. The grass covering those hills was a bit wilted from all the people tramping over them to set up more lights and cables and pedestals atop every hill with the nodes we'd selected from Abby's collection.

No wonder Argent had trouble attracting qualified

magic practitioners. My solitary translation in a darkened room was the proper environment for such workings. This circus... was not.

I spotted Sadakat first, her shell-pink hijab standing out from all the dark suits. Abby and I made our way to her side. "You have to dismiss all of these people, or this won't work," I said.

She cast me a rueful sidelong glance and a tired smile. "I know. I have told them this. But our security heads are insistent, and they have some legitimate concerns after Lahore, Melbourne, São Paolo, and Johannesburg."

"Johannesburg?"

Sadakat grimaced. "There was another attack last night."

I bit my inner lip to keep from cursing. Stupid. I was so stupid. Lung Di had warned me. I'd watched Sadakat and La Reina take off to deal with São Paolo, and it still hadn't occurred to me that I had tools at my disposal. "I have a set of sigils that might help ward against these attacks. I'll give them to you after we're done here. Where's La Reina?"

Sadakat looked up. "Patrolling. If our actions invite another incursion, she'll be more useful than this entire lot, no matter how well trained they are."

I nodded. Nobody could be trained for something like this. "How much weight do I have to bring to bear here?"

Sadakat's brows raised, and some of the

exhaustion lifted from her eyes and shoulders. "Mr Masters, where Shadow is concerned, you are the proverbial eight hundred-pound gorilla."

"Excellent. You lot!" I raised my voice and pointed at... everyone, really. I swept my arm to include the agents fiddling with the cables leading to the floodlights. "All of you. Finish whatever critical task you're about and then leave."

"Mr Masters." Agent Fuller exchanged a look with the agent he'd been conferring with – I recognized her as the young woman with the crush on Skyrocket. "The Academy has requested these security precautions to avoid another incident. Our presence is a requirement for our use of this facility."

"And your absence is a requirement of my assistance. Go. All of you." When he hesitated, I tipped my hat. "Or I can go. It makes no nevermind to me." I headed for the stairs.

"No, wait." Fuller's outstretched hand closed into a fist when he realized I'd backed him into acquiescence. He exchanged a few more words with his associate, and she left to round up the other agents.

In very little time, the rooftop was cleared of everyone but myself, Abby, and Sadakat.

"Old Man, some days I could just kiss you," Abby said into the descending quiet.

"I do hope you'll manage to restrain yourself, professor," I murmured in reply, watching a gold-lit figure descend, the tails of her duster rising with the currents caused by her churning wings. La Reina landed on the edge of the platform and came to join us.

"The area is clear," she said. "The veil is thin, but I don't sense demons amassing on the other side. You?" She gave me an expectant look. Accepted my nod with one of her own. "We'll summon the fire demon at the convergence of the seven nodes and the four quarters. That should contain her until we can secure her cooperation."

"You're certain this contract is binding? That she'll abide by the terms?" I murmured. From what little I knew about Asha, she didn't seem the sort to keep her word or follow the rules.

La Reina plucked a feather from her wing – one of the long flight feathers, gold-tipped and easily the length of my forearm. Jaw tense, she set the feather in the center of the geomantic diagram the Argent agents had crafted out of tape and chalk. "If she does not wish to permanently join my Host, she will. Let us begin."

La Reina's ritual was very different from the sorts of ceremonies I'd become accustomed to during my years in China. The numerology in particular had me cringing as she called the four quarters and invoked the protection of the four archangels as represented by the four elements and four and four and four.

"Not inspiring of confidence," I muttered as

I initiated my portion of the ritual. I chalked my translated sigils along the taped lines of the seven-pointed star that connected the seven hills and the seven bits of metallic junk that we had deemed most resonant with our quarry. According to Sadakat, their combined resonance would create a prison that Asha wouldn't be able to escape from without trapping herself permanently in one of the artifacts.

Assuming we were able to call her to our location in the first place.

"Turn off the floodlights," I instructed when I was done with the sigils. The lights flickered out, leaving us bathed only in the ambient orange glow of the city. I took my position in the north quarter, waited for my three associates to take theirs, and began reciting the verbal translation of La Reina's Enochian summoning ritual. I went slowly so as not to stumble over the Shadow speech. Shimizu's *Klaatu Barada Nikto* was forefront in my thoughts. I was *not* going to foul this up with a stupid pronunciation error.

The darkness around us thickened, grew heavier, taking on the cat-fur feel I'd sensed on the ground level. The ambient light receded. In the east and west, Abby and Sadakat shifted uncomfortably. Across from me in the south, La Reina held herself still and ready, only the sound of the breeze ruffling her feathers differentiating her from a statue. I rubbed the pads of my fingers against my thumb and continued reciting.

As I spoke the last syllable, something crackled along the tape lines, a quick *buzz-snap*! like the charge of an active bug zapper. I held still, searching the darkness as I knew the others could not. Except for a faint smoke that rose from the tape lines and smelled of ozone, I didn't see anything out of place.

"You said this would only work if she was in the Shadow Realms?" I asked La Reina.

She nodded. She, too, was looking around, wings raising and taking on a soft glow that was still too bright for me to look at. "We will have to try again later and hope she didn't sense this attempt."

"You didn't mention that was a danger," Abby said, enunciating each word with the care of the supremely pissed off.

La Reina's wings rustled and dimmed as she shrugged. "It is always a danger, especially with a trained practitioner, as I suspect she must be."

I looked around again. Granted, I had no idea what a successful ritual was supposed to feel like, but that bug-zapping charge hadn't felt like failure.

"Your chalk," I whispered to Sadakat. "Give it to me."

She cast me a puzzled look, but she handed over the chalk without argument. In the center of our circle, I scrawled out the string of sigils that had gotten us into this mess. The moment I chalked the final diacritical, I reached through the non-existent veil, grabbed what lurked on the other side, and pulled with all my might.

I emerged with a squirming armful. Nails raked at my face, knocked my hat askew. A braid thick as a rope whipped against my shoulder.

"Abby," I grunted. "*Someone*. Grab her. I need to close the veil."

Asha's struggling form was dragged from my grasp. I used my coat to smudge out the first set of sigils, then scrabbled for the chalk to scrawl a second set outside the boundaries of our circle, setting down the counter-ward so that she couldn't flee the way she'd come.

I sank back on my haunches, breathing heavily. My hat appeared before me. I looked up. Abby held it out to me, grinning wide enough to split her face.

"I owe you one, Old Man. We got her."

"This isn't getting us anywhere," Abby growled after an hour of Sadakat and La Reina explaining Asha's situation to her and the requirements for her freedom. Asha sat in the center of our seven-pointed binding, turning La Reina's feather over and over in her hand. She had met those explanations with silent composure, her gaze never leaving Abby.

And Abby, who had agreed to let cooler heads try to prevail, was finally losing patience with that steady gaze. She and I stood in the shadows at the edge of the observation platform, but that didn't seem to prevent Asha from noticing Abby's growing agitation. Every time Abby shifted position, Asha's full lips tightened with the hint of a smirk. When I placed a restraining hand on Abby's arm in response to her low growl, one of Asha's perfectly drawn brows lifted.

That seemed to do it for Abby. She shook off my hold and stalked forward, careful not to break the chalk-and-tape outline that seemed all that was necessary to keep Asha contained. "Forget it. Both of you. She's not going to do anything for us unless it's me doing the asking. Are you?"

"Professor Trent," Sadakat traded a wary glance with La Reina, "I do not think that it is wise for you to lead the negotiations, given your feelings regarding our guest." Both women frowned at me as though I'd failed in my job to keep Abby in check.

"Are you?" Abby repeated, glaring at Asha.

Finally, there was movement in the circle. Asha rose to her feet, twirling La Reina's feather like a child's toy. "Why should I agree to anything? You cannot hold me in this circle indefinitely. Not when we're in such a public place. And even if you could manage it, surely one of you might grow a conscience and question the ethics of such unlawful detainment." Her eyes passed over all of us, seemed to rest just a bit longer on me than on the others. Her taunting words hit home, my pragmatic side warring with the larger part of me that cared about things like due process. The only thing that kept me from smudging out the chalk sigils binding her was the knowledge that she'd known about the attack and used it as cover for her own illegal activities. She'd embroiled herself in this of her own free will.

Pragmatic rationalization. It's a skill.

"One of us might," I said. "If we did not all feel that we were offering you a fair and simple alternative to a messier and more prolonged legal process. You'll be freed once you agree to assist Argent's agents in recovering their stolen technology from the Conclave."

"Mr Mystic, you don't know the Conclave as well as you should if you think that is a fair and simple alternative. I might be better off trying my chances with your legal system. I'd definitely be better off as cannon fodder in the Host's army."

"You won't be," La Reina said, and the hardness of her tone made me shiver.

Asha took a step back. The smile she turned on Abby was brittle, lacking the confidence of her previous smirks. "All this for... what did you call it? A bit of stolen tech?" The smile widened when Abby flinched. "Really Abby? Is that really your wish? Is that really how you want to spend your one chance to make me do whatever you want? To give you whatever you want?"

"Shut up." Abby's voice trembled. "You don't have what I want."

"No. But I know where it is. I know who has it. Our father trapped, all this time..."

I must have gasped when I realized what she was talking about, what I suspected she was offering Abby to betray us. The carpet their father was trapped in. Asha's glance flicked to me. "And I believe I even know how we might–"

"Shut. Up." Abby's hand went to her side.

"Abigail!" I caught her elbow before her revolver cleared her holster. "You need to step away. Now."

"Let go of me, Masters," she growled. Not Old Man. Masters. She was talking to the person behind Mr Mystic. Which was fair. I wasn't sure Mitchell would have stopped her.

"Keep your weapon holstered, professor," I said.

Abby's muscles tensed, and she tested my grip a few more moments before relaxing and ducking her head.

"I wouldn't have shot her, you know," she grumbled. "No matter how fucking annoying she is, she's still family."

"Yes," I murmured. "And you only shoot strangers, as I recall."

"Fuck you, Old Man."

I glanced warily at Asha. If she'd been serious about the offer she'd made, then it was no wonder she looked unaccountably smug. Given everything that Abby had told me... "Abby, if she knows where that carpet is–"

"She doesn't know jack or shit," Abby snapped. I flinched back. "And even if she did, fuck her if I'm going to let her use that to get out of this. I'll find it some other way."

Shoving her way past La Reina and Sadakat, past the tape-and-chalk circle, Abby grabbed Asha by the back of the neck and slammed her to the ground. "Here's how it's going to be. You are going to sign La Reina's fucking contract, or I am going to wring your goddamned neck and nobody is going to care."

I hesitated on the edge of the ritual markings, appalled and helpless to do anything. "Abby, stop."

"Stay out of this." Abby pressed her knee into Asha's back, grinding her cheek into the trampled ground. "You will sign that contract. Got it?"

Asha clawed behind her head at Abby's forearms, eyes wide and white, feet kicking against the pavement. "Got it," she croaked.

Abby released her neck, but only to grab her braid at its base. She held Asha like a recalcitrant dog and shoved the feather into her hands. Hesitantly, Sadakat unrolled a thick length of golden parchment. Asha didn't even read it – how could she, with Abby jerking her head about by the braid? My niggling unease blossomed into full-fledged nausea as I watched Asha scrawl her name with the golden feather and did nothing to stop it.

"There. It's done. She's ours until this is finished." Abby shoved Asha to one side and stalked past the three of us to the stairwell. "I'll have Fuller round up the crew to start the cleanup."

Several moments passed in quiet and stillness.

La Reina and Sadakat watched the stairwell where Abby had disappeared. Asha sat in the center of the circle, head bowed, hands clasped to the back of her neck. A distant siren from somewhere outside the park broke our tableau. La Reina kicked the tape line, breaking it. Sadakat retrieved the fallen feather and rolled up the signed contract. Asha stood and sauntered out of the broken circle with a dignity that seemed as fragile as a soap bubble. Unnoticed, perhaps forgotten, by the others, I backed into the shadows behind one of the extinguished floodlights. The discomfort raised by the presence of shadow creatures was nothing to the sickness I felt now as I considered the full extent of the violence I'd just witnessed and the violation I'd just participated in.

EIGHT
Balancing Act

I escaped the Academy while everyone else was still busy with Asha. I spent several hours wandering Golden Gate Park, past the rose gardens and the tea gardens and the botanical gardens before meandering up to the bison paddock. I came out the other end between two of the windmills and turned north. The Pacific Ocean was a night-dark shadow to my left: all sound and darkness. I wandered past the ruins of the Sutro Baths and along the cliff leading to Land's End. The taffy-twisted boughs of California cypress supported evergreen thunderheads. Fog drifted through the tree breaks in sheets unwinding, dampening the city noise and traffic. The only sounds here were the rush and flow of the ocean and the lowing of a foghorn. Sometimes, I have difficulty telling the difference between the real world landscapes and the sorts of strange places you can stumble across in the Shadow Realms.

I meandered until I reached the shelf that held the rocky remnants of the Land's End Labyrinth. I'd been so disappointed the first time I'd come here with my grandfather. I'd been expecting David Bowie levels of awesome, not an ankle-high rock spiral covering an area no bigger than my local Starbucks.

It was just what I needed now, though. I paced the maze like a mandala, going over each step of my fall. My actions had all seemed so reasonable in the moment. I saw a chance to see my son, so I accepted Argent's invitation to the exhibit, all the while knowing that they weren't the friendly face they showed to the world. The shadows attacked a public place, and I thought, who better than Mr Mystic to investigate and assist? Abby needed my help, and didn't I owe her for… what? Shooting me? Not selling out my true identity to Argent? Each time I hit an obstacle, I took it as my cue to try harder rather than a hint that I might want to consider whether I should be trying at all. Going to Lung Di should have been a glaring red flag that I was straying far afield, but it had proved so very effective.

Idealism is just a series of compromises waiting to happen, he'd told me in Shanghai. I thought again of Asha's fear as Abby pinned her to the ground – a trapped woman. Afraid. Violently forced into a magically binding contract for no better reason than that her skillset was necessary. The justification that she'd deserved it for being in the wrong place at the wrong time made me ill all over again. I'd done that. I'd forced her into compliance, as surely as Abby, La Reina, or Sadakat. The road to hell looked remarkably like the past few weeks.

I found my way to the center of the labyrinth and sat on the rocky ground, not caring about the damage to my trousers. I rolled a pebble under my fingers and told myself that my clammy skin and shivers were due to the drifting fog and not my own self-disgust. I listened to the rumble of the surf at the bottom of the cliff, when I could hear it over the rush of blood through my head.

When the ground beneath me shifted, I assumed at first it was the product of a truck passing by. Until I recalled that I was easily a half mile from any road big enough for a truck. And then the shifting increased, a staggered back and forth strong enough that it would have knocked me over if I hadn't been sitting.

I don't know what self-destructive instinct prompted me to look across the veil when I should have been scrambling to find more solid ground than an erosion-prone ocean cliffside. But look I did and immediately regretted it.

If the Shadow Realms are an ever-present nightmare lurking just behind corners and under overhangs, the Voidlands are a place of mind-twisting wrongness. That's what lay just across the fog-thin veil. The Voidlands pressed against the

veil, against the land on both sides, powerful as a
tidal wave, insidious as an invasive root system. It
was the cause of the earthquake, seeping into the
cracks of the real world and thrusting them apart
like some eldritch horror version of frakking. From
somewhere far off – I couldn't be sure if it was in
the Shadow Realms or the real world – came the
creaking groan of shifting metal. I glanced north,
where the Golden Gate loomed in a dizzying double
image. In the real world, the span was shrouded in
thick fog, only the rust-red towers visible above it.
In the shifting border between the Voidlands and
the Shadow Realms, the bridge burned the mottled,
murky gold of its namesake. Black splotches broke
off from the leading edge of the Voidlands and
attached themselves to the cables and towers,
seeming to consume the bridge, to overwhelm it.
And then a light shone from somewhere further
east, siphoning off the darkness. The bridge flared
bright enough to burn my eyes, bright as La Reina's
wings. The void splotches seared away, leaving
only wispy smoke behind. The Voidlands retreated
out to sea, and I was left looking into the Shadow
Realms once more. They seemed almost friendly in
comparison.

I rubbed my face. Forced my senses to focus on
the real world. The earthquake had passed. I wasn't
certain how long it had lasted, how bad it had been. I
had to get home, check on Shimizu, find Mei Shen.
I'd been so busy faffing around with Argent that

I'd ignored her warnings about pending disaster. I hadn't bothered to follow up on my puzzlement as to why the Conclave would want Argent's tech in the first place, or what Lung Di's protections had been protecting us from.

I stumbled to my feet, turned about, trying to figure out how to retrace my steps to the entrance of the labyrinth. I'd been so focused on getting to the center that I hadn't paid attention to where I was going or how to get out. I stood a long time, irritated at the metaphor for being too on-the-nose.

"Fuck this," I muttered, pulling out my cell phone and tramping a straight line across the furrows until I reached the edge.

Jack was kind enough to pick me up at the Legion of Honor parking lot, and even kinder not to mention the early morning hour. The earthquake had woken him, though it wasn't nearly as bad as it had seemed – low fours, that was all. That was enough to unnerve me. Foreshocks. We'd had three of them that I knew of. How much worse would they get?

Jack took me to his place and fed me pancakes, loaned me a Giants t-shirt and green froggy flannel bottoms. He merely nodded when I told him that Mr Mystic was going to ground for a while, and that he should refuse all requests for contact.

"Missy," he said softly as I was climbing out the window and onto his roof. "Just… don't run away again."

I gave him a tired smile. It did seem like running away was becoming a pattern with me. "I'm not running away. Only a bit of a regroup."

"In that case, just remember you have friends."

Friends. I surrounded myself with them over the next several days. Shimizu came back from Sheila's couch, though she threatened to make it a pit stop on her way back to Iowa when I told her the earthquake thing might be a developing issue leading to the Big One. At least I could assure her that Lung Di's Shadownomicon was locked away in the garage and sigil-warded to a fare-thee-well until I could figure out how to return it.

Shimizu's departure should have been another hint that I was losing the plot. I buried myself in mundanity and minutiae as I struggled to regain my bearings. I read Patrick's most recent chapter draft for his dissertation, went to a Bawdy Tales night with Vess and Andrew, helped Mason and Luis price wedding venues, and put in double hours on our house maintenance day because I'd skipped the last one for superhero stuff. I visited the bridge and even took a peek across the veil while I was there, but the Voidlands seemed to have been burned back to a sullen roiling far off the coast.

At my instruction, Jack forwarded the warding sigils and my polite regrets to Sadakat. He informed me that, after a few calls, things went silent on Argent's end. I didn't hear from Abby on either my cell or Mystic's burner.

"I know you're shaken up by what went down at the Academy, but you can't keep not-doing anything," Johnny said during our Friday afternoon one-on-one. He'd taken me down for the third time with the same leg sweep, and I still hadn't worked out how to anticipate it or block it. There had to be a way, I knew. Johnny didn't hammer home an attack unless I already had the tools to counter it.

"I know," I said, kipping up to my feet. "But I'm not going to keep flailing blindly. I need to figure out the right action before I start acting."

We bowed and settled into stance. It was my turn to attack. I led with a series of quick feints. Johnny danced back, caught my foot when I tried to follow up with a front kick. I relaxed and pivoted with the movement's flow when he twisted my leg. He lost his grip and I rolled to my feet–

– And went down again from that same leg sweep.

"You should consider doing that on the mat as well." Johnny reached down a hand to help me up. I took it, but then knelt rather than standing for another round of Rock 'Em, Sock 'Em Missy.

I closed my eyes, running through each time Johnny had taken me down. Johnny knelt across from me, giving me time to work it out.

Sort of. I had the chattiest sifu known to man. "Why did you start helping Argent in the first place?" he asked

I shrugged, and then followed the movement into rolling my shoulders. I was so damned tight these days. Maybe I could wheedle a massage out of Vess when I got home. "It was a shadow attack, and shadow's my thing. I saw a nail, and I was all 'I have a hammer! I have a hammer!'" I paused, glaring at his poorly contained smirk. "And no, the hammer is not my penis. Asshole."

"Hey, it was your metaphor." Johnny nudged my knee when I continued to glare at him. "C'mon. Grab your shoes. Let's walk."

I swapped my taiji slippers for my boots, pulled my coat on over my workout clothes, and followed Johnny down to the street.

"Is there actually a problem other than your desire to be a solution?" Johnny asked once we'd turned onto Grant. He nodded at the door hawkers outside the emporiums and received respectful bows in return. The sidewalks were fairly crowded – not even the events of the past six months could put much of a damper on tourist traffic on a sunny Friday afternoon in June – but the *laowai* tourists shied away from the overeager door shills. The crowds were here to gawk, not engage. Certainly not to be tricked into buying cheap trinkets. The tourists wanted authenticity. The shopkeepers wanted to make rent. Observing the disconnect made me twitchy; I was neither fish nor fowl. This was why I usually took back ways to the *kwoon*. Why had Johnny wanted to come out into this?

I stamped my feet as Johnny and I got caught behind cluster after cluster of amblers. Johnny shot me an amused look and wove through the crowds like magic. Probably was magic. Become a Chinatown Guardian; never get caught in foot traffic again. There were worse job perks. Too bad I wasn't descended from dragons.

I caught up with him further down the block, dodging a girl and her pet chow. At least it had given me time to consider his question. "The Voidlands seem to be encroaching. Which seems to be causing earthquakes. I'd say that's two pretty big problems. And recent, which means they're probably related to Lung Di's defenses falling apart, which is what Mei Shen was trying to warn me about. The Conclave is staging coordinated attacks on our world, that's... four? And I guess five would be: why? Who are they working with, what do they want, and why?"

"Any of that have much to do with Argent?" Johnny had led us down the hill to the Dragon Gate. The grey day dulled the gleam of the two guardian dragons topping the gate and the cinnabar pearl between them. A host of sparrows burst out from under the verdigris eaves, chased off by a larger feathered intruder. Tourists clustered around the weathered grey columns with their phones and selfie sticks and the occasional serious semi-pro kit. Someone had set their toddler atop the head of one of the guardian lions, which was causing a bit of a backup among the people waiting to take pictures. Despite her parents yelling at her, the crying child refused to make an acceptable face for posterity. I resisted the urge to lift the child down and tell the parents off. Everything I saw these past few days seemed like another reminder that it wasn't always my place to intervene.

"The sigils at the Academy were most likely placed by someone inside Argent. And someone with high clearance has to be feeding the Conclave intel on Argent bases, but mostly... no. I got so caught up in their stolen tech and its recovery that I forgot that was their priority, not mine. What are we doing here?"

"Teaching moment. You'll see." Johnny leaned up against one of the supporting columns on the backside of the gate where fewer photographers were jockeying for a good angle. Something snapped, a building tension in the air that I hadn't even noticed, releasing energy like the breaking of a rubber band. The tightness in my shoulders drained away, leaving me loose and limp. I glanced over at the other three columns. The girl with the chow was letting her dog sniff one of them. At another stood an old man with a bright green snake coiled under his collar and down his arm like a scarf. I was pretty sure if I scanned the eaves, I'd spot the red-tailed hawk that had chased away the sparrows. Johnny wasn't the only Guardian of Chinatown, but I'd never noticed the others out and about. I nodded at the snake and wasn't sure if the tongue flick that followed was meant as *hello* or *piss off*.

Someone took the toddler down and gave her a ring-pop for being such a good girl. The irritated crowd drifted away once they'd gotten their shots, replaced by new groups who were content to make goofball faces at their cameras.

I hurried to follow Johnny back the way we'd come. The crowds going up the hill were thinner. People were being lured into the shops. Chatting. Laughing.

Well shit. "What the hell was that?"

"Chi realignment. People living here. People coming here. They're all here for different reasons. Usually things flow and it all works out. Sometimes the system gets gunked up and needs a bit of a tune-up." Johnny flicked my ear. "Or did you think I was just around here to kick ass and take names?"

"Hell no. I thought you were just a pretty face to fuel fangirl moe." Which earned me another ear flick.

"Lung Di's protections against the Voidlands weren't the only ones in San Francisco, though they were the strongest. The other wards are picking up the slack, which means they're falling out of balance more quickly and need to be realigned on occasion."

I could feel that realignment, the shift in energy. In flow. The crowds moved more easily, without the stops and stalls from before. The door patter as we passed rose and fell like a melody brought back in tune. It baffled me how I'd missed it before.

"My balance was off. That's why you were able to take me down. Each time, you maneuvered me into some sort of roll because you knew when I came up, my balance would be off."

Johnny chuckled. "She can be taught."

I resisted making a face. I'd sort of deserved that. I followed him back up to his studio and grabbed my backpack. The kids for his Lil' Ninjas class had already started trickling in. Johnny went into teacher mode, accepting their bows, greeting the parents.

I caught his attention briefly on the way out. "If you happen to see Mei Shen, tell her I'm sorry. Tell her I'm ready to hear what she and Tsung have to say. That I'm ready to help."

Johnny winked at me. "I'll make sure she knows."

The kids waved at me as I headed out. They knew me; sometimes I stuck around to let Johnny use me as his demonstration dummy. I waved back, feeling lighter, happier than I had in days. I had something that might resemble a direction. I headed out to the main drag to enjoy the restored flow of Chinatown.

I walked home on autopilot, diverting through the alley behind the house because while the news vans had mostly given up, you never knew when some erstwhile paparazzo would get creative in his stalking.

I was so lost in my thoughts that I almost ran headlong into the woman lounging against our back gate.

"As – ah – ha… Hi." Fuck. I backed up a few steps and weighed my options: bolt or play it cool?

I sucked at playing it cool, but it was too late to bolt. "Can I help you?" I asked, as though strange Indian women made a habit of hanging out at my back gate. As though I didn't know her immediately. Stupid. She knew who I was. Had to. Why else would she be here, smiling at me as though she wished I was on fire so she could refuse to spit on me?

Asha tilted her head, one perfect brow arching. "Really? You're going to cling to the pretense?"

My hands formed fists in my pockets. "Abby told you?"

"Abby wouldn't tell me if I had a piece of spinach in my teeth. What makes you think she'd share your secrets?"

"Then…" Shit, had I given myself away?

"We met before, you and I. When you were Mistra? You made quite an impression, you and your little asura. When I saw Mr Mystic at the Academy… well, it is not that difficult to put this and that together." She waved a languid hand at me, at the house behind her. "There are only so many Shadowborn sorcerers in the world, and few so naturally gifted."

Shadowborn? I wanted to ask, but I was already

feeling doubly off-kilter. Doubly exposed. I didn't want to talk to her any longer than I had to. Certainly not out here in the open, and no way was I going to invite her into my house. I was still making things up to Shimizu for the last femme fatale intrusion.

"Look, Asha. I'm sorry. About the other night, about what we forced you into. If there is any way I can make it up to you. Any way I could undo it–"

Her laughter cut my apology short. "Oh dear, you mean Abby was right? Mr Mystic abandoned us because he felt guilty?"

Laugh she might, but I remembered her fear and fury. Just because she didn't seem to hold a grudge didn't make my actions right or righteous. I straightened my posture, pulled my hands from my pockets to let them hang loose at my sides, seeking balance in becoming a little bit more my grandfather. "I am not proud of my actions or their impact on you, and I felt it best to remove myself before I continued to act in a questionable manner."

"My goodness, you're as uptight as that Skyrocket fellow. They should team you two up. Get you a radio show. Something... old fashioned for the whole family." She pushed away from the fence, searching my expression for a reaction. "Does this mean you have no interest in the Conclave's agenda anymore? Not worried at all about what they took?"

"I'm concerned about their activities, but

Argent's problems are not my concern. Especially when I can't agree with their solutions."

"Hm. And if I told you I needed your help to fill the terms of my contract? The one you helped force me into?"

I studied my feet, the wide cracks in the old asphalt of the alleyway. I used to play lava monster out here, jumping from patch to patch and pretending to teeter at the edges, a moment of poor balance away from falling to my doom. "If there's something you need of me, forward the specifics to Mystic's lawyer and I will consider it."

Asha nodded, smile fading. "Fair enough. I promise I'll be circumspect about this rather silly ruse of yours."

The tightness in my shoulders relaxed a hair. "My thanks."

"Oh, it's not a kindness on my part. It's just more valuable to me as a secret." She stepped aside to let me pass, smiling at my scowl. "You know it's my own fault, getting this close to Argent. I was practically begging for Abby to come after me, all for some Ida Redbird pottery."

I flinched at the rape culture rhetoric. I'd been guilty of it myself; I could hardly take her to task for it. And there was nothing I could say about it that wouldn't earn me more mockery. "I hope this gives you and Abby a chance to work out your differences. Good day, Asha." I slipped through the gate and shut it on the echo of more laughter.

NINE
The Rock

Sunday found me testing my new resolution for a balanced approach as I climbed too high on a too-old wooden ladder to clean the cobwebs from the eaves of our front landing. Living in one of San Francisco's historic painted ladies was pretty awesome, but you had to take upkeep seriously or you'd start to skew a little too Addams Family. A perfectly harmless house spider had bungeed down to say hi to Shimizu the night before. I'd offered to take care of the issue as part of my ongoing penance.

A penance I might die for. The ladder rocked as I climbed another rung above the recommended safety step so that I could reach the corner furthest from the door. Forget running with scissors. My epitaph was going to read *Missy Masters: Her reach exceeded her grasp*.

The ladder steadied underneath me, which surprised me so much that I almost tumbled off it.

I dropped my duster and grabbed at the top step before I followed the duster's tumble over the porch railing to the pavement far below.

Mei Shen grimaced up at me in apology, both hands on the sides of the ladder. "Sorry. It looked like you were going to fall."

"It's okay. Heart attack's a more dignified way to go." Keeping my grip on the top step, I carefully climbed down to terrace firma. Then I tossed caution after my duster and pulled my daughter into a rib-crunching hug.

For once, she returned it just as hard instead of trying to squirm away.

"You spoke to Johnny?" I hadn't expected to see her, not this soon, and certainly not without Tsung attached to her side.

"Yeah." Now she squirmed. I let her go. "He can be really annoying. But I figured we had tickets, so…" She shrugged.

"Tickets?"

"Alcatraz? The ferry? Mother, we talked about it weeks ago."

I remembered her talking about it, though nothing of any plans. Still, I wasn't going to let this chance go because of an early-onset senior moment. "Right. I just thought… with everything… let me change?"

I stored the ladder and abandoned Mei Shen as a captive audience to Luis and his ever-thickening wedding plan album while I rinsed off and layered up. I'd never been to Alcatraz. It was another one of those things you only did when family came to town, which was on my not-so-much list. But everyone talked about how cold and windy it could be, even in summer. When Shimizu's parents visited for Christmas, her father couldn't stop repeating that he'd left Oskaloosa to escape weather like that. It had been fun to watch Shimizu laid low by Dad humor.

"So, what did happen with Argent?" Mei Shen asked after I'd rescued her and we'd set off down the hill toward Fisherman's Wharf.

I dug my hands in the pockets of my coat and told her everything I'd been up to since the Academy, leaving nothing out. Not the stuff I was certain Argent would want to keep classified, not the subjugation of Asha, not even my meeting with Lung Di.

And yet, strangely, it was the Lady who seemed to catch Mei Shen's attention.

"You're sure she's not a member of the Conclave?" Mei Shen asked as we boarded the ferry. The crowds were thick enough that we had to go to the open top deck to find two empty seats together at the back of the ferry. Even at dock, the wind whipped past us hard enough to pull hair loose from my French braid. It would be even worse out on open water. I resigned myself to eating my own hair for the rest of the day.

"Who can say? I only ever hear them talked about

as a nameless collective. I don't think so, though. She didn't seem fond of them, and Templeton... he serves the Conclave, but he was afraid of her. Why?"

Mei Shen rose up on one knee, watching with interest as we pushed away from the dock. "You know about uncle's fading protections. David and I are doing what we can to restore them, but I'm untrained and his blood is diluted by many generations. I've heard mention of this Lady, but it sounds like she's much more powerful than I'd been led to believe. If she doesn't like the Conclave..."

"The enemy of my enemy?"

"Exactly." Mei Shen went to the rail as we came about, leaning over it to watch the engines churn the water. The wind blew her hair across her face as we picked up speed.

I might have joined her, but the bump of the ferry over the choppy waters was making my breakfast sit funny. I pressed my hand to my belly, grateful to the wind for drying the clammy sweat from my face and neck. It only got worse as we headed further into the bay. I gripped the edge of my seat as if that could steady me against the rocking of the boat, and bit my tongue for pride because... really? I was getting seasick on a damned bay ferry?

Pride gave way to nausea before we were halfway across to Alcatraz. "Mei Shen. I... I have to go below." If I was going to puke, it was going to be over a porcelain god, not over the side of the ferry.

Mei Shen's excited grin died when she turned to look at me, and she helped me down to the latrine.

Given the boarding announcements' warning of rough waters, I shouldn't have been surprised that the ferry crew knew how to deal with my situation. An absolutely lovely young park ranger brought Mei Shen cool cloths for my face and bottled water for me to sip after I'd emptied my stomach. When we finally docked and the ferry stilled, he told me to take my time until the nausea passed.

"You're welcome to return on this ferry, but most folks like to rest up a bit if they have this bad a reaction. There's a cafe, and they have Dramamine at the park station. Might make for an easier trip back?"

"Thank you so much, Dylan," Mei Shen said, giving him a shy smile that was pure theater. Great. I was dying and my daughter was flirting.

"No worries. I'll check in on you once the ferry's clear."

Mei Shen's smile disappeared when Dylan left us. She prodded me upright and toward the gangplank.

I stopped halfway down the ramp. My nausea had returned in full measure, but the ferry was relatively still. This wasn't motion sickness. I planted my feet against Mei Shen's prodding like Old Bessie being led to the abattoir.

"Mei Shen, we have to leave." The little dock and entry plaza looked perfectly safe. The most dangerous thing about it was the seagulls stalking tourists for whatever food they could snatch away. A knot of people clustered around the souvenir kiosk and ranger station – just arrived or waiting to leave. Most of our fellow ferry riders were already walking up the long drive to the main cell block. The wind on the eastern side of the island wasn't nearly as strong as it had been on open water. The midmorning sun shone brightly on the pale stone and crumbling concrete of the buildings.

But there was something else, a darkness only I could sense. I wondered if this was how the presence of the Shadow Realms felt to other people, this miasma of terror and despair surrounding the island, thin as a scream and thick as oil.

"It's fine, Mother. We'll get tea at the cafe and you'll feel better." Mei Shen tugged me forward. I stumbled, then balked again. I could feel the edges of the veil like cobwebs brushing my skin.

"No, you don't understand." I held her arm for balance and caught the brief tensing of her muscles, the guilty glance away. My daughter was good at lying – to everyone but me. I gaped at her. "You do. You do understand. You brought me here deliberately. You want me to go into that?"

How many times had Mei Shen faced off against me with that stubborn glower – times when she knew she'd done wrong and was doubling down by refusing to admit it? We inherit more than genes from our parents. "I need you to take me across it. I don't have the skill, and David won't take me. You're the only person I trust who has enough command of shadow to do it. I didn't know it would affect you like this." She frowned down at the water bottle crinkling in my fist. "It's only a ward. You should feel better once we're across."

"Across into what?" I hissed. The gangplank jostled under our feet, making my stomach roll dangerously. Dylan had finished whatever shore duties had taken him away and was heading up the ramp toward us. I could grit my teeth and tell him we were heading back with the ferry. I should. But Mei Shen had to have put me through this for a reason. "You're the one worried about trust? Try talking to me instead of lying to me. What's going on?"

"Nothing but a bit of recon. They won't even know we're here."

"Who? What is this place?"

"On this side? Alcatraz. Across the veil?" Mei Shen chewed her lip for a moment, then nodded as though coming to a decision. "It's the Citadel of the Conclave of Shadows."

Dylan was infinitely understanding when I told him that yes, I would be disembarking, and that I just needed another minute.

"You realize I have no fucking clue what I'm doing?" I hissed when he left Mei Shen and me alone again on the gangplank. "Your father's lessons in Shadow Realms matters basically boiled down to 'stay away', and my grandfather wasn't much more forthcoming."

And yet, my recent crash course in Shadow writing and summoning rituals had reinforced a few things I'd started to realize in Shanghai. Rituals and wards and other sorts of magic followed rules, which meant you could bypass them if you understood what they were meant to keep out. The wards around Alcatraz seemed to be a perfect example. Regular people could clearly pass through easily enough. Mei Shen couldn't, but neither was she affected by the nausea that had flattened me. She'd said it was because her blood was too thin – her blood on my side, inherited from my grandfather.

"So what happens if we trick the wards into thinking we're not connected to Shadow?" I mused, digging through my backpack. Somewhere in there–

"Hah!" I pulled out a Sharpie. I was tempted to do myself first and head down the ramp to protect Mei Shen, but if there was any validity to my blood theory, then she'd be more likely to get through safely than I would. "Give me your arm."

Mei Shen pushed up her sleeve, and I scrawled the Lady's ward across her pale underarm, cutting her off from her connection to the Shadow Realms. She shivered and swayed. "That feels… weird."

"Give it a go." I glanced back at Dylan, standing

at the top of the gangplank and watching us with a frown. I scrawled the sigils up my own arm, and my nausea quickly receded. Better than Dramamine.

Mei Shen took a cautious step down the gangplank, then another and another, picking up speed. She skipped down to the bottom and disembarked with a little hop. "It worked!"

My daughter, skipping and hopping her way into probable doom. Apparently, her brother had inherited all the good sense. I followed at a more sedate pace. Just as apparent, none of that sense had come from me.

"Now what?" I asked. The feeling of dread that had receded when I scrawled the sigils disappeared entirely the moment I stepped on land, a bit like I'd stepped out of a fogbank and into sunlight.

"Um. Tea?"

Mei Shen and I planned while I settled my stomach with some ginger tea – my own, dug out of my pack. The best the little cafe could offer was Bigelow. We agreed it would be best if I retained the sigils. They rendered me blind to the movement in the Shadow Realms, but I could sense something big and ominous looming behind my crappy Sharpie ward, and I didn't want to do anything to call its notice down on me. We reasoned that Mei Shen's thinner blood gave her some level of protection against the ward, so it might also keep her from being noticed. The fact that she was a dragon was also a big plus. Worse came to worse, I had my Sharpie on hand to renew her wards. We found a hand sanitizer station and she rubbed her skin red removing the protection.

As ready as we could be, we headed up the hill toward the cell house for our headsets and the tour.

Alcatraz deserved its reputation. It was a cold, cruel, eerie place, the sort of place that seemed to feed the Shadow Realms. The crumbling bits like the Military Chapel and the Officer's Club were the nicest parts. The gulls and cormorants had reclaimed them from human use, prisoners to nobody. Weeds and wildflowers burst free of the cracks alongside exposed, rusted rebar and window casings. Thick coyote brush grew up against the foundations, and streaks of white birdshit painted the crumbling stone walls. Yes, the most pleasant thing about Alcatraz was the birdshit-streaked walls.

Up in the main cell house, it was a different story. Grime covered both walls and windows, making everything grey and dreary even on a sunny day. Sound bounced strangely through the cell blocks, the wind a constant rise-and-fall of hollow notes.

I wasn't sure what it had been like when The Rock was a prison, but it remained an eerie example of state control even as a tourist attraction. A gaggle of pre-teen boys shuffled along ahead of Mei Shen and myself, some school group, but there was none of the roughhousing or jostling I'd expect. Everyone moved quietly from station to station under the steady instruction of the voices in their headphones. There was little conversation, no laughter. It was a well-ordered passion play of the systematic degradation of the human spirit, giving us all a taste of what might await us if we transgressed. Fear and remembered despair hung in the air, a miasma that weighed down everyone's shoulders and spirits.

The miasma here at Alcatraz was result of decades of suffering, evils large and small –gods knew we were aces at fucking ourselves over seven ways to Sunday without any supernatural support – but I was hardly surprised that the Conclave had noticed and cultivated such a place as its base of operations. Even the Lady's sigils weren't enough to completely disguise the taint of shadow in the air. I shuddered to think how it would feel if my connection to the Shadow Realms hadn't been blocked, and shot concerned glances at Mei Shen. Her smile had fled. She didn't blink enough, as though reluctant to close her eyes even for a moment, and her hand when she took mine was clammy.

We stopped in Sunrise Alley to give ourselves both a moment to breathe. The barred windows were opaque with grime, the so-called sunlight streaming through was diffuse and thin. This was the best it got.

"Anything useful?" I asked.

We'd agreed to wait until we'd left the island to discuss anything of importance, in part so we wouldn't risk being overhead and in part because neither of us wanted to stay in this place longer than we had to. But I needed to know if there was any point in pushing on.

Mei Shen pressed her cheek to the cement wall, earning us not a few concerned glances from passing tourists. I waved them on. Nothing to see here. Move along.

"There's a lot of overlap. More than I've ever seen anywhere else." She kept her voice low. "It's like they used the real world as a scaffolding to build permanence into the Shadow Realms structures. The cell block is all barracks. There's at least two knights to a cell all down the main avenues – Broadway, Michigan. These ones are empty, but I think they might be for servants? The light..." Her fingers crawled up toward one of the high-set windows as though seeking that light. I placed a hand on her back and soothed comfort and warmth into her tense shoulders. "... it rots the structures. I don't think they like it much."

"Solitary's on the other side. Sunset Strip. You think that's for more servants?"

Mei Shen gulped. "Or prisoners. We should check the dining hall and kitchens, but I don't think they will be bunked down with the rabble. And I doubt they'd keep anything valuable here where there's so much traffic."

They. The Conclave. "Then where?" I consulted the map we'd been given with our headsets. "The Officer's Club is a ruin. So that leaves what? The

ALYC HELMS 173

Power House and the Model Industries Building? Aren't there supposed to be catacombs?"

"Pretty sure those are just legends, mother."

"At least on this side," I said with gallows' cheer.

We exchanged a look of perfect understanding. We'd barely escaped Lung Di's catacombs when they collapsed. Mei Shen groaned. "Let's hope we don't have to deal with catacombs again."

"Times like these, I wish your uncle wasn't such a prick."

"Dining hall. Then let's get outside. I need to be outside." Despite her attempt to match my levity, Mei Shen looked as peaked as I imagined I had on the ferry.

The dining hall plan got dumped as we approached. Mei Shen's twitches broke into shrieks and jerk-limbed strikes at nothing. I caught her before she could start clawing at her arms. Her voice echoed above the quiet shuffle of feet. A few people around us lowered their headsets, glancing at each other, at me, as though waiting for someone else to help before they had to. Crowd dynamics at their finest. I hugged Mei Shen's arms close and dragged her away.

"Bee. She saw a bee. She's allergic."

Comprehension dawned, followed by relief at the restoration of the social order and a few nervous chuckles and kindly smiles.

Mei Shen was *compos mentis* enough to latch on to my excuse. "Bee. It was a bee. Damned bees."

She didn't stop shivering until I'd dragged her along Broadway Avenue and into the relative quiet and brightness of the administrative offices.

"Are we okay here?" I asked.

She nodded, gulping air.

"Are you okay?"

"I don't think we need to worry about the kitchens and the dining hall. It's some kind of breeding ground."

I shuddered and stroked her hair. I didn't care to consider how shadows replicated. "So. Not bees, then."

That earned me a laugh, albeit a shaky one. At least she was laughing. "No. Definitely not bees."

"Let's go outside."

The wind blowing across the flat parade ground outside the administrative offices cooled the heat in my cheeks and dried the nervous sweat. Mei Shen turned her face to it, eyes closed and knuckles white on the top bar of the chain-link barrier that kept us from tumbling to the rocks and the surf below. The wind was salt-heavy and biting damp, but a welcome relief after the stifling air of the cell block. Apparently not for everyone, as it chased all but the most determined tourists indoors after only a few minutes, leaving Mei Shen and myself mostly alone. Just us and the gulls. Across the bay, the Golden Gate Bridge stretched between the city and the empty Marin headlands, a clay-red cat's cradle. The fog was moving in, swallowing the bridge like some creeping, hungry kaiju.

"I think they must use this for drilling. At night, I mean. There are weapon racks." Mei Shen waved back the way we'd come. And then she stumbled back against the barrier fence, eyes wide and lips slack.

I uncapped my Sharpie, ready to re-inscribe the wards in the hope that the permanent marker was mightier than the sword.

Mei Shen's grip on my wrist stopped me. "The lighthouse. It's working."

"It's what?" I whipped around fast enough to get a neck twinge, but the old lighthouse rising above the parade ground wasn't doing anything beyond posing prettily for pictures.

"On the other side." Mei Shen's gaze flicked nervously around us. I could barely hear her over the wind. She held her hair off her face and looked back across the bay. "The light, they're using it to bolster the bridge."

"The who... the what, now? You mean against the Voidlands?" I followed her gaze, but all I saw was the fog-devoured Golden Gate. I scrubbed at the marks on my arm, wishing I could see whatever she was seeing, wishing I'd brought some sanitizer to remove the markings on the fly. I didn't know what I could do to stop another earthquake, but dammit I had to try.

The look Mei Shen gave me reminded me of her father at his most annoying, that timeless look that somehow conveyed both infinite patience and impatience. "What else? I cannot believe you've lived here all this time, and yet you had no idea the threat this city faces daily."

Parents take heed – even more obnoxious than having a teenager who thinks she knows everything is having a teenager who probably does know everything. Or at least a more sizeable chunk of everything than you do. "Maybe instead of training for the snarky comment, snort, and eyeroll triathlon, you can tell me about it in detail? After we get off this island?"

Mei Shen slumped against the fence and pressed her fingers into her eyebrows. "You are right. I should not blame you for what I refused to confide in you. David told me the same many times over. I have been… stubborn."

So much for suggesting we not do this here and now. "You've been upset with me. And for good reasons." I smoothed her hair, as much as the wind would allow.

"I know why you had to leave. I do not blame you for that."

For that. Not for that. "I should have said goodbye to you and Mian Zi."

She raised her head. Lowered her hands. "Would you have been able to leave if you had tried?"

Possibly not. That had certainly been my thinking at the time. "I should have said goodbye." I pulled her into my arms. After a moment of resistance, she returned my hug with rib-bending strength.

"So," I whispered into her wind-tangled hair after I'd gotten control of my tears and my voice. "What do you want to bet that whatever's powering that lighthouse has something to do with Argent's stolen tech?"

Mei Shen pulled away, wiping her eyes even as she chuckled. "Maybe we shouldn't have skipped the Power House."

The bridge had lost its battle with the creeping fog by the time we tracked back and exited the tour in the proper fashion so we could return our headsets. The exit spat us out into an impressive and slightly unnerving souvenir shop. It was the prison uniform onesies for toddlers that pushed it over the edge of respect, I decided. There was something more than slightly abhorrent about turning human misery into kawaii cuteness and then selling it at an obscene markup, even if the money did go to park restoration and maintenance.

Battling the current of a wave of newly arrived tourists, Mei Shen and I trudged back up the hill toward the Power House and the Model Industries buildings. I thought about Johnny's balance-of-place. Alcatraz's history going back almost two centuries was one of pain and human degradation, but not always. At the start – at least, the start of European occupation – it had been meant to be a home for a lighthouse.

"How long have they been here, the Conclave?" I asked Mei Shen, huffing because the hill's grade was a little too steep for easy conversation.

"The Shadow Dragon Triad avoided having much to do with the island, but even the earliest records indicate it was a place of darkness." She hugged herself to contain her shudder. "It is only in the past half century or so that there have been any signs of organization, which makes me think that the Conclave moved in around the time the prison was being closed down."

"Moved in. Or took over. But the lighthouse working, that's new?" I slowed as our progress was blocked by a gaggle of teenagers with their eyes and thumbs glued to their smartphones.

"I haven't come across any indication that it has been in use." A shadow of a cloud passed overhead. Mei Shen frowned up at the sky, flinching at whatever she saw that I couldn't. "We should not talk about this here. We should–"

"Look out!" Someone charged from behind me, tackling Mei Shen into the crowd of teenagers. Their tumble took down several boys with them under a rising cacophony of *What the fuck, man?*'s. I lunged after Mei Shen's attacker, grabbing two fistfuls of dark suit jacket and pulling him off her with mama grizzly strength.

I recognized David Tsung the moment after it was too late to pull my strike.

He doubled over my fist like a deflated balloon,

gasping for breath and grabbing for my forearms to keep me from striking again. I skipped back a few steps, not following up, but not quite willing to let my guard down, even if he was a semi-known quantity. "What the fuck?" I asked, echoing the boys around us.

"Run... The ferry... We have to–"

Mei Shen's shriek shut us both up. The boys who had been helping her to her feet scattered like startled sparrows, leaving her alone in the middle of the road, batting and flailing at something that nobody could see.

Nobody except David Tsung. "Get... off... her!" Still struggling with basic body functions like breathing, he nevertheless stumbled toward Mei Shen. I realized that whatever was attacking her, he could see it. Which meant he could fight it.

I stopped one of the kids from taking a retaliatory swing at him. "You lot, get out of here!" I shouted, pushing two more back. Tsung had grabbed at air and seemed to be running through a solo kata, but I could see the tension, the jarring impact of each strike, that indicated he was fighting more than air and imagination.

Mei Shen, too, and the reaction of the teenage boys was to nudge each other and smile as their understanding of the interruption went from crazy-guy-attacking-a-woman-that's-fucked-up to this-is-some-of-that-cool-flash-mob-shit.

At least, until Mei Shen grabbed her head and

fell back, heels scrabbling for traction on the road as something invisible dragged her away at speed.

"Get out of here!" I yelled at the boys, and sprinted after my daughter. Tsung followed not two paces behind.

Whatever held Mei Shen dragged her down the escarpment and through the doorway of the Power House. Her ass and kicking feet left a trail in the dust covering the concrete floor of the cavernous room. Scant sunlight filtered through the broken panes, but most of the space was grey and grim and cold as concrete. Even with the ward scrawled down my arm, I could sense the thickness of the shadows here, like smoke at the back of my throat. Whatever had Mei Shen, I still couldn't see it, which left me feeling as helpless as any tourist. I opened my pack, digging for the only thing I knew might help.

Tsung surged past me to deal with the entity attacking Mei Shen. I grabbed her ankle and popped the cap on my Sharpie one-handed. Ducking to avoid being kicked in the face, I started scrawling the wards up her shin. I managed two sigils before she was ripped from my grasp. She had her hands to her throat, her face red and edging toward purple. Tsung was flat on the ground, pinned by nothing I could sense.

I was useless to them. Helpless. And alone. Whether through disinterest or arcane discouragement, the crowds outside hadn't followed our scuffle. I was on my own against forces I couldn't touch or see.

"Fuck this." I left my pack spilling across the floor and scrambled to my feet, darting for the broken paned windows. I had nothing on hand to remove the Sharpie and no time to do it prettily. But experience told me I didn't need pretty. Padding my elbow with my coat sleeve, I slammed it through one of the window panes. If I survived the day, the National Park Service was going to get a hefty donation from Mr Mystic to assuage my guilt for the vandalism. I snatched up one of the shards that had broken free and shoved my sleeve up. Sending a quiet thanks to Shimizu for making sure I kept up on my tetanus booster, I slashed the jagged edge across the marks on my arm.

In the dimness that descended after my shredding of the ward, my blood shimmered like living darkness, like the Lady's skin and gown. Where before there had only been the noise of Mei Shen's struggles, now the cacophony of a menagerie of shrieks and wails deafened me. I watched in fascinated horror as my blood dripped to the ground, birthing a tide of strange, scarab-like creatures. Their shells glistened like candied apples, as bright as my blood had been dark. As bright a red as Mei Shen's shimmering skin in this place of darkness.

Mei Shen. I saw now that a half dozen Conclave knights had descended on us. Two had pinned Tsung. The other four held my daughter. Or tried to.

In the Shadow Realms, she was not quite human woman nor quite dragon. Her scaled skin glowed like coals, ruby bright on the surface, each one edged with darkness like soot – my blood mixed with her father's. Her limbs were lithe, unnaturally long, and the knights smoked and bubbled wherever their shadow flesh met hers. But there were enough of them, with enough single-minded determination, that they held her in spite of the smoke that rose from any contact. One of them had her pinned with an arm around her throat, and even as I got my bearings, I saw her eyes roll white and the glow of her skin fade.

"Help me," I whispered to the scarab swarm milling around my feet. My arm still dripped blood, birthing more of the creatures. I remembered Templeton, remembered what the Lady had said, reinforced by my days cramming over the Shadownomicon. Names. Names mattered here.

"You are the Blood-Dimmed Tide." I wasn't sure whether to cringe or take a queer, feminist pride in the first name that came to mind. But what was said was said, and the scarabs seemed to respond, growing brighter in response to being named. Louder. Hungrier. "Help me free my daughter from those bastards."

As eagerly as the blood had gushed from my arm, the tide of scarabs rushed forth. I followed in their wake, dribbling more scarabs behind me to add to their number. I hadn't been quite sure how useful a swarm of insects might be, no matter how menacing they looked. I should have had more faith in the special brand of awful the Shadow Realms seemed inclined to produce. The knights had released Mei Shen, dragging out rubbery sheets to bind her. Undaunted by their numbers or size, the scarabs swarmed over their feet and up their legs, moving like a single, bubbling pool of the blood from which they were formed. Three of the knights screamed and were silenced by a thick vanguard of scarabs sliding down their throats. The fourth knight danced about in a parody of a jig, trying to stomp the tide. A few scarabs were caught under boot, flattened like copper souvenir pennies, but they sprang back up the moment the knight stomped away and quickly overwhelmed him as they had his fellows.

The two knights on Tsung lost their hold. He surged up. The knight he shoved into the swarm was quickly overrun, and just as quickly the lump of that knight's body settled flat, as though he'd been devoured. I grappled the last knight. He made the mistake of trying to escape my hold by twisting my injured arm, releasing a second swarm of scarabs right into his chest. I turned away before I had to witness what they were doing to make him scream like that.

I wrapped my scarf around my arm. I needed my wits more than I needed a few more scarabs. With the knights distracted or downed, I rushed to

Mei Shen's side. Tsung was already there, already rousing her from her faint. She swayed, woozy.

"We need to get out of here." I looked around for my Sharpie, but I must have dropped it on the other side, along with my bag, which had my emergency stash of glow sticks intended for emergencies just like this. "Fuck."

"We can carry her out. If we can get to the ferry…" Tsung said, not realizing my reason for cursing.

I ducked to sling Mei Shen's arm over my shoulder, hissing at the burn of her skin, like metal heated in the sun even through several layers of clothing. Tsung grunted as he took the other side, but he raised no complaint as we helped a groggy Mei Shen out of the Power House.

Gone was the sunny day, the tourists, the white-wheeling gulls – although I thought I spied the black shadows of cormorants overhead.

Sure, Masters. Those are cormorants. Keep telling yourself that.

"Wards… can you…?" Mei Shen gasped. She regained her footing, still gripping my shoulder to keep her balance.

"Dropped my Sharpie. How'd you get off the ferry?" I asked Tsung, glaring at him over Mei Shen's head. Actually, "How did you know we were here?"

"Somebody booked the tickets on my credit card." His glare was all for Mei Shen. "I told you it wasn't safe to come here. I told you–"

"You can tell me all you want after we get out of here. Before–" A howl rose up all around us, horrible and hollow and pitched at the edge of hearing – Cthulhu's cover of whalesong's greatest hits. Mei Shen groaned and rested her forehead on Tsung's shoulder. "That. They've sounded the alarm."

I glanced down the dark ribbon of road that led to the ferry slip, now filling with Conclave knights flooding from the guardhouse. The coyote brush on the hillside to our right rustled, a thousand soft hisses roused by the eerie clarion. Whatever flapped above us darted down. We ducked, but not fast enough. Something sharp skittered across my cheek, like a record needle skipping. A few more scarabs dribbled to the ground and milled about in confusion.

"So much for the ferry," Tsung said, eying the gathering knights. They hadn't seen us yet, but it was only a matter of moments before the needle-beaked bird things drew down attention. The only clear route was the ruins running next to the road, the Officer's Club and the glass-black bay beyond that.

Watching the orphaned scarabs scuttle aimlessly gave me an idea. "Can you get us across to the real world?" Tsung hesitated. Nodded. "Then maybe a distraction to lure them away from the ferry?" I said and squeezed my scarf-bandaged arm. The pain helped me focus my whispered call. I'd done similar things to summon shadow in the real world, or when I called Templeton, but this was different. This wasn't an alien monster I'd temporarily bound to my will, or a friend who helped me out of his goodwill. This was something *mine*. Something of me, but separate.

I could contemplate the unsettling ramifications of that during the same later that Tsung was going to use to yell at Mei Shen.

Out of the shadows of the Power House came a shining, satin-bright flood of scarabs. Their hard carapaces clacked against each other, the rising crescendo of their chittering like an alien invasion. The orphaned scarabs at our feet perked up and joined my Blood-Dimmed Tide as it coursed down the black road to meet the gathering knights.

"You made a cockroach army," Tsung said, deadpan.

I scowled at him. "They're scarabs."

"Whatever you need to tell yourself to let you sleep at night."

Later. I'd also tell him where he could shove his opinions. Later. For now, I led the way down the escarpment into the roofless shell of the Officer's Club.

The blackened walls rose into the sky like decaying teeth sprouting from rocky gums. Beyond the rocks, the shadow reflection of the bay shifted in slow, thick ripples. The surface shone black as

pitch and nearly as viscous. Tsung and I helped
steady Mei Shen as we climbed down to the gully
that had once been the ground floor. I frowned out
at the waters. I was even less eager to test them
than I would have been if we'd stood on the other
side of the veil.

"Where's a raincoat raft when you need one?" I
muttered.

"Now what?" Mei Shen asked, then answered
her own question. "I can fly us out of here."

"No!" Tsung and I said in tandem.

"You'll only draw attention and pursuit," he
explained.

"And you're woozy enough that you might crash
us into the drink," I continued, because it looked
like Mei Shen might argue with Tsung's logic.

Mei Shen crossed her arms, a sure sign that she
was digging in for an argument. The next stage
would be her doing what she wanted to do anyway.
Which was probably why she and I had ended up
here in the first place, with David Tsung rushing
to the rescue. I needed an alternative that didn't
require waiting and hoping my scarab army could
lure the knights away from the ferry platform. I
picked at the scabbing-over scratch on my cheek
and released another drop of blood.

It was smaller than the others, barely larger than
a Japanese beetle, the runt of my scarab swarm. He
balanced on my fingertip like a cabochon agate.

"Hey. Um." Names. "Rover." Ugh. I sucked at

this. "Red Rover? Is there somewhere we can hide? Or some way off this island? A boat? Something?"

The blood scarab circled my fingertip, then its carapace opened up to reveal shadow-thin wings, and it flitted off into the thick coyote brush at the base of the wall.

Holding my breath in case my luck gave out, I slid down the incline and dug into the brambles. A narrow stairway of tarry black stone descended into the earth, ending in a rusted grate. Rover hovered above one of the crossbars as though waiting until I'd seen him, then he flitted off again into the darkness beyond the grate. The tiny ember spark of his carapace quickly faded in the shadows.

I tamped down on a eureka-style shout. My little scarab had led the way to the legendary catacombs of Alcatraz.

"Hey!" I hissed up at Mei Shen and David Tsung, still engaged in a contest of wills that Tsung would never win. "If you two are done flirting, I think I've got us a way out."

TEN
The Hard Place

The initial intestinal twists of the damp cave gave way to a long, smooth-walled corridor that glistened dimly in the soft glow of my scarab and Mei Shen's scales. The smoothness of the walls and the uniform shape of the passage confused me until I reasoned that this was not man-made nor water-carved, but the ecofact of some long-gone – and disturbingly large – seaworm of some sort.

At least, I hoped it was long gone. The fear that it might not be kept Tsung, Mei Shen, and myself moving with little conversation. None of us wanted to call the attention of something awful by talking too loudly.

I was only able to track how long we followed my little red spark by the creaking of my knees and the double-fisted tension in the small of my back. Walking was my main mode of transportation around the city, so if I was getting sore, then however far we'd gone, it was far. It was only when my thighs started burning and my breath shortened that I realized we were walking up an incline and probably had been for some time.

"I think we're out from under the bay," I whispered, a weight of fear lifting now that I wasn't imagining several million gallons of seawater – or the Shadow Realms equivalent – crashing down on top of us.

"Can you get us out? Either of you?" Mei Shen asked. I pressed my hand against the red-dim wall illuminated by her glow. Shook my head. Tsung was already shaking his.

"Not enough light to get to the other side," I said, cursing again that I'd thrown aside my backpack in my rush to get to Mei Shen. So many things I could have used – my glow sticks, my cell phone. Instead, I'd led us into a tunnel that still might lead nowhere. Stupid, stupid.

"I can't even tell what's on the other side," Tsung said, which made me feel a little better. At least I wasn't the only member of the poor-planning brigade.

"Rock. I'm not sure there's even a tunnel on the other side," I said. Up ahead, my little Red Rover was bobbing and flickering strangely.

Mei Shen scraped a claw along the wall. "How can that be?"

"Whatever creature made it only exists on this side." I reached for Red Rover just as he flickered and winked out.

I stumbled to a stop. Mei Shen crashed into me, and Tsung behind her, pushing me forward. My face smooshed into a vertical bed of spongy black fungus and underneath that, a wall of solid stone.

"Ack!" I shoved back, my hands slipping on the fungus-covered wall. The crushed fungus exuded an odor of old tires and brackish water. I scrubbed at my cheek, which did little good given my hands were covered with the same slime. "Dead end," I said. Overcoming my reluctance to touch the fungus again, I poked through it with one finger. There was no sign of Red Rover. Poor little guy.

"Is it?" Mei Shen raised a hand. Her scales were dimmer at her extremities, but her long, curved claws gleamed the mellow gold of antique pearls. Instead of the corridor roof, the area above us opened up. We stood in a sunken carbuncle in the floor of what seemed to be a narrow crevasse running perpendicular to our passage. A lazy flicker of red flitted down and landed on my shoulder, shadow wings tucking neatly away under his shining carapace.

"Good job, little guy," I said, and got a little wing flutter in response.

"Which way?" Tsung asked, already searching the walls of our carbuncle for the best route up and out. The fungus-covered wall didn't offer much in the way of purchase, but he was tall enough to catch the lip and strong enough to pull himself up.

Tsung caught me when I jumped, hauling me up

to the lip so I could climb. We both assisted Mei Shen, grimacing at the heat of her scales.

"I could try flying us—"

"Too narrow, and we don't know how high the passage goes. We don't want you getting stuck or injured," Tsung said before I could weigh in. Just as well. I didn't want to point out that in this place, Mei Shen's touch was uncomfortable for both of us. Too uncomfortable for her to fly us around for any length of time. That was the sort of disturbing bit of knowledge I'd prefer to dissect over tea and biscuits.

"If I'm reading Rover correctly, one way's as good as another?" I held up one fungus-damp finger, testing the air. "That way?"

"Why?" Mei Shen asked, peering in the direction I'd pointed.

"Because I read too much Mark Twain as a kid? There's a breeze."

With no good argument against it, we left the carbuncle and headed along the crevasse toward my elusive breeze.

"I think we may have chosen poorly," Tsung said some while later. The ache in my spine and knees had moved down to my feet. My toes throbbed. My arches cramped. My legs felt like they were held together with rubber bands, like one of those little plastic figures that collapses when you press the button in the base. I kept on keeping on only because I knew that once one of us flagged, the other two would quickly follow. Sorry, Anne Robinson, but I was not going to be the weakest link.

However, if Tsung's words were preface to him giving up and asking for a rest, I was fine with nudging that along. "What makes you say that?"

"See that darkness up there?"

I snorted, too tired to dredge up a real laugh. Outside the glow of Mei Shen's scales, there was nothing but darkness. Even Rover had buried himself somewhere in the folds of my coat. "Gee, which darkness is that? The pitch black, the oily obsidian, or the velvet depths of nothingness?"

"The Voidlands."

Any urge to laugh drained away. I skidded to a stop, looking ahead and trying to see what my brain clearly didn't want me to see. "That's not funny."

"I'm not laughing."

No, I didn't think he was. Now that I wasn't concentrating on setting one foot after the other, I could see what he meant. Between the velvet and the obsidian was an absence of light so deep that I could only measure its existence by holding up my hand for foreground comparison. Seeing the Voidlands through the protection of the veil dimmed their awfulness. Now I was being forced to confront it head on, and my mind was twisting itself into a pretzel in its attempts to not comprehend.

I had been in the Voidlands. Once. During my

rescue of Mei Shen after her uncle had kidnapped her. I still wasn't quite sure how I had made it out, other than using the insanity of the place to trick myself into thinking I was sane long enough to escape it. What else could explain the swarm of Templetons that had bubbled up to drag me out? I still wasn't sure how much of my perception of that experience had been real and how much had been pleasant alternatives to whatever I'd really experienced. I was pretty sure I'd tried to end the world by opening the bridge to the essence of not-being. It had seemed like a good idea at the time. Which was the problem.

"We should head back," Mei Shen said, interrupting my moment of gibbering terror.

"What an excellent suggestion," I said. We all retreated several steps before turning to hurry back the way we'd come.

Only to collide again a moment later when Tsung stumbled to a halt. "We've got company." Sure enough, several raptor shapes soared ahead, a slightly dimmer grey than the sheer walls that trapped us. They swooped down the crevasse like patrolling TIE-fighters. A screech of discovery from one of them jolted me out of my inaction.

"Shit. Run!" I hesitated in following my own directive. There was only one way to run that wouldn't put us in the path of the raptors.

"Which way?" Tsung asked, stymied by my hesitation. I glanced back at the Void. Even worse than entering voluntarily would be to be driven into it in terror.

"The tunnel. Back the way we came!" And hope for a miracle, I didn't bother to add. I sprinted as best I could along the uneven ground. No need to tell anyone that pretty much either way, we were screwed.

We ran beneath the raptors, close enough to see that they weren't raptors at all. They were gargoyles. They howled and wheeled about, nearly colliding in their confusion as we changed course. It gave us a few moments' lead, but that wouldn't be enough.

It also gave me a good look at what we were facing, which wasn't always a good thing. The gargoyles' bodies were heavy-boned and muscled, vaguely doglike. Their skin was dark as weeping stone and looked just as solid. Their pinions spread wide, a canopy of bone-shot shadow, and they rattled with every downbeat. If Tom's rocket pack and the *Kestrel* stretched credulity with how they managed to fly, then the gargoyles snapped it like tired Silly Putty. They weren't aloft by their own design, but by the will of another. A powerful will. That was the way of things in the Shadow Realms. Nothing kept its shape longer than an echo, unless someone with power willed it so.

My experience with the Blood-Dimmed Tide and Red Rover was still new and unfamiliar. Until now, the most I'd managed to craft was a half dozen or so amorphous blobs. I didn't have the power to sustain something as complex as these gargoyles for any length of time. Only the Conclave could command a half dozen flying gargoyle soldiers of bone and shadow.

"Masters, there's nowhere to run!" Tsung panted beside me. He was right. We'd already walked this path. The walls were too high and sheer to scale. This was why, as a rule, I avoided the Shadow Realms. It was a place of impasses.

Like now. Keep running, or stand and fight a losing battle?

The first gargoyle plummeted into a dive, taking the choice from me. I dropped and rolled, but the talons snagged my coat, jerking me half-aloft. I raised my arms and struggled out of my coat.

There was a screech of pain and fury as a second gargoyle swooped down, right into Tsung's roundhouse kick. The creature was knocked aside with a rattle of bone, but Tsung landed with a wince and a gasp, favoring his foot.

"What are these damn things made of? Granite?"

Another dove for Mei Shen, and her claws cut through its wings, sending severed bone spurs flying. They clattered against the wall, the rattle of bone drowned out by the gargoyle's screech of pain.

"Or tofu," Mei Shen said with a pleased little smirk, holding up her gold-gleaming claws. "You run. I will fight these."

Tsung and I shared a rare look of perfect agreement. Yeah, like either of us was going to leave her alone.

We didn't have time to argue with her. Five more gargoyles were diving down on us, their pinions snapping close to their bodies as though wind resistance was an issue. Which it wasn't. They were just shadow on wings of shadow diving through more shadow. This place was nothing else.

Except maybe perception?

"Go for their wings." I willed my own shadow into shape. It was nothing compared to the complex constructs attacking us. Just a gently undulating veil, only a little more corporeal than the shadow around it.

That's all the kraben had been, really. That's all I needed.

On my command, the veil rose up behind the attacking gargoyles and wrapped around one of them. Head on, the gargoyle would have torn through the tissue-thin veil with momentum alone, but from behind the veil could wrap, and wrap, and bind those wings close. Howling its fury, the gargoyle plummeted to the ground. I fell to my knees, exhausted even from the small effort of keeping the winding sheet under command.

Another cry came from my left – human. I glanced over. Tsung had wrenched back the wing of one gargoyle – it hung askew as though broken – but another gargoyle had seized him from behind and was launching aloft.

"David!" Mei Shen screamed. The other three gargoyles had surrounded her, keeping her trapped in a cage of bone wings and shadow without coming within range of her claws. All three were knocked back by a long, sinuous tail as she transformed into a full dragon.

Light exploded through the crevasse like an M-80 going off in an old coffee can, blinding me and, I could only hope, the remaining gargoyles. It would have been so easy to use that light to step back into my own world, but there was nowhere to step. Everything on the other side of the veil was stone. And I couldn't leave Mei Shen.

Though apparently, she had no such qualms about leaving me. By the time my eyesight cleared enough that I could tell my real foes from the dancing blobs of my blown-out rods and cones, Mei Shen was a streamer of red-gold light diminishing into the distance, and the five gargoyles she'd left me to deal with had recovered and were closing in.

Well, fuck. I suppose there was one way to follow Mei Shen and Tsung. Not that it looked like I had much of a choice.

I put up no resistance when one of the gargoyles caught me with clawlike hands and launched aloft, wrenching my arms with every wing beat. We were flanked by two more, and the two with damaged wings limped behind, tearing my coat to shreds between them. There but for the grace of God went I?

We crested the lip of the crevasse. The landscape beyond was carved with deep ravines, like the claw marks of some long-gone leviathan. They all led in the same direction. Ahead of me, the gargoyle carrying Tsung banked, Mei Shen's red-gold streak in close pursuit. My captors trailed in their wake. We flew over the claw-mark ravines, heading toward the looming Voidlands. The leading edge cut across the landscape like the event horizon of a black hole; nothing beyond that dark curtain was visible, nor did I particularly care to see what it hid. In the rush of contained terror that followed that realization, the destruction of my coat barely mattered.

Wherever we were headed, God's grace didn't mean squat.

The gargoyles banked again before we crossed over into the Voidlands, their path paralleling the leading edge. The claw-marked landscape gave way to a primordial forest of trees the size of small skyscrapers. No surprise, really. A glance across the veil told me we were somewhere in north Marin. I suspected we were seeing the Shadow equivalent of Muir Woods. It settled some of my fear. At least they weren't returning us to Alcatraz.

Rather than flying over the trees, the gargoyles wove through the spaces between them. I lost sight of Tsung, and I could only track Mei Shen by the glow limning the black-barked trees.

At least, until we broke into a clearing ringed by trees grown so close together that the only access seemed to be through the upper branches, where the trunks narrowed slightly to create space. Down below, a collection of structures was wedged into the clearing. It had the look of a Burner camp. Small tents of silky shadowstuff were set up in concentric circles. Offset from the center of the camp stood the only spot of color to be seen, a yurt of actual canvas, desert pale against all the darkness.

Tsung had been dumped in the center of the clearing. The gargoyle that had carried him disappeared into the upper branches of the trees. Mei Shen landed, forming a protective circle around Tsung's crouched form. The light from her coils illuminated lurking shadows all around – the camp denizens come out to greet our arrival.

The moment my gargoyle dumped me, I moved, hauling Tsung to his feet with one hand and grabbing the searing end of Mei Shen's tail in the other. Using her light, I tried to pull us back across the veil.

We didn't go anywhere. My connection to the real world slipped away like I was trying to grab air. I dropped Mei Shen's tail, cradling my burned hand to my chest. Tsung shot me a confused glance, but I shook my head. I didn't dare explain just how bad our situation was, in case the gargoyles could manage more sentience than animal howls. At least Mei Shen's internal brightness seemed to be keeping the gargoyles and the shadow troops at bay.

The opening of the yurt was thrown back, and a familiar figure stepped out.

The Lady's skin was dark as anything in the Shadow Realms, but unlike the rest of this place, it carried an internal luminescence similar to Mei Shen's. Except the Lady's skin burned like a black hole, if a glimmer of light could escape that sort of gravitational pull. Her hair coiled like a living thing, and shadow trailed off her limbs when she moved. Instead of the gown of living shadow that I'd seen her wearing when we first met, she was dressed in black and grey camouflage military fatigues, a combat knife strapped to her thigh.

Tsung gaped. I seconded the feeling. I didn't know whether to be relieved or more terrified on seeing her. She wasn't the Conclave, true, but the enemy of my enemy was not always my friend.

"You are disturbing my people," the Lady said to Mei Shen with the cool censure of a librarian telling a patron to hush.

Mei Shen's coils folded in on themselves until she was a dragon-scaled girl again and we were left in relative darkness. "Your people took mine."

"My hounds secured you before the Conclave could find you. They are not precisely tame, but they meant you no harm. I cannot say the same of the Conclave's new master." She inclined her head to me. "Hello again, Missy."

"This is the Lady I was telling you about," I whispered to Mei Shen. Then, to the Lady. "Thank you. The timely rescue was much appreciated. We'd appreciate it even more if you would let us go."

"Yes. Of course. My hounds will take you outside the camp wards if that is your wish." She waved an elegant, long-fingered hand as though my request and her offer were of little interest. "But your companions… this girl shares blood with the Shadow Dragon. As does the man, though it is further removed." She turned her hungry, intense gaze on Mei Shen, only flicking to Tsung as an afterthought.

While I was busy worrying about what danger the Lady might pose to my daughter, Mei Shen was busy being insulted on Tsung's behalf. She stepped in front of him, facing off against the Lady. "I am Lung Mei Shen Mi, niece to Lung Di. David Tsung is his bloodline and my consort."

"Consort?!" I blurted. Forget the Lady, Mei Shen should be more worried about me. "Does your father know about this?"

Mei Shen cast me a glare of perfect teenage disgust. "Not now, mother."

Oh, definitely now. "Since when are you old enough to be taking consorts? And you–" I rounded on Tsung. "You are way too old for her."

To his credit, Tsung squirmed and looked decidedly uncomfortable. "It is in name only. Purely ceremonial. To help strengthen her claim."

"I don't care if it's meant to qualify you for the consort tax credit. You are not–"

"Mo-ther!"

"You are her mother?" The Lady's soft question broke through our moment of family drama, reminding me that for all her seeming friendliness, she was an uncertain ally. We weren't out of the woods yet. In more ways than one.

"You couldn't tell by the way she ignores my very reasonable concerns?"

I paid no heed to Mei Shen's disgusted huff and eyeroll, nor did the Lady.

"Yes. I understand that the relationships between mothers and daughters can be... fraught." The Lady touched long, segmented fingers to Mei Shen's brow, ignoring the hiss and shadow smoke that rose from the contact. "I had perhaps thought to keep you. You would be much use against the Voidlands. But as you are blood, you are free to leave with your mother." Her smile was like the glimmer of darkness between stars. And oddly indulgent. "You and your handsome consort."

"Don't encourage them," I muttered under my breath.

"Thank you," Mei Shen said loudly, as though the vindication made up for the implicit threat that the Lady had been intending on keeping them.

"If I may, Lady," Tsung said, brow furrowed. "You indicated you are working to contain the Voidlands?"

"In the Shadow Dragon's absence, someone must. And I do not like the methods the Conclave employs, nor the price they hope to exact."

Mei Shen and Tsung exchanged a look that left me feeling very much the third wheel. This was the secret Mei Shen had been loath to share with me.

"We share similar goals, and I hope our methods are more palatable than the Conclave's," Mei Shen said. "Perhaps you don't need to hold us to secure our assistance. Will you show us?"

Showing us, as it turned out, required a gathering of what seemed like half the camp – gargoyles, spiky goblinoids, a few of the manta-like kraben, and a dozen other denizens of Shadow that I had neither name nor description for. They armed themselves with a variety of equally mismatched artifacts from my world. Several of the goblins carried trash that looked to have been liberated from a construction site – bent rebar, nail-studded boards, coils of razor wire. A pair of ambulatory octopodes wielded a Louisville Slugger between then, passing it from tentacle to tentacle as they rolled along. The Lady's army was nothing like the organized, faceless regiments of the Conclave knights.

The Lady led us through a narrow passage bored out of one of the skyscraper trees. "It is not often that the Conclave sends scouts this far, nor that creatures of the Voidlands escape its pull, but I prefer to prepare for both eventualities."

Cheering thought, that.

We marched, a few dozen strong, toward the ever-present absence that was the Voidlands. It felt like walking down a steep hill, even though the ground was level. I ignored the pull in favor of gently interrogating our guide.

"You said the Shadow Dragon had been the one to hold back the Voidlands," I said to the Lady, frowning at Mei Shen. At least she had the grace to duck her head, and her luminous scales seemed to tint slightly pinker. "I thought he was holding back the Conclave."

The Lady moved gracefully around trees and through brambles that had the rest of us, even her own people, struggling. "He was a check on all powers at the borders. The fulcrum that held them in balance, if you will. He was not particularly well liked for it. If not for him, I would have destroyed the Conclave decades ago, before they were this much of a nuisance. But I do not think any of us fully appreciated his... service."

Just as well. If Lung Di knew he was missed, even grudgingly, he'd be insufferable.

"I am trying to revitalize his wards," Mei Shen said. "But I do not have his power."

"Nobody does, child. The Shadow Dragon is a Leviathan, and it took more than one such to contain the heart of the Void. But you know that, do you not? Being of that bloodline? I do what I can to ward against the encroachment of the Voidlands; the Conclave tries to siphon them and shape them into something they can control. Others do their part, knowingly and unknowingly. It is not enough. Ah. Here we are."

We emerged from the trees and stood at the edge of a dead zone. Some of the trees had fallen over into the encroaching curtain of darkness. Others had bark turned ashen and desiccated where it faced the leading edge of the Voidlands. Some of the largest, oldest, trees still stood tall, bisected by that same edge. I wondered if they would fall before they were engulfed.

The black fungus from the carbuncle covered almost every surface. The air stank of fresh asphalt burning in the sun.

In a space between two of the fallen trees, a headless white figure faced the void, swaying. Blue-bright stars eerily illuminated the lace and tulle of her gown, and a knot of blood-red light pulsed at the center of her chest.

"Estelle?" I gaped at the sight of the goff bride Shimizu and I had made.

"Who?" Tsung said.

"I... nothing." I turned to the Lady. "That's why you wanted her?"

"A simulacrum crafted by a shadow mage is a powerful artifact. And this one triply so for the form she takes and the name you used to shape her."

Right. Because brides and ghosts were both liminal, border creatures. Apparently ghost brides were even better. And ghost brides named after stars... I'd hit the trifecta of symbolism without even intending to.

"But how is she lit up?" I picked up the end of the Christmas light cord, which trailed along the ground behind the ghost bride.

"By me. You may have named her, but I am giving her life."

Wait. Life?

The swaying I'd written off as the effect of a breeze became a full-fledged turn. The headless figure raised an empty sleeve and dipped into an awkward curtsy.

I shrieked, cast the plug away from me like it was a snake, and leapt back.

Mei Shen caught me. I think she might have been stifling giggles.

"Shut up," I grumbled, collecting myself and pulling away from her overheated scales before I burned myself again. Brat.

The Lady led us along the narrow no-man's land between trees and void's edge, from waypoint to waypoint – a pachinko machine, a fiber-optic Christmas tree, a glowing inflatable bunny the size of an elephant.

"And all of these draw their power from you?"

Tsung asked when we stopped at a cabinet aquarium that had to be over two hundred gallons. It was filled with luminous anemones and iridescent cichlids whose scales glowed almost as brightly as Mei Shen's in the UV of the tank's lights. "How are you still standing?"

The Lady shrugged, as though it was nothing of note, but I noticed our escort shifting, choking up on their weapons. The ambulatory octopodes squeezed together until they looked like one creature with too many tentacles. "I am no leviathan, but I manage. It would be easier with assistance."

"Then why have you not allied with the Conclave?" Tsung pressed. "Whatever your differences, surely this is–"

"Those men," the Lady spat. "They know nothing of danger, nor of obligation. They were only ever freed of that prison because of my goodwill, and the first chance they had, they turned against me because they fear women. They fear me. They have done all they can to overthrow me ever since."

I might not have made the connection if I hadn't spent the morning on an Alcatraz tour and the afternoon trying to escape it. "Wait. Three men. About… fifty years ago?"

The Lady nodded, shoving through the undergrowth with more force than needed. One struggling sapling creaked, groaned, and fell slowly into the squelchy cushion of the fungus surrounding it. "Even so. One had a touch of Shadow upon him. The other two were brothers of my bloodline, greatly removed. Three ingrates. Three fools. I will let the Voidlands end them before I join with them. And if you are foolish enough to seek them out, I will have naught to do with you."

I pressed my lips hard together. It wouldn't do to laugh in the face of such fury. I fell back and braced myself against the tarry trunk of a fallen tree. More of the scorched-asphalt smelling fungus covered it. Even the spongy slick surface and the stink couldn't dampen my amusement. I released it under the guise of a coughing fit.

"Mother?" Mei Shen's hand hovered above my back, a comforting heat. She exchanged a worried glance with Tsung. I waved away their concerns and regretted it when my waving sent a waft of eau de burned rubber in my direction.

"It's fine. I'm fine. I just... I think I know the identities of the Conclave."

I explained as we trailed the Lady back to her camp, about Frank Morris and the Anglin brothers, John and Clarence. About the years they spent digging with spoons through the porous stone at the back of their cells, of the raft made of rubber-backed coats – or was it? Kraben skin had that same rubbery quality – and the nighttime escape. I told them about the disappearance, the presumed death, the conspiracy theories and reported sightings over the years. The *Mythbusters* episode.

"Seriously, Tsung. You've never seen *Escape from Alcatraz*?" I muttered.

Mei Shen, at least, could be forgiven for her lack of pop culture knowledge. "It makes no sense. They could have gone anywhere, and they went back to the place they escaped?" she asked.

I shrugged. "It closed less than a year after their escape. Wonder if they had something to do with that. Or maybe they just took advantage of it."

"And the chance to assert control over what once controlled them?" Tsung mused. "Men have done stupider things for similar reasons."

I gave Tsung a long, searching look. He flinched and looked away before I could read more than my own biases and suspicions in his expression.

I stopped trying when Mei Shen dug a burning elbow into my side. "Ow. Okay. So, Frank Morris and the Anglin brothers go back to their thieving ways. This time, it's tech from Argent – gonna go out on a limb and say they used that proprietary energy technology to get the lighthouse up and running."

"And they are using that to siphon off bits of the Voidlands to make their knights," Mei Shen murmured.

It made a horrible kind of sense. The Conclave knights weren't like any other Shadow denizen I'd encountered. They were solid. They bled. They could cross over to our world on their own. "The knights go back long before Lung Di abandoned his wards, but given what you saw in the cell block at Alcatraz, I can believe the Conclave has stepped up production."

We came to a fallen tree at least two stories tall and covered with black fungus. Our conversation stumbled to a halt while we waited for the Lady's gargoyles to carry us over it – even Mei Shen, though she could have flown herself. But that would have lit the entire forest up with her light, and we'd already drawn enough attention.

"What about this new master the Lady mentioned?" Tsung asked, more to Mei Shen than myself. "We hadn't heard anything about that."

"Guess we could, y'know, ask," I said. We were approaching the ring of trees that sheltered the Lady's camp. A crowd of residents who had been left behind scurried out to greet our return. I pushed forward toward the Lady, sidestepping a goblin, ducking under a kraben wing, hopping a few trailing tentacles from the ambulatory octopodes. "Pardon, Lady. We didn't mean to upset you with… our…" My apology dribbled to a stop as I saw the creature leading the welcoming committee. "T-Templeton?"

"Hi, Missy!" And then the rat astonished me even more, splaying out his paws before the Lady and burying his nose in the mulch in something very like a bow. The gems set in the leather gauntlet fastened around his front leg caught the light from Mei Shen's scales.

The Lady knelt and set a proprietary hand on his flank, looking up at me. "You know my lieutenant. I hope you will not challenge me over him?"

Challenge her? "Er. No. Templeton is free to do what he wants."

The Lady stood. "You are an odd creature." She glared down at Templeton. "And you were instructed to stay and observe."

"I have news," Templeton said. It was strange to see him being so solemn. But his solemnity broke when he looked up at me, all sparkling eyes and ratty grin. "I'm a spy, Missy. I'm sorry I couldn't tell you before."

"S'okay," I said faintly. Of all things, I hadn't expected to see Templeton here. And I certainly hadn't expected him to be a double agent for the Lady. Maybe I should have challenged her for him. He was going to get himself hurt. Or worse. "Spies have to keep secrets."

"And share their news," said the Lady. "Inside. To shield us from hunting eyes." She made her way through the passage, and we all squeezed after her. The motley guard scattered once we'd reached the safety of the warded clearing, but the Lady didn't stop until she reached the yurt at the center of her camp and motioned us all to enter.

The inside of the Lady's home was like no place I'd ever seen in the Shadow Realms. It was warmly lit with a hodgepodge of lamps and lanterns – paper and colored glass and cut tin. It was cozy. There was color. Granted, mostly dark jewel tones. It came from a collection of junk that would make any thrift-store hoarder drool with envy. A full suit of dented, tarnished armor listed against a taxidermied bear with patchy brown fur and dusty glass eyes. A brass samovar filled with peacock feathers permanently depressed the jagged keys of a folding harpsichord. The photo that she'd made off with of younger me with my missing tooth and my spotless gi was propped up on the scratched lid. Threadbare carpets covered the ground, the central one picking out the gruesome slaughter of a unicorn by a pack of hounds. The vermillion of the hounds' blood and the silver-gold of the unicorn's seemed to float a breath above the carpet, so vivid were they in comparison to the other, muted colors of the weft and weave.

The Lady sat in a high-backed chair that was rendered more thronelike by her presence. "Report," she told Templeton, who had settled in a hunch of ratty obeisance at her feet.

Templeton hadn't quite gotten the knack of serving two mistresses at once. He worried his tail between his paws and looked back at me. "He knows you were there. He knows who you are. He has your scent. You left your backpack."

I glanced at Mei Shen and Tsung, but they looked as mystified as I felt. I suffered a twinge of panic that Templeton meant that someone else had guessed the connection between Missy and Mr

Mystic, but there was nothing in my bag to lead to that connection. Even Jack's number on my phone was coded and went to a burner. "Who?"

The Lady responded for Templeton. "The Conclave's new master. He has been hunting, and now he has found you. I suppose it was inevitable. You should remain here. It will be safer."

Safer from what? "Who is this master? Who's hunting me?" Until today, the Conclave had left Mr Mystic alone, and they didn't know about Missy at all.

"The great cat. The shadow cat." She tilted her head. "Though I suppose it can be said that all cats belong partly to the Shadow Realms and partly to Alam al-Jinn."

A shadow cat? Or... no. *The* shadow cat.

The cat. I only knew of one feline who had it in for me. Lao Hu.

"Tiger," I muttered.

I was so fucked.

ELEVEN
Worst Laid Plans

After a quick breakdown of what had been in my backpack, Mei Shen and Tsung agreed that it would be suicidal for me to return home. We could hope that Lao Hu had no great knowledge of how the real world worked, but Frank Morris and the Anglin brothers did, at least well enough to plan successful raids against Argent in cities across the world. If they were helping Lao Hu, he'd have my home address, most of my friends and former flops, the Dragon's Pearl and Dojo d'Cho. Anything related to Missy Masters was a danger. I didn't even dare bring Jack into it. Friends don't let friends get on the bad side of the chthonic expression of feline cunning and caprice.

"You could come with us. David and I can keep you safe," Mei Shen said, worrying my hand between hers. It no longer burned. With the Lady's help, we'd crossed over into the real world. My daughter looked like a normal young woman again.

Young woman. I was going to have to force myself to get used to that as a concept.

My prediction had been correct on our location. The Lady's camp stood in the heart of Muir Woods, only a few hundred yards from the visitors' center. The redwoods seemed puny in comparison to their Shadow Realms counterparts, but the fresh scent of sun-warmed bark and broken evergreen needles was welcome. Mist still sat in the hollows and low places, despite the day pushing past morning. We'd gone all night in the Shadow Realms, between walking the length of the bay, our capture, and our time touring the Lady's wards.

We stood at the parking lot dropoff, saying our goodbyes next to the town car that Tsung had called using the lone payphone. I smoothed Mei Shen's hair. "I suspect I'm safest in the Lady's camp. I'm more worried about you and Tsung. What are you going to do?"

"Sleep?" Mei Shen huffed softly. "Continue to work on my uncle's wards. After seeing how the Lady's wards work, I wonder if I'm going about it all wrong."

"What do you mean?"

"That slimy black stuff that was growing on everything? She's using it to gather energy from the Shadow Realms itself. She isn't powering the wards. The Shadow Realms are."

Well, that couldn't be sustainable. It was already

decimating the forest. "We are *not* covering San Francisco in black mold," I said. I was putting my foot down on that as a Bad Idea.

Mei Shen giggled, and I couldn't help but join her. We were well past sleep-deprived city and heading toward loopyville. "It would solve the housing crisis and the whole tech-bro problem. No more families being evicted out of Chinatown," she said.

"No. Black. Mold. I expect Tsung and I will be in agreement for once."

Mei Shen sighed and pulled away. "I wish…"

"What?"

She hugged herself, chewing her lip, before blurting, "It doesn't help that you refuse to use his name."

I wanted to argue, but she was probably right. It may have been unconscious. It was also deliberate. "I don't like him."

Mei Shen's barked laugh caused several passing hikers to give us odd looks. "Yes. You have made that abundantly clear. You. Mian Zi. Father. And you have made it clear that you think less of me for thinking well of him."

Again, it was hard to argue with hard truths. I held out my hands. "Can you at least understand why we're all so worried?"

"No. Nothing is as clear as any of you have taught me it was. My uncle has done bad things. He also held the Voidlands at bay when nobody else would. And that he isn't doing so now is because of what you and Father did."

Ouch. "You mean giving birth to you."

"I do not regret being alive. And I accept the responsibility you both have placed on me. But I no longer blindly accept that either of you knows what is best. I will determine that for myself."

Well. Shit. Maternal pride was a fucked up thing. I pulled her into a hug before I could start bawling. "I can live with that."

David Tsung finished conferring with the driver and came around the front of the car, scuffing at the gravel to announce his approach. "We should go. Are you sure you won't come with us?"

I gave Mei Shen a final squeeze before releasing her. We both spent a few moments wiping eyes and noses. "The Lady knows more about what's going on than anyone. She can protect me until I come up with some kind of a plan to deal with... all of this."

"Right. Anything to add to your care package?" We'd discussed what I would need: a few changes of clothes, including a suit and hat in case Mr Mystic was needed. A few burner phones and a tablet. Cash. Food and water. He hadn't raised a fuss at any of my requests.

Dammit. I was going to have to start trying not to disapprove. "I think I'm good."

"Right then. Six pm. I'll tell the driver to wait in case you get... delayed." He held open the door for Mei Shen before climbing in himself.

"Thanks. And... David?" I caught the door

and pretended to ignore his stunned look and
Mei Shen's small, pleased smile. "At the risk of
setting feminism back several decades and horribly
offending my daughter's sense of independence in
the process... take care of her."

David nodded. I still didn't trust him, but I
believed him when he said, "With my life."

Wandering Muir Woods for a while would have
been a nice break from the darkness of the Shadow
Realms and the stink of heated rubber and burning
asphalt, but I was exhausted, and paranoia had me
peering through ferns and jumping at every loud
noise that echoed through the busy hub. Templeton
had assured us that Lao Hu knew who I was, but not
where I was. The assumption among the Conclave
was that Mei Shen and I had escaped by flying across
the bay. Before vanishing into the water, my Blood-
Dimmed Tide had apparently covered that section of
the island with a blood scent so thick that not even
Lao Hu could track through it. Small mercies there.

I used the money pooled from Mei Shen and...
David to buy a couple of overpriced bottles of water
and a few packaged meals from the visitors' center
café before wandering up one of the trails to the
spot where we'd stepped through earlier.

Templeton, bless him, was waiting for me on the
other side when I slipped back through. And with
him—

"Rover!" I exclaimed. Possibly too brightly, as

my voice echoed through the night-dark forest, bouncing oddly off the huge trees. Templeton flinched and glanced around nervously. I ignored him in favor of holding up my hand for the flitting spark to land on. Rover's carapace – a few shades darker than Mei Shen's scales, but no less shiny – closed with an impressive snap for a critter no bigger than my thumbnail.

I should not have been this happy to be reunited with a bug I'd only just met. Or made? "I thought he got shredded by the gargoyles," I explained to Templeton, shifting Red Rover from the back of my hand to my shoulder. He perched there like a shiny, bloody ladybug pin.

"I thought he might be one of yours. He looks like the others." Templeton sounded positively grumpy, which I thought might be due to my shouting while Lao Hu was on the hunt. He turned and trundled back in the direction of the Lady's camp. There was something odd about his gait, the way his coat bristled along his back and his tail swished in agitation.

Could Templeton be jealous?

"Hey." I hurried to catch up with him, bumping his flank gently with my knee. "You're still my favorite guy. My Rat-Friday."

He glanced up at me, and I realized that his gait was because he had his paw, the one with the jeweled gauntlet, clutched protectively to his chest. "Even though I serve the Lady now?"

"Are you kidding me? I'm proud of you for that. Although I don't understand why you're doing it."

"Because of..." Templeton glanced around, but there was just us, the trees, and the black fungus creeping over everything. "*Him*," he hissed.

Him? Lung Di?

Or. No. Him, Lao Hu. Tiger. "You became a spy to protect me?" Shit, I was going to cry again. I really needed to eat and sleep.

We came to the tree with the hidden tunnel, and Templeton led the way through. The ambulatory octopodes were standing guard on the other side with their Louisville Slugger clutched between them. They waved us past after a few watery blinks.

Templeton seemed to relax once we were in the safety of the camp. "He took over the Conclave so that he could hunt you, and in return he taught the Conclave how to use the light to shape the voidstuff more quickly. I couldn't help hunt you. You're my Missy. So I came to the Lady and said I would serve her if she would protect you."

I stumbled to a stop just outside the yurt, the edge of the flap wrinkling in my grip. "Oh, Templeton."

"I have to go back now. But you are safe."

"But..." I struggled with my protective urge. What I'd told the Lady was true. Templeton wasn't mine to order about. He made his own decisions – even if many of those decisions seemed to be for my benefit, something I didn't know how to curb. This was why I tried not to call on him too often. I didn't want him putting himself at risk to help me.

"I'm safe here now. I could challenge the Lady for you—" I fell silent when his whiskers drooped. Shit. "Rover. Red Rover." I plucked the little scarab from my shoulder. "Go with him. Stay hidden. Help him as though he were me. I place you and all the Blood-Dimmed Tide under Templeton's command. Understand?"

Rover flashed and fluttered down to land on Templeton's gauntlet, settling above the opal in the center like he was another jewel.

"He is... very pretty," Templeton said, snuffling at his new gem. "Thank you, Missy."

I crouched down to hug him. "Don't do anything stupid. Keep yourself safe."

He nuzzled my cheek. "I will return when I can with more news," he said, and trundled away admiring his new pal. It didn't escape my notice that he hadn't made any promises about his safety.

Feeling pretty surly and with nobody present on whom I could fairly vent my irritation, I shoved my way into the Lady's yurt.

The Lady sat on her throne with the shreds of my coat spread across her lap. She seemed to be picking it apart into pattern pieces with a pair of embroidery scissors. I really didn't want to know what place it would take in her collection of junk. I dragged the bench away from the harpsichord, straddled it, and dug in to one of my boxed lunches.

I devoured most of a tofu wrap with peanut sauce before I started to feel vaguely human again. I washed it down with one of my bottled waters, ran my tongue over my teeth. Lordy, I needed a toothbrush.

"These wards you've created. Mei Shen says you're tapping in to the Shadow Realms to power them. Eating away at it."

"All wards must be powered by something." The Lady had changed out of the fatigues and… well, I could hardly say back into her gown when the gown seemed to be made of the same stuff that she was. She'd finished picking apart my coat and started piecing it back together with patchwork bits of fabric and silver thread. Was she… mending my coat?

"All wards?" I asked. I knew big wards seemed to need it. Lung Di had imprisoned Lao Hu and the other Guardians of China – and all the Chinatowns – to create his barriers. That was why Lao Hu had it in for us. But… "Even the little ones, like the one you scraped into my wall?"

"Little wards require little power. Great wards require great power. Few things are powerful enough to fuel the wards that hold back the Voidlands. So I use the potential of this land. It is not without cost, I admit."

I used a wet nap to clean my fingers and thought about that cost. The Shadow Realms scared me, but they had their place and their function. They were meant to be a buffer between the Ten Thousand

Things and the source that could not be named. At least, that had been Jian Huo's way of explaining it. Lung Di had made what was on the other side of the Voidlands sound a lot more terrifying and, having seen it for myself, I was inclined to agree with him on that point.

"Could something else... someone else... power it?"

The Lady paused mid-stitch. Light from the lamps flashed off her needle and the silver thread. "Such as?"

"Lao Hu?"

She knotted off the piece she was working on and started on another. "I can't imagine the cat being amenable to that."

"Wasn't planning on asking him," I muttered. Though that wasn't precisely true. He was my last resort if my plan A fell through. "What about another realm? You mentioned the realm where the Djinn come from? Alam al-Jinn? You're familiar with it?"

The Lady stopped her mending again and leaned forward while I fidgeted on my bench. "So you suggest, instead of devouring this realm, that we substitute another?"

"No. Not exactly. Look, the best solution would be a balanced approach. The Voidlands are encroaching because something on the other side is pushing. They're out of balance. The Conclave–"

The Lady hissed and drew back. I held up a hand.

"Hear me out. The Conclave has figured out a way to redirect that energy. But it still has to go somewhere, so they're making more and more knights. I think we can all agree that's going to be a problem, especially if you keep weakening the foundation of your power in your own attempts to push back the Voidlands."

"I will not work with those men. They take everything that is precious."

"And I'm not asking you to. They're not exactly my favorite people, what with being allied with Lao Hu and all. I'm just suggesting a more balanced exchange. We figure out how they're siphoning off the void, and we feed that energy into Alam al-Jinn, which is also out of balance. The void gets burned off safely, then we use the surplus energy from Alam al-Jinn to ward off the weakened Voidlands."

The Lady sat back in her chair, long fingers stroking a ragged gash in my coat. "We will need to take away the Conclave's stolen technology and subvert their lighthouse to our use."

I sighed "Yeah. Well, I can't seem to avoid getting embroiled in that mess. Might as well do it for the right reasons."

"How do you propose to gather the energy of Alam al-Jinn?"

That, at least, I had an answer for. "What do you know about the Djinn and their ability to travel through unalloyed metal?"

•••

As it turned out, the Lady knew very little about the Djinn. No surprise, really. But she did have a wealth of ideas about how to connect a new network of Alam al-Jinn attuned nodes to the existing mishmash of wards.

"– and that point would act as a terminus, creating a synergy between my vanguard, the Red Gate, the Shadow Dragon's shrine, and the Conclave's Citadel."

She placed markers – bottle caps from a jar that had been stuffed between the greaves of the suit of armor – on a cheesy cartoon map of the city that we had spread across the carpet. She had strange names for some familiar places, but with the map, I was able to follow most of them.

"Right, so we need a node at Land's End to connect what you have along the coast with the Golden Gate Bridge, Chinatown, and Alcatraz." I scanned the map. Seven locations, aligning with the seven hills, with additional terminus nodes at the lighthouse on Alcatraz and the labyrinth at Land's End.

Nine. I liked nine. Nine was a number I was vastly comfortable invoking in a ritual. "Is that it? Do we actually have a workable plan?" I stifled the urge to laugh. To point out it was too easy. To point out that something was bound to go wrong.

"There are still many details to be worked out. The shadow sigils will need to be paired with Djinn markings. We will need to acquire these nodes of yours. Any impurities will eventually create blockages that must be corrected. We will need to devise some sort of ritual to align and awaken them. And of course, we will need to subvert the Conclave's hold on the lighthouse and divert it to our use."

"Right. Details." I yawned as I again traced the lightning bolt path from the lighthouse to Land's End. Terminus to terminus. For the next steps, I'd need a phone and a prayer in hell that I could avoid Lao Hu's notice while I connected the people who needed to be connected.

I yawned again and glanced at an old windup alarm clock I'd dug out from the Lady's hoard. It was the kind with two bells on top that I could have sworn only existed in cartoons. I'd ballparked the time when I set it, and I was confident that David's delivery driver would wait all night if he had to, but I didn't want to put him out. Besides, the sooner I met up with him, the sooner I could crash out and sleep for... oh, days, at least.

"I need to go out again," I told the Lady, rising and stretching. Walking all day the day before and then spending a chunk of the afternoon kneeling over the map made my legs creak.

"Then I will go with you," the Lady said, rising as well.

I gave myself a few moments to come up with a response more diplomatic than "the hell you will."

"Um. Are you sure that's... you stand out, a bit. And there will still be a decent number of hikers around to notice you."

"I do not need to stand out. I am able to walk the light realms without drawing notice." She lifted my mended coat from the chair, a mad patchwork of shreds and silver threads now, and slipped it on.

Great. Just peachy. But I was too tired to argue, so I just shrugged and led the way back to the spot where I'd met Templeton.

I was not too tired to raise a protest when the Lady and I stepped into the real world and I realized I was facing a doppelganger of myself.

"Holy, what the everloving – ack!" In my stumble backwards, my feet found a helpful log and I tumbled over it. The ferns rustled as I displaced them, and the ground squelched soggily under my ass.

"Is this not adequate?" The Lady... my twin... reached down a hand to help me. Now that I could take a moment to look, there were subtle differences. Her hair was a darker red than mine and didn't catch the light. The hollows beneath her eyes and cheekbones seemed more sunken, more shadowed. And of course, the coat she wore looked like some ragged custom fairy version of the original.

Great. She wasn't just my twin. She was my evil, gothy twin.

"That's uncanny as shit is what that is." I reluctantly let her help me up. Her fingers still had that overlong, double-jointed quality, which didn't help at all with the uncanny. "Can you just... at least change the rest of the clothes up? We're only going to attract more attention with the Doublemint Twins bit."

After some coaching, the Lady was able to shift her clothing so that we were more complementary than identical, and her features, which was unnerving enough for me that I had to look away. But eventually, we got her sorted. Exhaustion was forming a sort of buffer around my reactions. I just couldn't seem to sustain the will to care about anything for longer than a few minutes. We hiked down to the visitors' center and parking lot, the Lady taking in the world outside the Shadow Realms with the same wide-eyed wonder that she'd explored my apartment. I guess she didn't get out much.

The driver was late, because of course he was. I sat on a bench at the parking lot dropoff while the Lady wandered, peering at cars, poking at tourists – or maybe that was the other way around. I struggled to keep my eyes open, waved at the hikers who were meandering back to their cars. The golden afternoon sunlight streaming through the canopy mellowed and dimmed as the sun dipped below the tree line, and still no driver. My shoulders hunched higher and higher at having my back exposed to a mountain's worth of trees and ferns. Exactly the sort of terrain Lao Hu was suited for. Even the squirrels were making me jumpy by the time a familiar blue Fit looped around the passenger dropoff zone and pulled into one of the short-term spaces near the front of the lot.

"Shimizu?" I hopped up from my bench, torn between irritation and relief. I'd been expecting a stranger. I shouldn't be this happy to see a friend. "I'm going to kill Mei Shen for letting you put yourself in danger like this," I shouted, even as I hurried around the front of the car to hug her as she climbed out.

She squeezed back just as hard. "Like I gave her a choice. It was me or Jack, and I won the rochambeau."

I giggled. "Nothing beats rock?"

"You know it. Here, before I forget." She snagged the strap of an overnight duffel sitting in the passenger seat and passed it to me. "The suit bag and hatbox are in the back. And I hear you might need some stitches?"

I lifted my bound arm, digging out a toothbrush one-handed. "It's fine. You are the best."

"Yeah, you can – holy fuckballs!"

I looked behind me to see the Lady approaching, groaned and rested my head against the doorframe. "Yeah. Tell me about it."

"Is... how is... I... need to sit."

I shut the car door and escorted her to the bench. The Lady loomed above us, looking vaguely bemused. Also, vaguely threatening.

"She looks like you."

"Really? I don't see the resemblance at all."

They both glared at me. Apparently, sleep deprivation made me think I was more hilarious than I actually was.

"I am the Lady. You are Missy's companion."

"Er... friend. Roommate," I clarified.

"Yeah, we're not together or anything," Shimizu said. Her focus bounced back and forth between us like we were playing tennis. "You're the one who took Estelle, and now you're using her to hold back the Nothing," she said, then, to me, "Mei Shen brought me up to date."

"I am. Would you like to see Estelle?" the Lady asked.

I put my hand on Shimizu's arm. It was dangerous enough her being here. I was not dragging her into the Shadow Realms, even if there was a headless ghostly bride at the end of that gothy rainbow. "No."

"But–"

"There's mold."

"Er..."

"Slimy black mold covering *everything*."

Shimizu shuddered. "Okay. That's a big nope."

"You should really head back. The Lady came to protect me, but it isn't safe with Lao Hu on the prowl." I gave her another hug, one-armed this time. "But thank you for coming and bringing all this. You are the best of friends. Even if you take stupid risks."

She stood and palmed her car keys. A dozen charms dangled from them – bunnies and foxes and waving cats. I noticed the Lady eying them hungrily. "Well, we all have to do our part to save the world. Do you have a plan? You know, to save the world? Mei Shen seemed to think this Voidlands thing was pretty bad. Maybe even worse than the Tiger thing. Cause. You know. Earthquakes."

"Pretty bad. Getting worse." I smiled at the Lady. "And I think we do have a plan. I'll just have to work around the whole Tiger thing."

"You know, if you need me to do anything..."

I considered. It would be a lot easier if I had a pair of trusted boots on the ground. Someone who could wrangle the cats – er, people – while I was in hiding. "I might. This is going to be hard enough to pull off without bringing in Argent."

"You're not going back to them?"

"They want their tech. I suspect they'll look on the rest of this as not their circus, not their monkeys. And honestly, after what went down at the Academy of Sciences, I'm not sure how much I trust them."

"Not even Skyrocket?"

I laughed. "I wish he was involved. He would have put a stop to that whole debacle with Asha." Maybe that should be my new ethical compass – what would Tom do?

Shimizu's frown dampened my amusement. "He's not involved? Not even in some, I don't know, top secret capacity where you say 'I can neither confirm nor deny' but we both know what you really mean?"

I shivered. The evening was growing chilly and

the Lady had stolen my coat. "I haven't seen him since the initial attack on the Academy. Why?"

Shimizu shook her head. "It's probably nothing. Just... he hasn't been doing the talk shows, and he always does the PR after something like this. And then... he canceled on the Oskaloosa Founders Day parade this year."

"The parade?"

Shimizu waved her hands, keys and charms jangling. "It's silly, I know. Everyone is trying to be understanding–"

"The parade that Skyrocket hasn't missed since Tom's grandfather first strapped on a rocket pack and managed to *not* burn off his own ass?" I clarified.

"Well. Yeah."

"Fuck." I shoved off the bench and yanked open Shimizu's passenger door, tossing the duffel in the seat well. "Lady, I'm sorry. I need to go back to the city."

"I do not think–"

"Missy, what are you–"

"I know where the Conclave has been getting its intel on the secret Argent facilities. I know what they took at the Academy," I said. "They have Skyrocket."

I climbed in and slammed the door. Abby was going to answer for not telling me sooner. Stolen fucking tech my ass.

TWELVE
Short for Stormtroopers

The Lady argued – vociferously – against my leaving, but the confrontation I needed to have with Abby wasn't the sort of thing that could be conducted by phone. When I wouldn't relent, she snaked into Shimizu's back seat and refused to budge. "I have given my word to the rat. I will not go back on it."

Fair enough. It was an awkward, mostly silent ride back to the city. I dug a legal pad out of my care duffel and wrote out my findings and plans in a car-shaken hand, everything we'd discovered over the past several days. The Lady's tension eased somewhat once the sun had set. She pressed her cheek to the back window in open-mouthed wonder when we crossed over the Golden Gate Bridge.

"It is one of the great workings," she murmured, and I didn't think she was talking about technological achievement. I chanced a glimpse across the veil into the Shadow Realms, and just as quickly looked away when I sensed the Voidlands shoving up to the span like an overconfident tech bro at a queer-friendly bar.

I had Shimizu drop us at a boutique hotel just off Market. The Mark Twain was the sort of place where the refreshed Victorian decor struggled to deserve the high prices. I wasn't worried about the money. David had included a credit card in my care duffel. I just had to hope the Conclave wasn't tech savvy enough to track my passport.

Abby responded almost immediately to my vaguely worded text requesting a meeting the following morning. I keyed the Lady and myself into our room, dumped my duffel next to the door, and collapsed face first onto one of the double beds.

"Wake me in the never," I mumbled into the duvet.

The mattress depressed. The Lady, sitting at my side. I turned my face and barely missed burying my nose into her thigh.

"It occurs to me that I may be of more use than mere warding. If Lao Hu seeks you, then let us give him something to seek."

"Bfhuh?" I asked, the duvet taking the brunt of my question.

"If you allow me command of them, I may take your swarm of scarabs and lay trails through this city that would confuse even the hunter among hunters."

I opened one eye and craned my neck so that

I could see her face. My face. Sort of. "Templeton must be the greatest spy of all time."

She looked away, rose and left the bed for other parts of the room. "He… has been very loyal."

I was an ass. Being tired made me an ass. I closed my eyes and pressed my forehead into the duvet once again. "Sorry. What I meant to say was yes, please and thank you."

"Very well. You call them the Blood-Dimmed Tide, yes?"

I mumbled assent into the bed. I was already regretting that one. It had seemed an appropriate name at the time.

"Then I will use that to summon them and begin anon." I heard her puttering about – warding the room, maybe, or possibly setting aside things to steal later. Just as I was drifting off, I felt her stroke my hair. "Sleep now, child."

Later, I thought muzzily. Later we could have a chat about boundaries. And I could worry about why the Queen of Air and Darkness seemed to be hitting on me.

Later didn't arrive with morning. The Lady was absent when I woke. Hoping she'd been around the real world enough to know how to take care of herself, I showered, dressed in my suit and hat, and headed out to ream Abby a new one.

The legal pad I'd used to make my notes made a satisfying slap when I tossed it on Abby's desk. The bullish expression she'd worn when I entered her office faltered. She lifted the pad, skimming the first page of spidery writing. "I thought you were out, Old Man. What's this?"

I closed her door, threw the bolt, before sitting. "Everything I've learned about the Conclave and their operations over the past few days. In the spirit of an open sharing of information. Now why don't *you* tell *me* about Skyrocket?"

Abby lowered the pad slowly, lips slack in surprise. I watched them as she attempted to shape and then discarded several replies.

"Better yet," I continued softly when she remained at a loss. "Why didn't you tell me about Skyrocket?"

She finally settled on, "How did you find out about that?"

"At the risk of sounding clichéd, I am asking the questions here. The Conclave knights drew him off and took him during the Academy attack, yes? He was always the target. They've been using him to get information on the other Argent facilities so that they can steal more of Argent's power technology, like the tech that fuels Skyrocket's jetpack. Have I missed anything?"

Abby stood and looked out the window behind her desk. She'd cleared away the boxes that had been blocking it. Most of the shelves were now filled with books. The wooden blinds painted her in stripes of light and shadow. I glanced uneasily behind me at the locked door. The reminder of Lao

Hu was the last thing my nerves needed just now.

"That about covers it. And I didn't tell you because I couldn't. I keep your secrets. Argent has their secrets, too."

"It would have helped me to know."

"Helped you before or after you walked out on us?"

I rose to my feet, torn between storming out and storming over to shake her. "I might not have walked out if I'd known Tom needed my help."

Dust puffed off the blinds when she snorted. "Someone's ethics are pretty damned pliable." She ran a finger along the blind. Dusting it off on her khakis, she turned to me, palms up in apology. "Sorry. Look. We haven't had much progress since you left. I get why you left. Hell, I even maybe respect it a bit. But does this mean you're back?" She tapped the notepad and raised her brows in a positively plaintive look. On anyone else, I'd have said it was begging.

Well, she was working with her obnoxious, estranged half sister, her judgmental and disapproving ex-lover, and a devout Muslim theurge who likely viewed both Abby and Asha as shayatin. Unclean, at best.

"No," I said, for the slightly vindictive pleasure of watching her slump. "You have a leak. Someone set those sigils at the Academy. Someone who was on site at the time of the attack. I don't trust Argent." I took my seat again and nudged the legal pad towards her. "However, I am putting together my own rescue mission. You, La Reina, Asha, and Sadakat would be a welcome addition. The rest of Argent is on need-to-know status."

Abby took the pad and began reading my notes more carefully. "Oh, Dunbarton is going to love that."

Once I'd walked through the issues and my solution with Abby, I left her to explain it to her companions and requisition what we needed from Argent. I spent the rest of the day in my hotel room, making calls, making plans, talking myself hoarse, explaining again and again until I had my patter down cold.

That evening, I gathered my rosebuds in the board room of Tsung Investment Capital, a more unlikely group of allies than I'd ever thought to see in one room.

David and Mei Shen sat together on one side of the long, oval table, and beside them, Johnny Cho. David managed to maintain the bland expression of a corporate executive as his receptionist escorted the Argent contingent into the conference room. Mei Shen was his opposite, staring unabashedly at La Reina – who, for her part, regarded Mei Shen with a similar intensity of fascination. Johnny kept passing his hand over his mouth. I suspected he was working hard to keep from busting a gut.

The Argent crew settled at the opposite side of

the table, La Reina shifting uncomfortably in an
executive chair that had not been designed to fit
someone with a full set of angel's wings. A few
murmured words from David to his wide-eyed
assistant, and a backless typing stool was rolled
in for La Reina's comfort. Asha, like Johnny,
seemed to be fighting to hold back her laughter.
Abby, in a perhaps unconscious reflection of my
mood, looked half-ready to smack upside the
head the first person who gave in to situationally
inappropriate levity.

Neither of us need have worried. Any urge
to levity was banished when Jack and Shimizu
arrived, and behind them, the Lady, looking like a
gothed-out version of Missy Masters.

Johnny leaned far back in his chair, absently
ruffling his hand through his red-tipped purple
spikes, as though checking to make sure his brains
hadn't escaped while he wasn't paying attention.
After a moment of puzzlement, Mei Shen whispered
a soft "aaaah" and leaned over to whisper in David's
ear. Abby ping-ponged looks between the Lady and
myself, rubbing her jaw and muttering, "Now that's
just plain uncanny."

Next to Abby, Asha's smile had drained away,
her warm, dark skin paling to a putty shade, but
it wasn't me that she turned her look of dawning
horror on. It was La Reina.

La Reina, who was already rising off her rolling
stool, wings raising, vanes taking on a soft,

threatening glow that made my belly flip with fear and hunger.

"What is *that* doing here?" La Reina spat, a growl of mixed fury and disgust. The Lady watched her, transfixed.

For my part, I had difficulty finding my voice around the yearning to reach out and embrace the implement of my destruction. "Sit down," I whispered, clutching the back of my chair.

"You did not say your help came in this form, or I should never have agreed to this. Do you even know what that is? I would be doing the world a favor if I banished it back to the plane from whence it came."

The Lady reached a long-fingered hand towards La Reina's growing light – I hoped it was only my imagination, the smoke rising from her skin. The sight of my dark reflection reaching so eagerly for that light broke my paralysis.

"La Reina de Los Angeles," I barked. Several of the others jumped. La Reina didn't so much as blink. "The Lady is my guest. I did not invite her here to put her in danger. You will sit down and dampen your wings, or I will banish *you* back to the plane from whence you came."

It was an empty threat. I didn't know if such a thing could even be done, let alone how to do it. I prayed that she didn't know that.

La Reina's wings dimmed and drooped. There was something almost like fear in the look she gave me. "… You wouldn't."

"Try me," I snapped.

After a moment's more hesitation, she shrugged. The remaining light snuffed out, and her wings relaxed against her back, a tawny feathered cape once more. She resumed her seat, and Sadakat leaned close to whisper to her, much as Mei Shen had whispered to David.

I turned to the Lady, who was blinking as though waking from a slumber. I gave her an abbreviated bow. "My apologies, Lady."

She pressed her scorched fingers together, open and closed. "Fascinating," she murmured, and sat.

I took a moment to collect myself. I'd missed my calling as a cat herder. Before the silence could get any more uncomfortable, I unfolded two maps – the city and the island – and spread them across the table.

"I've already explained to each of you that we are facing a set of interrelated issues. The Conclave's abduction of Skyrocket," I nodded to Abby's crew, "and the expansion of the Voidlands, which also happens to be the reason the Conclave wanted Skyrocket."

"And Lao Hu," Mei Shen said. "Do not forget him."

As if I could. "Lao Hu's vendetta is against me. I would rather it not expand to the rest of you. The Lady has been kind enough to leave false trails throughout the city today. Let us hope that's enough to distract him." I refrained from elucidating. If La Reina had issues with the Lady, then I suspected her feelings regarding my blood-scarab army wouldn't be that much more welcoming.

I allowed myself a small smile at that thought, unseen by the others, thanks to the shadows pulled over my face. "Once we receive word that Lao Hu has left to hunt for me, Mr Wentworth and Ms Shimizu will head to Alcatraz to deliver the first terminus node and set the sigils that will allow us to pass the wards surrounding the island. The Lady will lead her people in a feint while Mr Tsung collects the node and primes it at the lighthouse. Asha and myself will free Skyrocket, meet Mr Tsung at the lighthouse, and the four of us will escape via the node."

"The rat believes your man is being held in the northernmost part of the citadel. Here." The Lady's finger ticked against the Alcatraz map.

"The Model Industries Building," Asha said, nodding. "Shouldn't be a problem. In, out, and then I'm done."

"Asha," Abby snarled.

"Those are the terms of my contract. I get him off that island, I'm done." The smile she gave Abby was sickly sweet. "Perhaps you should have asked for my help nicely."

"Bitch," Abby muttered. She crossed her arms. Mules could take lessons from that jutted jaw. "I'm going to Alcatraz with you."

"No," I said.

"I didn't ask, Old Man–"

"And I didn't offer you a choice, Professor Trent. I need you elsewhere."

"Argent's interest ends at Skyrocket."

Sadakat placed a hand on Abby's arm before she could rise to face off with me. "There I must disagree, Professor Trent. These Voidlands are a grave danger. Grave enough that if the Conclave had not made us their enemies, Argent might have considered working with them. As it is, we must accept... other allies." Her worried frown encompassed not just the Lady, but David and myself.

La Reina's wings rustled, but she kept to her tight-lipped glaring. Only Johnny and Mei Shen escaped her stinkeye.

Abby's glares were all for me. "Fine. Where do you want me?"

"You – all the rest of you – will wait at the terminus nodes we are setting up around the city. Once the lighthouse node has been attuned, Asha will take us through to Rincon Hill, where Professor Trent will be waiting to help us attune that node."

"You expect us to attune the others?" Sadakat asked, frowning at the map, and then at our motley assembly. "Many here do not have the power or the skill..."

"I will be handing over my name to each of you," the Lady said softly. "So that you may summon me to the next point and the next." She tapped each hill in turn. "I will be the one to activate the nodes and attune them to Shadow."

I leaned forward, forcing La Reina and Sadakat's attention. "I trust you won't look on this as a weakness to exploit later?"

Sadakat flinched and exchanged a long, silent look with La Reina. I tamped down on my fidgets. This was not going to work if I couldn't trust everyone to do their part. Finally, Sadakat nodded. "You have my word."

La Reina followed suit. "And mine."

I relaxed. Slightly. "Thank you both. Once the Lady has attuned the node at Rincon Hill, Mr Wentworth will summon her to Coit Tower on Telegraph Hill, and so on to–"

"Wait," Asha said, frowning at the map. "The Lady is attuning the nodes to the Shadow Realms. Who is attuning them to Alam al-Jinn?"

I hadn't anticipated La Reina and Sadakat's resistance to the Lady's help, but this hurdle, I had. "I was rather hoping you might."

The conference room rang with Asha's laughter long enough to make everyone fidget. "Oh. Oh dear, but that *is* amusing. No."

"I understand your reluctance, but there must be something–"

"There is no incentive in this realm or any other that could convince me to bind myself to a set of Voidland wards."

"I'll do it," Abby said. Her scowl deepened at Asha's renewed laughter. "I wasn't joking."

"Oh, Abby. You'd need to exit and re-enter each node. Even the purest metals pose a danger then. And even if you're spared attuning the lighthouse, that leaves eight nodes for you to travel through. You don't have it in you."

"If you can do it, I can do it."

"You'll get yourself trapped, halfblood," Asha snarled.

Abby brushed under her arm, where her gun would be if I hadn't told her to leave it at home. "Well, that's one way to get me out of your hair for good."

Tetching and rolling her eyes like a surly teenager, Asha sank back in her chair. "Oh, fine. I will do it." She leaned back further to address Sadakat behind Abby's back. "We can discuss my *generous* compensation package later."

Leaning as she was, Asha missed Abby's slight smile and the wink she threw me. I tipped my hat as though to say "well played."

La Reina stood, tapping each ritual spot on the map. "You only have seven on the ground. Who will do the summoning at the final node?"

"I will," I said. "I'll have my motorcycle waiting at Rincon Hill. There should be time for me to get across the city so that the Lady and I – and Asha – can close the conduit that we opened at the lighthouse."

"And the city on both sides of the veil will be safe once more," the Lady concluded.

"Yeah. No more earthquakes. At least, no unnatural earthquakes," Shimizu said. I could have kissed her for reminding us why we were all here.

I leaned over and retrieved the maps, folding them carefully. "You all know what you need to do to prepare. Are there any questions?"

Sadakat already had her tablet out and was tapping away. "Argent has approved our requisition of the purified titanium, but it will take at least a day for La Reina and me to identify the nine purest samples."

I walked them to the door. "Work as fast as you reasonably can. We need to be ready when Lao Hu moves."

"Just keep that shit far away from me." Asha's voice echoed down the hall as the Argent contingent departed. "Although... purified titanium? How much of that do you think Argent would approve as my payment?"

I stopped Johnny as he made his way out. "You were oddly silent," I said, wondering if that meant he thought my plan was a good one, or doomed to fail.

He hitched a shoulder. "My part is fairly simple. Wait at the cable car museum for the call, integrate this set of wards with the various existing networks. I'll see if I can arrange some backup if you don't mind. The other guardians have a bit of experience with this sort of thing."

I sighed, relieved. He didn't think the plan was a disaster. "I didn't wish to impose on them, but I would welcome their assistance."

Johnny nodded, grin cracking his solemn mien. "You know that any plan with more than three moving parts is doomed to failure."

So much for winning his approval. "Thank you for that rousing vote of confidence," I deadpanned, ignoring his cheerful parting wave.

Mei Shen and David had reopened the Alcatraz map. The Lady had cornered a rather terrified-looking Jack to correct his sigils. Which just left Shimizu and myself in the doorway.

"Bye-bye, boys," she murmured under her breath.

I found it impossible not to answer the call with the appropriate response. "Have fun storming the prison."

"Seriously, though. Do you think this will work?" she asked, sounding more worried than Carol Kane.

I found myself wishing the following line wasn't quite so accurate a reflection of my estimation of our success. "It will take a miracle."

The next two days were a demonstration of a controlled descent into insanity – mine. I returned to the Lady's camp and holed up in her yurt lest I undo all her hard work of laying false trails.

With David driving the Lady down to the city and Shimizu and Jack waiting to hop onto the next Alcatraz ferry at a moment's notice, my main sources of contact were otherwise occupied. The Lady's camp was empty save for a few gargoyles. The rest of her army was waiting in the crevasse at the mouth of the long passage.

I spent most of the time considering the myriad of ways my plan could go wrong.

Thankfully, the Lady and David were in the camp when Templeton arrived with the news that Lao Hu had caught the scent of his quarry and gone on the prowl. David shunted across to the real world to make the go call, and we four took the gargoyle express to the mouth of the Alcatraz passage.

There seemed to be more to the Lady's army than before. More gargoyles, more kraben, more goblins. I spotted at least five pairings of ambulatory octopodes, though only the one pair wielded a baseball bat. And Estelle, the headless ghost bride, walked among the mob. As did my Blood-Dimmed Tide, with Templeton and Red Rover at its head.

When I asked, the Lady waved an elegant hand. She'd taken to wearing her version of my face when she was in the Shadow Realms. And my mended coat. "I have diverted the power I'm drawing to them, and recruited what new allies were available. If it leads to our success, we will be grateful for it. If we fail, then it is all moot."

I donned my hat, deepening the shadows beneath

the brim – my version of my grandfather's face. "Every battle should begin with a bit of cheerful nihilism, I suppose," I said, and waved for her to precede me into the passage.

"Says you," David muttered, passing me. "King Henry can keep his honor. I'll take the ten thousand extra forces, thanks."

I chuckled and followed before I could be swallowed up in the army at our heels. We few, indeed.

Any urge to laugh had been crushed by the weight of stone and darkness and fear by the time we reached the other end of the tunnel. We stopped at the soot-dark grate that led to the overgrown bowels of the Officer's Club. It had not changed in the few days since David, Mei Shen, and I made our escape. The foliage grew dense as any jungle; the crumbling walls rose to a cloud-racing sky as dark as a photo negative. I couldn't see any of the raptors, but I heard them rustling above, creaking and cawing at each other over the hollow sound of the wind.

"We will draw the knights north first," the Lady said as her army squeezed past us and took cover under the brambles. What had seemed many in the narrow crevasse and the narrower passage now seemed too few. "They will think we are making an attempt to steal their power source. That will give Mr Tsung time to set the node and lay down the sigils. Then we will retreat to the south."

I patted Estelle's shoulder as she passed me. The lace cuff of her thrift-store bridal gown caressed my cheek in response. "And Asha and I will recover Skyrocket and meet you both back at the lighthouse. Assuming she shows. Where is she?"

Asha had listened to our description of the tunnel and said she'd make her own arrangements for getting to Alcatraz. I didn't like it, but she wouldn't be budged.

"It is only a matter of time before we are discovered and lose the element of surprise," the Lady said, following her army out into the overgrown hollow. "We cannot wait long for her."

"And you don't have to," whispered a shadow, detaching itself from all the other shades lurking under the black scorched walls. Asha pushed up a pair of high-tech goggles and pulled down the mask covering her lower face. The rest of her was covered in dark, form-fitting tactical gear similar to what she'd been wearing at the Academy. "Took you long enough to get here."

I was surprised Abby had any teeth left. If I'd had to deal with Asha's smiles all these years, I'd have long ago ground mine to nubbins.

"And now we go," said the Lady, even as the raptors nesting in the top of the walls took to the blackened skies with screeches and caws of alarm.

David, Asha, and I pressed back into the mouth of the passage, watching the Lady's army surge up the escarpment and over the lip onto the road.

Raptor bodies rained down as the gargoyles noisily dispatched the early warning system.

We watched until the raucous cries of the Lady's army faded north to a distant roar. David roused and crept out of the passage. I grabbed his arm. "Be safe."

His glance flicked down to my hand and back to me, bemused. "You care?"

Only slightly less annoying than Asha, I decided. My teeth were doomed. "Mei Shen will never speak to me again if I get you killed."

David nodded. "I'll be as safe as I can while still being effective."

I released his arm, chuckling. "Keep that up, and I may start liking you myself."

"That's the plan." He winked and departed.

"And now we wait again," I muttered.

"There is no need," Asha said. "Among the many things they have been stealing from Argent, the Conclave has managed to take some of their purified titanium stores as well. I can sense it. North. Likely in the same building where they are keeping Skyrocket. I can take us there directly."

I stepped back before she could take my arm, paranoia prickling all down my spine. "That wasn't the plan."

She rolled her eyes. "It is a *better* plan. And one I could not have suggested until I was close enough to know the titanium was here, so it is not as though I deliberately kept it from you." She spread her hands. "Come. You're the one who helped bind me. Don't you trust me?"

I didn't want to. Because I had helped bind her. The sounds of battle had receded entirely. It was just us two in the hollow. Possibly just us on this entire side of the island. We would be safer sticking to the original plan of sneaking north along the road.

"How do you propose we get to it? It is not like there's much in the way of unalloyed metal lying around, and what with wishing to avoid building resonance, I doubt you brought any with you."

"No, but you did." She cocked her head to one side, her hip to the other. "I would have thought you stupid not to. As apparently you think me stupid. Did you miss the part where I can sense it?"

Oh. Right. I told the part of me that was howling suspicion to shut up. I'd already decided to trust Asha. It made little sense to start doubting her now. I dug into a pocket of my overcoat, the one not stuffed with glow sticks for a quick escape from the Shadow Realms, and pulled out a vacuum-sealed package that contained a bar of Argent's purified titanium.

Asha smiled and took the packet, cracking the seal. "Excellent. Now, hold on to your hat, Old Man. This may sting a bit." She took my arm, grabbed the bar of metal, and the world erupted into smoke and flame.

•••

In my time I have feared the Shadow Realms even as I sought to master them. I have cringed in gibbering terror from the Voidlands. I spent fifteen years in the timeless peace of a spirit realm that was as close to heaven as I'm likely to come, and I have been seared by the reflected light of whatever heaven La Reina serves.

I have never felt a realm burn me down to the very core of my being like Alam al-Jinn did. It wasn't flame scorching my skin to crackling char. The heat erupted from within, the marrow of my bones cooking my muscles, my flesh. Even the air in my lungs was fire as I screamed.

And then... it was gone. I stumbled to my knees from the sudden absence of pain, ran frantic hands over my face, my arms, expecting charred bits of me to slough off. Nothing. I was fine. Whole. The shadows I used to conceal my face had been seared away, but other than that, my jaunt through Alam al-Jinn hadn't harmed me in the least. Only the memory of the pain remained, and my mind was already scrambling to rationalize that away.

"Yes, the first time's a bit rough," someone said. Asha. She caught me under the armpits and helped me to my feet. "Probably worse for you. Oh, we have company."

Her bright comment was all the warning I got before a fist slammed into my gut. New pain replaced the old. Only Asha's hold on me kept me from staggering back and keeling over. She pushed me upright and shoved me forward into the fight. "Go get 'em, Old Man."

Another fist came at me. I danced aside – well, stumbled really – using the moment of transition to catch my breath and bearings, and to assess the trap Asha had led me into.

We'd emerged into a darkened cavern, its walls covered with bubbles of dimly glowing light. No. Wrong. The walls were too even, the bubbles too square and regimented. Building. Windows. A warehouse. I put my back to a wall lined with grey-cased commercial generators that hummed loudly enough to make my teeth and bones ache. The thing looming before me was larger than any Conclave knight I'd ever faced, but built along the same lines. Shifting, organic plates shielded its body rather than the usual semi-medieval armor that most of the knights wore.

Asha crouched behind the knight beside a toppled stack of crates. One of them had burst open, and a fortune in Argent's purified titanium bars rolled across the floor. She was digging in her bag, or possibly shoving the titanium into it. The knight didn't give me much time to worry about what she was up to. It picked its way towards me, off-balance thanks to a network of wrist-thick cables that ran from the generators at the far end of the room, past me, and out the open door. I could hear screams and howls from outside – the Lady's army?

The knight cleared the cables and charged me again. I dodged under its arms. So, big and armored, but not that bright.

A second knight rose up from behind the crates, blindsiding me with a running tackle. We rolled across the floor of the warehouse. I came out on the bottom, thick cable crossing under my back. The knight pressed down. I could barely catch my breath much less find any leverage to flip him off.

"Asha!" I dug my fingers into the crack between two of the plates. Impossible. If there was a weakness there, I wasn't going to find it before I was crushed to unconsciousness. "A-sha!"

A boot connected just below the plate I was scraping at. Not mine. The knight grunted and sagged to one side. Asha hopped over my legs, raising something black and gun-like. Light flashed strobe-fast with a frenetic ticking sound like a Tesla coil on speed. She shoved her hand against the shoulder of the reeling knight, and he went into convulsions.

Before I could reassess who was on whose side, the first knight roared and launched himself at Asha's back. I tangled his limbs with my legs, tripping him before he could reach her. The carapace covering him didn't offer much in the way of weakness, so I improvised. I snatched up the cable digging a groove into my back and flung a loop of it around his head. Glomming onto his back like an Atreides riding a sandworm, I dug my heels into his shoulder blades and pulled for all I was worth. My palms burned from the scrape of textured metal weave against my skin. I only loosed my hold when the knight flagged and fell to the floor next to his still-twitching friend.

I stumbled off him, wiping my burning palms on my trousers. Asha shook her taser, clicked the trigger a few times. It failed to emit even a faint tic-tic. She grimaced and tossed it aside. The clatter of plastic on cement echoed loudly in the cavernous room. "This place. Sucks power worse than a smartphone app hogging the GPS. Which makes me wonder," she tapped one of the grey-cased generators. "What sort of juice is powering these lovelies?" She glanced over at the knights. "We should dispose of them."

I backed up a few steps, nearly tripping over one of the cables. "I don't think–"

Asha huffed and drew a black-bladed combat knife from a back sheath, plunging it beneath the neck armor of both knights with surgical precision. She wiped the blade on her own thigh when the knights dissipated into pools of shadow. "We really don't have time for squeamishness," she muttered and headed for a door half-hidden by the grey-cased machinery.

Right. Right. I tried to rationalize that they weren't people. They were shaped by the Conclave, possibly from remnants of the Voidlands. Probably using the same energy coursing through those generators and cables. Even so, I stepped around the spot where the knights had fallen. "I thought for a moment that you were going to–"

"Betray you? I know." Asha laid a hand flat on the steel door, tapping her fingers over the metal and along the seam of the doorway, up to an electronic keypad. "Don't worry. I'm used to it."

I pulled the shadows back around my face, using that to recover my equilibrium. "Even so, I apologize."

"The amount of this purified titanium Argent is going to be giving me in payment, I can put up with a bit of suspicion." She tapped the keypad. "The door, the generators. All of this is real. None of it is created from shadow. They brought it here from the real world."

I studied the door, the generators and cables. "Perhaps it's part of the technology they've been stealing from Argent's facilities?"

Asha nodded. "Must be. We can't take it all."

"We are here for Skyrocket. Can you get through?"

Asha opened one of the pouches in her combat vest and drew out several small tools that looked like no lock picks I'd ever worked with. She unscrewed the face of the keypad with a tiny screwdriver and covered the insides with a mist from a stainless steel can of aerosol. "Old Man, I've yet to meet the door I couldn't get through."

I kept watch on the front door and the room

behind us, trusting her to know her business better than I could. The sounds of battle from outside had faded, leaving only the howling of the wind in their wake. Other than the two oversized knights that had met us, the Conclave's warehouse seemed to have been left unguarded.

"There should be more resistance. The Lady can't have drawn everyone away," I said. Asha's answer was the buzz-chunk of a pneumatic lock springing open and the click-sigh of a sealed door opening.

Another, more ominous, click followed.

"I'd say that's a yes," Asha said, rising from her crouch and raising her hands. I turned to see a man on the far end of a long-barreled rifle. A man who looked vaguely familiar, and far younger than he should have.

"Frank Morris," I said, stepping between the gun and Asha. Whatever her flaws, she hadn't signed on to get shot, and she'd already done more than I'd expected. And, of course, I needed her to attune the nodes to Alam al-Jinn. Pragmatic chivalry at its finest. "You are looking very well for an octogenarian. Though I suppose I can say the same for myself."

"You!" Morris backed up a step when he spied me, but the room on the other side of the door was small, no place to run. A control panel covered the wall beside the door, blinking with lights like it was pulled out of Mission Control. More crates were stacked against the wall behind Morris, framing another steel door. He'd have to turn his back on us to use the keypad if he meant to escape via that route. He must have realized that even with the rifle, the odds were not in his favor. The barrel lowered slightly such that my kneecaps were in more danger than my gut. "You're working with *her* now? After what she did? After what she almost did?"

I chanced a quick glance back at Asha, who still had her hands raised and looked as puzzled as I was. She arched a brow and gave me a barely perceptible shrug.

"Beg pardon?" I faced Morris again. I hadn't been exaggerating. He looked much as he had in his mugshot from 1960 – dark hair cut sharp and square, equally sharp nose, jaw, and cheekbones. He wore a suit much like mine, black tie on white shirt under black tailored mohair that gave off the faintest sheen. We could have been brothers, for all that we'd never met.

"Clarence and John figured you for dead when you went missing a few years back, but I always knew it'd take more than a little dustup with that bitch to take down Mr Mystic. Never figured you for working with her."

I breathed out and couldn't breathe back in again. It was worse than when the knight had gutpunched me. The hum of the generators became a high whine, and black shadows crowded at the edge of my vision. Frank Morris knew what had become of Mr Mystic. And so, it seemed, did the Lady.

I found my voice, or rather, I gave in and let Mr Mystic take over while the part of me that was Missy continued to reel. "Strange bedfellows, you might say," I murmured. Behind me, Asha shifted, the hand obscured by my body sinking into her pack. "I could hardly come to you when you were stealing from old allies and working for new ones."

"What, you mean the tiger? We don't work for him. He's obsessed with some China girl. Ling Bing Big Bang or something. What do you care about that?"

I let anger give me focus. "*Lung Bao Hu Zhe*," I corrected softly. "And I care because she is... a friend. As is Skyrocket. Where is he?"

The rifle barrel came up. Morris sighted along its length. "You got shit taste in friends these days, Mystic. Demons and China girls and now that thing. You got any friends who're human?"

"It would appear not." I dropped to the ground at Asha's signal, but she was already gone. One of the titanium rods clattered to the floor. The rifle went off over my head. Before Morris could fire again, the crates in the room burst open in an explosion of wood, packing material, and shining rods of metal. Asha lunged from the center of the explosion, smoke rising from her black body suit. She caught Morris' rifle when he spun to face her, slamming the butt into his nose with two brutal thrusts. Tearing it from his hands, she whipped it around so he was in her sights.

"Don't shoot him!" I scrambled to my feet and wrenched the barrel down and away. Asha glared at me, and for a moment I thought she might go for her combat knife instead, as she had with the knights.

She didn't. She wrenched the rifle from my grasp and rendered Morris unconscious with three quick, sharp strikes.

"Leaving him alive is a mistake," she muttered, passing me the gun and stepping over the body. She dug out her tools and went to work on the next door.

"I am well aware," I said. Gingerly, I set the gun aside and searched for something to bind Morris. After a quick scan, I gave up looking and used his tie. The silk knotted tightly enough that I wasn't too worried about him escaping. "If he has any information on what happened to my... on... Mr Mystic's disappearance..."

"Hey. I get it. I've done stupider things for family."

I glanced up sharply, question on my lips, but the door locks clunked and Asha was already pushing it open. "There's our... well. Shit."

"What is it? Is he hurt? Is he..." I pushed up behind her, shoving the door wider in case she was struck by some stupid impulse to protect me from whatever was in the room. And then I stopped, because what was in the room made no kind of sense.

There were more monitors, more cables, more generators. Tom was laid out on a table in the middle of the room, stripped to the waist like a subject in some mad scientist's lab experiment. The cables ran from his gut, his arms and legs, his head. There was no blood. No gore or viscera. Just shining metal bones and softly glowing fiber-optic muscles and skin-covered panels hanging wide open.

Morris' crack about my friends made more sense in the face of this. Skyrocket wasn't human. He was a robot.

THIRTEEN
Escape from Alcatraz

"Did you know about this?" I whispered, following Asha into the room. She was muttering, lifting cables, glaring at everything. At my question, she turned that glare on me.

"That the Conclave was using him as their personal Energizer bunny? No. How the hell could I have known that?"

"That is not what I meant, and well you know it," I growled, picking my way towards the table. She'd known. Abby had known. They'd all known. And they'd chosen to leave me in the dark.

"Abby said... after he was trapped and drained in the Shadow Realms on your mission, they improved his power source with the most updated tech. So his ego identity wouldn't be endangered again."

"His ego identity." My nails cut into my palms.

"Meaning he ignores or misinterprets any stimuli

that might make him realize… what he is."

She couldn't say it either. I forced my fingers to relax. "So the only ones who didn't know about this are Tom and myself."

Asha snorted. "And the rest of the world."

I grimaced. I'd reached the table. "Tom?" I leaned over him, touched his bare shoulder. His skin was warm. It had color. But there was no animus to him. I found myself hoping this was some hoax, some elaborate decoy with the real Tom hidden behind yet another door, until those caramel brown lashes fluttered open and a hint of that famous Colgate grin curved those lips.

"Hey, Old Man. They put you in charge of the rescue mission?"

I was going to be ill. I looked away for just a moment, thankful for the shadows disguising my face. I was not nearly a good enough actor to hide my revulsion. I tried not to let it creep into my voice. After all, this wasn't Tom's fault. "As though I gave them a choice. Tom, can you… move?" I had to do something for him. But what? I was no master of technology. Hell, I was prone to strutting around if I managed to hook up my internet without mucking it up. "Can you help us disconnect you?"

Tom shifted, and the cables shifted with him, the lights on the consoles flashing yellow and red. They went back to green and white when Tom slumped back down onto the table. "Naw. They got me trussed tighter'n a Christmas goose."

"Trussed?" I glanced up at Asha.

"I did warn you," she said. "Don't worry. They must have suspected this might be a possibility. Sadakat gave me the keys to the car. Hey, flyboy."

"Hey, pretty lady." Tom turned his smile on Asha. "Now this is what I call a rescue mission. Almost don't mind being tied up if you're doing the untying."

"Uh-huh. Well, I've received worse propositions. Skyrocket model T-301, executive override, enter safemode, authorization key Oskaloosa Rockets."

All expression drained from Tom's features. His eyes closed. "Awaiting senior agent authorization," he said in a monotone.

Asha poked me. "That's you, Old Man."

Me? "Er. I'm Mitchell Masters and I authorize this safemode," I said. There was no way it should work. I wasn't my grandfather, and I had no official status with Argent. And yet after a few moments of nothing more than digital noise, Tom's eyes opened again and he spoke with no trace of an accent: "Safemode engaged. How may I assist you, Mr Masters?"

Asha winked at me. "TC-301, we need you to run a class C diagnostic and walk us through how to safely uncouple you and get you going again."

With Tom's guidance – or rather, TC-301's – we were able to remove all the cables rather more quickly than I'd expected. And a good thing, too. Whatever time we'd gained by traveling through

Alam al-Jinn, we'd certainly lost it cutting Tom loose. Once he was free of the cables and his panels were all closed and sealed, Asha set him on a reboot cycle. She poked around the stolen machinery while I retrieved Tom's rocket pack from where it had been stashed in the corner.

"If you want Morris to live, you should drag him out of here," Asha said, her voice muffled by the server cabinet she was digging behind.

"Why?" I asked. I'd given up trying to lift the rocket pack onto the table next to Tom. It had been all I could do to drag it across the floor, and I'd left long scrapes in the concrete with my efforts. The damned thing was heavy. Clearly, Tom needed a robot's strength just to stay upright while wearing it.

Asha held up a small black box with green blinking lights. "Fulfilling my contract. Nothing belonging to Argent stays in Conclave hands. Since we can't take it with us." She crawled out from behind the server when I remained unable to do more than gape dumbly at her. "Alcatraz go boom."

"You can't blow up Alcatraz!"

"Only on the Shadow Realms side of the veil."

Ah. Right. Of course. I still didn't like it, but we were too short on time for me to argue. Who knew how much longer the Lady's forces could continue to distract the Conclave knights, or when Lao Hu might return, or where the Anglin brothers had got off to. "No damage to the other side?" I asked, laying Frank Morris out so I could lift him into a fireman's carry.

"Possibly a bit of crumbling masonry. Some broken windows. Nothing worse than any of the tremblors we've been having. Promise."

"Fine. Is Tom..." I peered through the doorway into the lab. I could barely look at him for fear I'd start staring.

"Should be cycling up. Hey, flyboy." She snapped her fingers above Tom's nose.

His eyes opened. He groaned and sat up, cradling his head. "Tell me there was another guy."

"Yeah. And you should see him. Come on. You're going to sleep through your own rescue." Asha shoved his leather flight jacket, buttondown, and undershirt at him.

He pulled the clothes on quickly, covering a physique that apparently owed nothing to nature and everything to science. "Sorry, ma'am. Shouldn't have had to see that."

"Oh, I wasn't complaining," Asha said, giving him a friendly leer. "Grab that hunk of tin you call a rocket pack and let's get out of here before the place blows."

"Yes, ma'am." Tom hopped off the table, energy already returning now that he wasn't being used to power half the island, including the lighthouse. He lifted his pack and strapped it on – the pack I'd barely been able to drag across the floor. On his way out, he took Frank Morris from me, shrugging the man over his shoulder like it was no matter.

"Bloody hell," I muttered under my breath, jogging after Tom and Asha. I wasn't certain what amazed me more. Tom's inhuman humanity, his quick recovery, or the fact that we'd actually bloody done it.

We jogged along the road past the Conclave's black-walled citadel, keeping low but meeting none of the Conclave's forces along the way. When Asha's windup kitchen timer dinged, we took cover behind a low wall. Moments later, the entire island shook with the percussive blast of the Conclave's laboratory blowing sky high. Heat washed over us, and light such as I hadn't seen in the Shadow Realms since we crashed the *Kestrel* on a rolling plain somewhere east of Shanghai. That was when Tom must have come to the attention of the Conclave.

Well, we hadn't left them much to salvage from the *Kestrel*'s crash, and I doubted they'd salvage much more now.

"Well, damn," Tom whispered, shifting Frank Morris' unconscious body to his other shoulder. "You weren't just kidding about the place blowing."

"What can I say, flyboy," Asha purred. "I'm thorough."

Dear lord. I couldn't tell if she was serious with her flirting, if she was doing it to set Tom at ease, or if it was her way of taking the piss out of me.

"Let's just hope the explosion draws attention so the Lady's forces may escape. We should move."

I rose, and Asha, but Tom remained on his knees, grimacing.

"Tom?" I asked. His color was fading, his arms trembling. The last time I'd seen him this peaked was in his recovery bed in Jiu Wei's temple. Whatever surge of energy he'd enjoyed after we uncoupled him, it was fading fast.

Tom shook his head. "Just give me a moment, Old Man. Don't know what it is about this place, but it tuckers me out right quick."

At the rate he was tuckering, I had my doubts that he'd make it to the lighthouse. "Tom, I'm going to send you across to the real world," I said, thankful that the light of the explosion was bright enough to make it possible. "You'll probably startle a few tourists. Don't stop for photo ops. The Conclave knights might be able to cross over and drag you back. You get to Argent HQ in China Basin, you make sure they bind Mr Morris with everything they've got, including the shadow wards I showed them. I want to question him when this is all over."

"You got it, Old Man." Tom shrugged Morris higher and lurched to his feet. "This fellow really that dangerous?"

"Dangerous, maybe. Slippery, yes. He's one of the only men ever to escape Alcatraz."

I don't think I'd ever heard Tom say a curse word stronger than damn. I blinked when he did so now. "Yes. Well. Go on, then. I'll see you on the other side." Using the fading light of the burning laboratory, I opened the veil and shunted Tom and Frank Morris through. With any luck, Tom would recover as quickly as he'd been drained.

Which just left myself and Asha again, with half an island between us and where we needed to be.

"So. That's my contract fulfilled." She rubbed her wrists as though they'd been sprung from invisible shackles.

I tensed. "Is this the part where you turn on me?"

Asha studied me in silence for longer than I'd have liked before a slow grin curved her lips. "Do you realize this titanium is so pure that I can carry it without worrying about resonance building up? That I could probably hop through it safely a good half dozen times? And do you know how much Argent agreed to give me?"

"As much as you could stuff in your bags before we blew up the Conclave's lab?"

"Oh, that's just extra. Come on, Masters. I'm capricious and a bit vindictive, but I'm not *stupid*. Let's get off this island."

Aside from a few lone shadow creatures – not even full knights, just half-shaped monsters that wouldn't last more than a few hours – Asha and I met little resistance on our run to the lighthouse. I realized why when we came around the far side of the citadel and nearly ran headlong into a sea of Conclave troops laying siege to the lighthouse tower.

"Shit," I muttered, flattening back against the wall.

"You just had to send away our air support," Asha said, peering around me to get a better look at what we were facing.

"Shut up." We both knew Tom could not have carried a tune, much less the both of us to the top of the tower. But since when had pragmatism or facts kept Asha from her one true love: snark.

I studied the ebb and flow of the troops. "Right. Here is what we'll do–"

"Save it, Old Man."

Another round of searing heat followed Asha grabbing my arm. Memory had dulled the incandescent edge of pain that ripped through me, making me think it had been more bearable than it was. We emerged into blessed cool, and I hit the floor, limbs twitching, dry heaving to try to expel the fire that had burned inside me, however briefly.

"Missy!" David knelt at my side, hands hovering over me as he looked for some ill to fix and found nothing wrong. He glared up at Asha. "What did you do to her?"

Asha leaned against the lantern. One glass panel hung open, and inside where the bulb should be, a fist-sized orb of titanium flickered with orange flames. "Her?"

David flinched and gave me an apologetic look. "Shit. I–"

"It's fine. She knows. She's just being an ass." I

let him help me up and fixed my glare on Asha. "A little warning would have been appreciated."

"Didn't expect it to be that bad the second time." She studied David and myself. "I don't think your kind does all that well in Alam al-Jinn."

A soft tread sounded on the metal spiral of stairs. "Then it is a good thing that I will not be traveling through your realm," said the Lady as she joined us. "Where is the rocket man?"

"Skyrocket. I sent him back over to the real world. This place was..." I ran a hand over my lower face to catch myself from making the same mistake David had. "He'd had enough of it. He took Frank Morris with him."

"So it really was him. Them. The three?" David asked, looking up from the pack he'd been securing. It was then that I noticed the sigils ringing the lantern, a hard, silvery script sunk deep into the lighthouse platform.

"So it would seem." I watched the Lady walk the circle, making a final check of the sigils that she and David had etched into the onyx-black stone. "He seemed to be under the impression that you and I should not get along," I told her.

"Were you truly your grandfather, we would not."

"Why?"

"He took something from me. They all did."

I'd had enough with the cryptic. "What?" I snapped.

Asha cut a hand between us, breaking my glare. "I hate to interrupt, but perhaps we can have this riveting conversation after we're away from the demon army? Just a thought."

"I need to attune this node to Shadow," the Lady said. She pulled out the combat knife that she'd been wearing when we met at her camp.

David shouldered his pack of ritual supplies. "And I need to cross over so I can make the call to Professor Trent and the others."

He fell still – we all did – when the Lady put her arm over the circle and ran the knife along her skin. Ichor black as coagulated blood oozed up from the long cut. I rubbed my arm as phantom sympathy pains shot up it.

David cleared his throat. "I'll need a... your name. For the summoning."

"Yes, of course." The Lady stared at her falling blood. "It is Anne."

David must have said something. I vaguely registered a flare of light when he left. I think Asha might have jostled my arm to snap me out of my daze. I paid her no mind. I was fixated on watching that oozing blood sluggishly gloop down onto the sigils, watching the script catch and burst into dark flames. They raced around the circle and flared at the center where the titanium burned, dampening the orange flames into a smoky gleam. The air around us vibrated like the center of a Tesla coil. It stank of sun-warmed asphalt.

"Anne?" I whispered.

The Lady took her scarf – my scarf? – and wrapped it around her arm. "Yes."

"And you knew my grandfather."

"Yes."

I shook my head, even as I spoke aloud the next logical step. "And he took... something... from you."

The Lady's gaze bored into mine. "Yes."

"Are you–?"

"The call comes. Later, I will explain."

And she was gone. I stared at the place where a moment before the Lady had stood. Eventually, Asha's elbow jostling got through to me.

"– don't snap out of it, I am going to slap you."

"Wha–?" I blinked at her. Didn't she realize? Didn't she comprehend? *Anne*.

Abby had been right. It was strange that I'd never questioned. Never wondered.

"Just... nothing. Put your hat on. It's time to go."

Asha dragged me, stumbling, over the activated ritual circle to the darkly glowing titanium orb. The thunder of many boots echoed up the circular stairwell. The Conclave knights had broken in. They were coming.

I donned my hat and let her drag me through fire once more.

FOURTEEN
Seven and the Ragged Tiger

Rincon Hill isn't much of a hill anymore. A century of development has leveled it until all that remains is a small rise of hardscrabble ground framed by towering office buildings and bisected by the last on-ramps and off-ramps before the 880 feeds onto the Bay Bridge on the way to Treasure Island.

The first thing I noticed after the screaming pain faded was the rumble of the 880 traffic overhead, the thump-thump of tires crossing bridge seams at sixty miles per hour. The second thing I noticed was a soft, heavy weight landing on my back, pressing me down into the grime and dirt of a vacant triangle of land. Jagged pebbles and bits of shattered glass and grit pressed into my cheek as the weight bore me down. Above me, much closer than the bridge overpass, a rumble started up loud enough to make my body vibrate.

Shit. I had a pretty good notion of what – or who

– was sitting on me.

"I thank you, firespawn, for bringing my quarry to me." Lao Hu's voice rumbled right above my left ear. My fingers scraped through the dirt as I searched for some way around my helplessness. "You have spared me an annoying hunt."

"And you helped me out of a very annoying – and binding – contract." Asha's voice came from somewhere behind me. All I could see from my tiger-trapped vantage was the slope of the verge leading down to an underpass, my new motorcycle parked on the sidewalk on the other side of a chain-link fence. The grimy freeway wall cast a shadow across the ground just beyond my reach. Asha's booted feet moved into view. "Though of course I would still appreciate payment."

"As we agreed. I will deliver it to you after I've dealt with this one and her master." Something soft and meat-scented nuzzled my hat off my head.

I twisted as best I could under Lao Hu's paw so that I could see Asha when I told her off.

Abby beat me to it. "You vindictive bitch! I should have known you'd pull something like this–"

"Oh, I'm the bitch?" Asha strode out of my line of sight again. Lao Hu growled when I stretched to try to track her. "Who enslaved someone else to force their cooperation? Oh. Right. Not me."

"So that's how you rationalize selling us out? I hope the payoff is worth it."

"Lao Hu has kindly agreed to retrieve Father's

carpet. So yes. I would say that it is worth it."

Silence fell, save for the roar of traffic and Lao Hu's purr. My shifting about had inched me closer to the stripe of shadow cast by the overpass. I kicked my feet to distract attention from my creeping hand.

"What of the nodes?" said a new voice, the Lady, speaking to Asha. So at least Abby's summoning had worked. "Will you still help us attune them?"

Asha's laugh was as grating as the grit and glass beneath my cheek. But it also provided another welcome distraction for Lao Hu. My fingers dug further forward.

"Let me introduce you to a colorful little phrase called 'not my circus, not my monkeys.'"

"Does that mean no?"

"Yeah. It means no."

"Then I have no use for you."

My quest to touch the overpass shadow became moot. The shadow darkened and expanded to encompass everything around me. I heard the beginnings of Asha's screams, but they cut off as I took the escape offered and dove into the Shadow Realms.

Not that it helped any. Lao Hu was still an immovable weight on my back. The world around us had gone ink dark. In place of the overpass, a massive tangle of roots ran down to the glass-still waters of the bay. I closed my eyes and concentrated.

Lao Hu's paw cuffed my head. "Silly *Lung Bao Hu*

Zhe. You cannot escape me. Didn't you learn before that I walk in many realms? Mortal, Elemental, Spirit. And I walk in Shadow too."

I flinched at the faint prick of claws flexing into the meat of my shoulder through layers of trench coat and mohair wool. "Yeah. Got that. Counted on it, actually. 'Cause you know who else does? Them."

From under the roots and over them, from the water and the sky, came the remnants of the Lady's army. My Blood-Dimmed Tide rode the crest, a thin line of crimson foam. Estelle flew with the gargoyles, a ragged banshee of lace and light.

Lao Hu lunged off me to meet the onslaught. I rolled away, dug a glow stick from my pocket, and cracked it. Moments later, I was back in the real world. I snatched up my hat and scrambled away from the giant cat who appeared to be attacking the air.

"Masters!" Abby grabbed me and hauled me further away to the questionable safety of the ritual circle. This one was sunk into a five-by-five pit dug into the hill, orange safety cones rimming it and a pile of gravel backfill waiting to fill it. The sigils were embedded into the bedrock in hardened black tar. At the center, another titanium node glowed with fire and shadow, already attuned to both realms.

"Asha?"

Abby glared at the Lady. "I don't know. Not sure I want to. What the fuck is going on with the tiger?"

Lao Hu fought the air, leaping, snapping at nothing behind him, slamming his paws against the freeway wall.

"Cats. They walk in many worlds," I said.

"He battles my army. They will not hold him long." The Lady cupped my cheek, "You must attune the nodes."

I shivered. I had too many questions for her. Who had named her Anne? Why had she shaped herself to look like me? What had my grandfather taken from her? Why had she taken the picture of a younger me? None of my questions were important at the moment. "You expect me to do it? But how? I don't know how–"

"Blood is the quickest key. Blood is the thread that links all things. Your blood is my blood. It will be enough."

"But what about Alam al-Jinn?" With Asha gone, we were screwed. The suggestion that Abby do it had been a ruse to trick Asha's cooperation. Nothing more.

"For that, you must entice Lao Hu to follow you to each node. I will ensure there is blood."

Her hand slipped from my cheek, pulling the shadows around my face for me. She stalked towards Lao Hu, fingers lengthening and thickening until they were curved talons, the sort that could reach from under a bed or a car and take you out at the ankles. She lowered into a feral crouch, and any resemblance to me slid from her skin like water. She was the Lady once more, in her cobweb-mended coat.

"Go," she said, and lunged at Lao Hu.

I went.

I crouched low over the body of my motorcycle, weaving through the noontime traffic that choked the Embarcadero. Horns honked at my passage, people on the broad sidewalk waved. I even got some bells from one of the restored F-line streetcars as I passed it by. If I'd been worried about Lao Hu being able to follow my trail on the bike, I needn't have. If he couldn't track me by scent, a few hundred pedestrians would be able to help point the way Mr Mystic had gone. I could only hope that he wanted me badly enough to leave the pedestrians alone.

I skirted Levi Plaza and ditched my bike in a cul-de-sac between office buildings on Sansome. No help for it. I'd have to climb the stairs on foot. I started them two at a time, but by the time I'd crested above the office rooftops – the halfway point, by my reckoning – it was all I could do to keep dragging myself up at a fast walk. My breath burned in my throat, my side ached. I wasted too much time glancing behind me, wondering when Lao Hu would catch up to me, wondering how I was going to lead him to five more nodes. Six, counting Land's End. Wondering how I was going to escape him after that if I did manage the rest.

Wondering if the Lady had managed to escape. The Lady. Anne. My grandmother's name. My... grandmother?

No. I knew better. Mitchell Masters didn't have the best track record with the truth.

"I don't. Bloody well. Have *time* for this shit," I rasped, using the surge of frustration to push myself up the last few flights of stairs and out into the parking lot for Coit Tower.

"Missy?" Jack was waiting in the center of the parking lot turnabout. He rushed across the empty lot to steady me as I staggered at the top of the steps.

I tore my hat off, bracing my hands on my knees and trying to heave in enough oxygen to satisfy my burning muscles and lungs. "Missy. Mystic. I don't even fucking know anymore." I ripped away my wig, careless of the pins, and threw it to the ground. Wind cooled the heat coming off my sweat-slicked hair. I blotted my brow against my shoulder.

Jack stopped a few feet away. "What can I do?"

"What do you know?" I hadn't entirely caught my breath, but I forced myself upright, forced myself to move past him. The grass circle in the center of the lot had been torn up, leaving another five-by-five pit surrounded by orange safety cones and a mound of gravel backfill. I jumped down into the pit. Hard black sigils like the one at Rincon Hill were embedded in a circle around an inert node of titanium. Jack's car was parked just on the other side of the pit, the only car in the lot. Bless Argent for coming through.

"Professor Trent called. Told me about Lao Hu and Asha. That you're the one attuning the wards now. And you've got to lure Lao Hu into doing the same."

"That about covers it." I jammed my hat atop my head. It felt a little loose without the wig, but at least I wasn't fighting off a pounding headache or heat exhaustion. "I need something to cut myself with."

Jack handed me a utility knife, the sort used to open boxes and protective packaging. Well, at least it was sharp. I dithered a moment over where to make the slice, settled on the forearm that I'd already slashed up a few days past. I shoved up my sleeve and sliced through a few of the stitches Shimizu had pestered me to sit through. I let the blood drip onto the prepared sigils, and they flared with smoky fire, the same flames that had lit the Alcatraz lighthouse and the Rincon Hill node.

Now I just needed Lao Hu to follow.

"What else can I do?" Jack asked, voice only shaking a little bit. He rarely got to see Mr Mystic in action. Usually, he just dealt with the fallout.

"Get the hell out of here. Tell Shimizu to clear the house." Russian Hill was my next stop, and I wanted it empty when I got there. "I don't know if Lao Hu's taking hostages, and I don't want to give him reason to try."

I headed for the stairs, but something, some shift

in the shadows among the trees, gave me pause.

"Down!" I tackled Jack out of the way just as a half ton of pissed-off jungle cat launched at us.

Lao Hu sailed over our heads and across the pit, claws tearing up grass and concrete as he tried to stop his slide. He slammed into Jack's car.

"Go!" I shoved Jack ahead of me, scrambling after him. I glanced back. Blood streaked along the grass, and a bloody smear ran along the dent in the side of Jack's car. At the center of the pit, the node flared brighter, a marriage of flame and shadow. Good enough. Time to get the hell out of Dodge.

I raced after Jack and made a running leap for the stairway. I covered half a flight in that first jump before catching the railing and using it to shift direction. I hit the landing and jumped again, vaulted over the next rail down and then the next after that. Going down was so much easier than going up. I'd almost caught up with Jack when I heard the scrape of claws above me.

I couldn't lead Lao Hu to Jack. I balanced on the next rail and made the long leap to the rooftop patio of the neighboring office building. I took out a few plastic deck chairs before I managed to roll to my feet. A low, fifties-modern penthouse covered the other half of the rooftop, a long bank of mirrored windows reflecting the tiger on my tail. I slammed through the access door and into a communal kitchen area. A girl with Disney-villain hair – silky black threaded liberally with silver – shrieked at my entry. Her Cup O' Noodles went flying into the air.

"Apologies. For both myself and the tiger," I said, slamming my palm against the lift call button and blessing whatever gods looked after me that it opened immediately.

"T-tiger?" she stammered, but I was already in the lift, frantically pressing the close-doors button. They slid shut on the sound of breaking glass and another shriek.

I burst through the main doors of the office building and revved my bike into motion just as the screams on Sansome started up. Evidence that Lao Hu had opted for the long jump down from the rooftop. I nearly kneed asphalt leaning into the turn onto Sansome, back tire fishtailing like crazy as I straightened and kicked into high gear the wrong way down a one-way street. A glance in my mirror told me that Lao Hu was closer than I'd ever want him to appear.

He may have been several hundred pounds of bloody-minded murder, but I walked this city every day and rode it when I wasn't walking. I knew it better than he ever would. I cut up Union and across Washington Square Park, passing the Pagoda Palace. Took Filbert to avoid the inevitable snaking line of cars coming down Lombard. Crested the hill leading to Mystic Manor–

– and screeched to a shredded-rubber stop at the gauntlet of news vans clogging my street.

"Bloody hell," I muttered. My wild city ride must have brought the B-rollers out in force, save that now they were A-rollers, and they were about to get front-row seats.

Something inevitable as death sideswiped my rear tire, sending my bike – and me – spinning into the line of cars parked perpendicular to the steep incline of the street. My bike wedged under a hapless little Fiat just as I jumped free. I landed on top of the Fiat and hopped up the rising line of car rooftops. Launching over the crowd of scrambling news people and cameramen, I sprawled atop the van for KRON-4. I slid chest first to a stop, hand clamped to my head to keep my hat in place.

A few intrepid reporters took the chance to fire off a few asinine questions – *Mr Mystic, are you working with Argent again? Do you have any thoughts about the attack on the California Academy of Sciences? Have you heard the reports about a tiger running loose through the city?*

The questions ended in screams when Lao Hu landed among them. He ignored the scattering reporters, claws digging into the sides of the van I was crouching atop. They shredded the metal like it was chiffon.

"Yes. Tiger. Thank you so much for pointing that out to me," I snapped at the last questioner before diving off the other side of the roof and sliding under the carriage of another van parked askew in the middle of the street. I squeezed through the gap between two more vans parked bumper to bumper, using them as obstacles between myself and Lao Hu. I needed to scale the front face of the house up to the widow's walk where we'd set the next node. And then blood it. Get Lao Hu to do the same without getting myself eviscerated like the side of that van. Or getting the bystanders killed. Or, or, or.

I managed to haul myself over the low, cast-iron guard rail rimming the widow's walk without accidentally impaling myself on it. I was already digging in my pocket for Jack's knife so I could impale myself intentionally when I realized I wasn't alone.

"Hello, Missy." Jian Huo, father of my children, love of my life, and dragon with truly shit timing, sat at the little iron patio table where the housemates sometimes took tea. "Sifu Cho indicated you might need some assistance."

He was dressed in his usual hanfu of red, green, and gold brocade, thick black hair coiling down around the legs of the white-painted patio chair like a living thing. He stood and pulled me to my feet, kissing me even though I was a sweaty, breathless mess. I was fuzzily aware of the flashes from below as half the local news stations and papers got pics of Mr Mystic making out with some strange man on the rooftop of his old house.

I pulled away, blinking confusion. "Please tell me you're here to pull my ass from the fire?"

Jian Huo sighed. "You know I cannot fight Lao

Hu. His grievance against Lung Di is legitimate. But I can... delay." He smiled gently and pushed me behind him, setting himself between me and the tiger crawling over the guard rail of the widow's walk. "Lao Hu. Such pleasant circumstances that bring us together this day."

"Lung Huang. You stand between me and my quarry," Lao Hu growled.

Jian Hua's pleasant smile faded, leaving behind the blank mask that had always unnerved me more than any frown. He folded his hands into his sleeves. "I stand between you and my bride."

"And your brother's champion." Lao Hu padded to one side. Jian Huo shifted to block him, and I remembered I had shit to do other than gape at a pissing match between gods. I used Jack's knife to reopen the cut on my arm and let my blood drip onto the rune circle at the center of the widow's walk. Lao Hu had already paced a line of bloody paw prints across the other side of the circle. The flaring node dimmed to a dull gleam. We were good to go.

Now I just had to get out of here and figure out a way to run faster than a tiger.

Jian Huo, still blocking Lao Hu's path to me, bowed slightly from the waist. "She is also that. Which reminds me. I believe you owe me a game of wei-qi."

"Now?"

Jian Huo's smile peeked through again. "I cannot

think of a better time for you to pay this debt." He waved a sleeve over the rickety patio table, and a wei-qi board appeared.

I could have kissed him again, save that I didn't want to take my chances getting that close to Lao Hu. Later. I'd thank Jian Huo properly later.

I hoped. I was racking up a lot of laters. I backed up to the far side of the widow's walk and climbed over the knee-high guard. Lao Hu's golden glare burned a hole into my gut, but he knocked the other chair aside, sat at the table, and carefully plinked his first piece down onto the empty board.

"I need a cell phone and another motorcycle," I told Johnny when I arrived at the Cable Car Museum just off Nob Hill. As with Coit Tower and Rincon Hill, Argent had managed to get the place shut down and cordoned off.

Johnny let the heavy glass-and-wood door slam behind me. He dug in a pocket and tossed me a phone with a Giants case – his – and led me up the half flight of steps to the main floor of the museum. A row of grooved flywheels, painted cast iron and taller than Johnny or I standing, dominated one end of the cavernous room. A web of cables spanned above us, and above that, a steel support girder crossed over the flywheels. The destination of each cable was spelled out across the girder in old-timey text: Powell, Mason, California, Hyde. This museum had once been the heart of a burgeoning city, and the cables and rails still spread throughout San Francisco like a great ferrous vascular system.

One of the great workings, the Lady had called the Golden Gate Bridge. The cable cars were another, and I was here to pour new blood over old.

The cement flooring in front of the cable spools had been jackhammered up, the node and ritual circle sunk into the resulting pit like the ones at Rincon and Coit Tower. I had to give it to Argent. The resources they could pull together with only two days' notice, and the willingness they had to throw those resources at a problem merely on my say-so, was endearing me to them in a way that all of Sylvia Dunbarton's coaxing and cheek kisses never would.

A chow sitting at the edge of the pit barked as Johnny and I approached. A red-tailed hawk winged down from the steel girder. I couldn't spot him, but I suspected that somewhere nearby lurked a pretty emerald tree boa.

"I don't think I can manage a motorcycle on this short notice," Johnny said. "What happened to yours?"

I jumped into the pit and bled onto the sigils, watching darkness bloom in the center of the node. "You know how cats like to bat their toys under furniture? Apparently with tigers it's motorcycles under cars."

Johnny winced and gave me a hand up from the

pit. "The way you go through bikes, your lawyer friend's going to stop letting you get them."

"Right now, I'm not feeling that picky. My kingdom for a Segway." I squeezed Johnny's hand when he would have let go. "Thank you. For calling in the big gun."

"I just don't understand why you didn't think of it."

His soft comment brought me up short. Why hadn't I thought of it? I'd been quick enough to go to Lung Di for help with the shadow translations. But I knew the answer already. Even after that kiss on the widow's walk, I still wasn't sure where I stood with Jian Huo. Or where I wanted to stand. Why did I feel more welcome asking his asshole of a brother for help? Because Mian Zi had called me dishonored, and La Reina implied I was a demon, and I was starting to wonder if they might both be right.

"Did you know?" I asked Johnny, who'd been my sifu most of my life. "About the Lady? About... me?"

"Shit, Masters." He freed his hand from mine and ruffled his hair. "Now is not the time for this."

Which was as good as a yes. I looked away so I wouldn't have to look at him. "Fine. You're off the hook for now. But you don't ever get to ride my ass for keeping secrets from you again. Got it?"

"I'm certain I won't have any problem finding other reasons to ride your ass," he said, half joking, half gentle, as though he realized just how fragile things stood between us.

I let myself fall into a laugh. I didn't have the luxury of alienating friends just now. "Right. Sure. Now, Lao Hu has to bleed on this or it won't–"

"We will make him bleed," Johnny said. "Now get going. It's a long walk to Lone Mountain."

It was, and I didn't have any superpowered friends waiting for me there. "Don't you get killed too," I muttered, giving Johnny a hug. "Give me a boost."

He lifted me up until I could grab a cable. I hand-over-handed it to the crossbeam, ran the girder like a balance beam to the upper walkway, and slid out one of the roof-level windows.

I needed to make sure Lao Hu could track me. I didn't have to make it easy for him.

I ate through half my supply of glow sticks on the run to Lone Mountain, skipping back and forth between the city and its reflection in the Shadow Realms. I tried calling up the Lady's army as I had on Rincon Hill – a gargoyle in particular would have been a welcome ally at this juncture – but either the Lady had reasserted control, or her army had been decimated. I found myself hoping for the former and dreading the likelihood of the latter.

My bright idea to stutter my trail between realms seemed less bright when I got to the wooded rise on the west end of the SFU campus and realized that my Shadow Realms jaunting had drained Johnny's phone of all juice.

"Fuck," I muttered. And then, louder, "Olly olly, oxen free!" hoping that Sadakat had decided to ignore the call to beat feet. How the hell was I supposed to find the node in this mess of trees and underbrush?

"I could be misremembering my childhood game lore, but I believe that's what you shout when it's safe to come out." David Tsung's voice came from the trees to my right. I shoved through them and stumbled down a steep slope to the curve of a service road. David stood at the curb, pit dug into the asphalt on one side of him, and a shiny Triumph parked on the other. My old bike, the one I'd told Jack to dispose of after Argent had its way with it.

"I hear you requested wheels?"

I restrained my joy. Barely. Johnny and I could hug. David and I were not on hugging terms. Though I was well on my way to revising that bias.

"Sadakat?" I asked. I had to make a new cut on my opposite arm. The original was a coagulated, oozing mess. I held the freshly dripping cut over the pit.

"Dealing with the reports of a tiger loose in the city. I hear Skyrocket has given an interview or two as well."

I let myself slump against the side of my bike. Just a moment to catch my breath. "He made it safely out, then? Good. Any news on Abby or the Lady?"

"Professor Trent made it away. She's said nothing about the Lady or Asha." He set a hand on the seat of my bike, possibly as close as he dared come to giving me an encouraging pat on the shoulder. "You should go before Lao Hu catches up."

I let out a deep, shaking breath and straightened. "Can't. There's no way to guarantee he'll attune the node unless I'm here to make him do it."

"I can–"

"You are not fighting him." I considered listing all the reasons why – I was a better fighter than David, and I was stronger with shadow even if I wasn't as thoroughly trained. And for better or worse, my daughter cared about him, which made him mine to take care of. But I knew none of those arguments would wash, and I didn't want to waste energy fighting about it. "I need you to go to Land's End and make a few adjustments to the ritual circle there."

That caught his attention before he could give me lip. "What sort of adjustments?"

"You helped Lung Di craft the wards he used to trap the Guardians in Shanghai, yes?" At David's hesitant nod, I grinned. "Good. Here's what I need you to do."

After I'd sent David on his way to do my dirty work, I rolled my bike further down the road. Not too far, just out of the immediate line of fire so Lao Hu couldn't take it out. I left it running for a quick getaway and settled myself down to wait. I stood as close to the pit as I could manage while keeping a healthy distance from the trees lining either side of the road. Lao Hu was already a master of stealth. I didn't need to give him the additional advantage of cover.

Even with that extra space and my constant, 360 degree scanning of the trees, Lao Hu managed to sneak up on me.

"I know what you are doing."

I spun and nearly fell into the ritual pit. Lao Hu crouched flat on a low limb of one of the trees branching over the service road. His long tail dangled like an orange and black striped bellpull. The tip curved into a little "j", waving and twitching even as the rest of him held perfectly still.

He could have easily pounced on me from there before I'd even noticed him. Wouldn't have taken a whisker's twitch of effort. Still could, now that I thought on it. I backed away slowly, putting the pit between myself and Lao Hu.

"What I'm doing? Trying to stay alive?" Now that I had a moment to examine him, I realized he looked a bit worse off than I was. The fur at his shoulder was stained dark and matted, and two of the claws on his front paw had been torn free. His pads were caked with blood and grit.

He lapped at his injured paw, long pink tongue curling around the pads, cleaning the wounds. "I am older than the tread of mortal feet on this ground. I have felt it shake and tremble under the fluctuations of the Voidlands before. You seek to bind back what was never meant to be bound so that... what? These piles of stone and wood won't crumble and crush those within?"

"Yes. Aren't you a Guardian? Aren't you meant to do the same?"

Lao Hu stretched to the ground, his body long and lean enough that his hind paws remained balanced on the tree limb even as his forepaws touched the pavement of the service road. His claws flexed, leaving bloody footprints on the asphalt. "I take a longer view than you. Death is necessary to life. The fire clears the forest, and the Void washes away what has been built up and leaves the world clean for new growth."

Dammit, why did every god I meet have to be a philosopher? I circled the pit, keeping it between me and the stalking tiger. "So you don't think this surge from the Voidlands is unnatural? You don't think Alam al-Jinn burns out of balance with the other elements?"

Lao Hu paused in his stalking circle, tail tip twitching. "Perhaps."

That was yes enough for me. "Then help me. Attune the rest of the nodes with me, and when we reach the last, I'll... I'll submit myself to your vengeance." I tried to keep the tremble from my voice. I didn't entirely succeed.

"An interesting proposal, but... no."

Lao Hu leapt for me, but I'd been watching his

haunches. I dove out of the way, back-kicking into his stretched-out body. I missed the wounded shoulder I'd been aiming for, caught him lower in the ribs. I rolled to one side, curling my leg close to my body before his snapping teeth could catch it.

Back on my feet, I jumped across the corner of the ritual pit. The node at the center flickered only with shadow, which meant Lao Hu hadn't spattered blood on it during his leap. Fuck. I was going to have to stick around for another pass.

At least Lao Hu didn't make me wait long for it. His hind quarters shimmied and he lunged for me again.

I was already leaping towards him. I ducked under his claws and teeth, caught his tail as we passed. My arms nearly jerked out of my sockets as we enacted a hands-on-tail demonstration of physics in equal and opposite reaction.

Lao Hu's yowl ripped through the air. We both went tumbling into the pit in a tangle of flailing limbs and thrashing claws. I managed to twist and land on top of him, using elbows and knees to stay that way until I could grab the lip and heave myself out.

One wild claw caught my shoulder, dragging me back down into the pit. I kicked back, felt my boot connect with something, and the fabric of my trench coat gave way. I scrambled to safety, running for my bike with my shredded coat flapping behind me. Pain coursed down my back in twin lines of fire. I jumped on my bike and shredded rubber getting out of there, tiger fast on my tail.

I hit a wall of fog halfway up the slope of Twin Peaks and had to slow, in part to avoid slamming into oncoming traffic, and in part because I couldn't be sure how much of the clouding at the edges of my vision had to do with fog, and how much was due to blood loss. I reached the figure-eight road that infinity-looped around the adjoining peaks. My bike fishtailed to a stop at the narrow, hourglass-shaped meridian at the center. It took me three tries to engage the kickstand. I nearly dropped my bike before I managed it, and the effort to keep it wrenched upright sent a wave of fresh warmth coursing down my back. I thought for a moment pain had me seeing double, but no. That was Mian Zi standing next to his sister. I choked on a giggle, which jostled my shoulder. I swayed with the pain.

Mian Zi and Mei Shen came up on either side, supporting me. "'Cause… twin peaks. Get it?" I told one of them. Maybe both of them. They were trying to make me sit. I struggled against them. "I have to attune the node."

"Mother, you're hurt. Let me see." That was Mian Zi, he of the soft voice and gentle hands. He removed my hat and set it aside, then tugged gently at my trench coat. I whimpered when the fabric was pulled from the claw marks slashing down my shoulder.

"Mei Shen?" I looked for her, but at some point she'd disappeared. Maybe she'd never been there? "No. The node. Where's…"

Mian Zi held me when I would have gone looking for the pit. Luckily, I didn't have to look far. We were sitting on the edge of it. "Stop moving. I need to take this off carefully or you'll—"

I didn't have time for gentleness. I tore my trench coat off, and the suit coat underneath, wadded them, and threw the bundle into the pit beside us. The node dimmed with shadow, then flared bright with fire, before settling into a smoky beacon with fire at its center. I sagged against Mian Zi, getting blood all over his nice suit. "There. See? Lao Hu was nice enough to bleed all over me."

"Good. Now may I see to your wound?" Fabric tore. Mian Zi wasn't even bothering to remove my shirt, just using the rents made by Lao Hu's claws and ripping them wider.

I pushed at him. "I don't have time for this. I have to get to Mount Davidson."

"Mei Shen is distracting Lao Hu—"

"No." I twisted to go after her, to stop her, and had to take several moments to breathe through the pain. "He'll hurt her."

"He is not that stupid. His quarrel is with our uncle. You stand in the way as Uncle's champion." More ripping fabric followed, and the soothing pressure of something binding my wounds tightly closed. The pain still pulsed deep in my muscles, but I no longer felt the gaping edges of my wounds shifting against each other. I stopped resisting and let Mian Zi do what he could.

"Mei Shen and I have the blessing of the Nine," Mian Zi was saying. "We have Lao Hu's blessing. He will not forswear his own pledge. He will not offend our aunts and uncles by causing us harm."

I leaned into him. Just a moment. I just needed a moment of not fighting or running or having to figure things out along the way. "But... before... you said I dishonored myself. Doesn't that mean you're... by helping me..."

"I... may have been harsh in my anger." His hand stroked my brow, cool as water. It washed away some of the pain, and I wasn't sure if it was due to magic or just the knowledge that my son didn't despise me. "You are our mother. We should honor you in all things."

I pulled a face at that. Sometimes the cultural divide that separated us was harder to face than the divide caused by my own mistakes. "I think I'm more comfortable with you kicking me to the curb when I mess up."

"I will leave such things to Mei Shen." He hugged me, careful of my shoulder. I sank into it for a moment before – carefully – squirming away.

"I have to go. La Reina is waiting." I looked down

at my shirt, half of it stained bloody and one entire shoulder gaping open. My suit and trench were hopeless. I'd dumped my wig several nodes ago. I took my hat from Mian Zi and set it on my head. "You think she'll notice I'm not quite myself?" I said in a Dick Van Dyke mockery of Mr Mystic's usual accent. Oi, it's a jolly 'oliday.

Mian Zi's lips twitched. "I think she might."

"Shit." I touched my face, my exposed braided hair. I'd always been so resistant to cutting it or dying it black, and now I was reaping the consequences of that reluctance.

"Here. This might help?" Mian Zi took off his suit coat and helped me into it with minimal shoulder jarring. It was a bit long in the sleeve, but close enough to pass.

And it reminded me of something. The Lady. I touched my face. If she was… we were… connected by blood, then it stood to reason that I might be able to do anything she could do. Didn't it?

I closed my eyes, passed my hands over my hair. My features I could disguise with shadow, but–

"Even better," Mian Zi said softly.

I opened my eyes. "It worked?" My hair felt the same to me. Whatever I'd done had to be illusion. A trick of the light. Or, rather, a trick of shadow.

"See for yourself." Mian Zi swiveled the mirror on my bike. My gut rolled. I looked like what I'd always pretended to be: Mr Mystic.

And now it was time to act like him. "I must be

on my way," I murmured in his voice.

"Go." Mian Zi helped me onto my bike. "We will do what we can to give you time."

The stairway pass-through between houses and the hiking trails circling Mount Davidson weren't made for motorcycles. I didn't care. I shredded my way up the steps and looped around the curve of the mountain. My tires kicked up dirt and rocks as I rode up the narrow, ungraded path to the massive white marble cross at the summit.

La Reina scowled at me when I roared up to her and cut the engine. Her wings puffed and settled. "You have no respect for what is holy, do you?"

The wooziness of pain and blood loss had faded somewhat thanks to whatever Mian Zi had done, but I still lacked anything resembling patience at being told off just now. "Upsetting gods seems to be a bit of a hobby of mine."

"Hm. So it seems. I called for backup. You look like hell."

Like hell. She didn't know the half of it. I'd refined my shadow illusion to hide the worst of my injuries and exhaustion. I could afford to look weak in front of my kids, but La Reina was Argent, and I was still Mr Mystic. Now more than ever.

"You are too kind. Shove aside." I was used to the drill by now – the construction cones, the neatly dug five-by-five, the gravel backfill, the ritual sigils burned into the rocky substrate with hardened pitch, the titanium node at the center. I hopped down and stomped around a bit, but whatever blood had coated my boots from kicking Lao Hu, it had long scraped off. The node flared with shadow flames thanks to my own blood spattering about, but there was no orange-flame brightness to counter them.

"Bollocks."

"What?"

I levered myself out of the pit. "I'm going to have to fight him again." I peered down the hill. Would he come up that way, following my trail? Or, knowing what I was up to, where I was likely headed, would he circle around and come from the trees that surrounded the cross on three sides? I passed a hand over my eyes. They itched with exhaustion. When La Reina's hand landed on my uninjured shoulder, I jumped.

"Are you allowed help?"

Forget my previous irritation. She could castigate me all she wanted. "Are you allowed to give it? On the disrespecting holy shrines front, getting into it with an ancient cat god so that you can use him in a blood ritual is not precisely... hm. I suppose it would be problematic to use the word 'kosher' in this instance?"

"Decidedly so. And he is not God."

Not your god, I kept myself from saying. I was not so foolish as to look a gift-angel in the Metatron. "In that case, I would welcome–"

I didn't get the chance to say what I would welcome. Lao Hu burst from the trees. I tackled La Reina to one side, but he wasn't going for us. He slammed into my motorcycle, sending it rolling down the steep incline in a series of crashes and groans and a spray of broken plastic and metal bits. I cringed at the noise, fighting fury and helplessness. Now, even if we managed to get Lao Hu to bleed on this node, I had no way to get to the last node at Land's End.

I scrambled to my feet, circling to one side of Lao Hu while La Reina looped the other direction, splitting his focus. Lao Hu rolled and came up snarling, all orange and black fur, yellow teeth and yellow eyes. Or, eye. The other was swollen shut, the fur on that side of his face matted, the white ruff under his jaw stained a rusty color. Mei Shen must have done that. My gut clenched around the fear that he might have injured her in return.

I flexed my wounded shoulder, testing how much movement I had, how much I could push it. Even that slight movement sent a deep pain shooting through my back and arm. I bit down on a hiss. Not much, then. This was going to have to be a kicking fight.

"My offer still stands," I told Lao Hu. I widened my half of the circle to put the ritual pit between us. "Help me attune the last two nodes, and I'll be your catnip."

"You offer to make a bargain with me when

you have no coin," Lao Hu said. I forced myself to keep an eye on him and not to glance at La Reina creeping around his blind side. "You are wounded. You have no way to flee." His whiskers twitched. "And your friend must think I'm stupid."

He lunged to one side, paw swiping at the air where La Reina had stood. She was already aloft, great wings flattening the fur along Lao Hu's back and sending leaves and dirt flying in little vortexes. She raised a sword that glowed with copper fire and hurt my eyes to look upon. Lao Hu's too, by the way he hissed and spat. She brought the sword down, driving him towards the pit. I moved closer to the edge, making myself bait.

Lao Hu was too cunning for that tactic. He feinted to one side, then bolted the other direction when La Reina brought her sword down to block him. His claws dug great furrows into the hard-packed ground as he scrabbled around the pit. His back legs kicked up a spray of dirt, leaves, and wood chips. I lowered to a half crouch. He bounded off the cross and came at me. Falling back, I planted a boot in his gut and flipped him over my head and into the pit.

And got dragged in with him when his claw snagged my trousers.

We were a mad tangle of kicking, clawing, biting, until suddenly I was alone in the pit, flat on my back and staring up at a receding Lao Hu. Great, tawny wings seemed to sprout from his shoulders, giving him the look of a flying sphinx. Save for the part where he dangled from his ruff like a giant kitten.

Not for long. He twisted in La Reina's grip, biting, bringing his huge claws up to shred her wings. She screamed, the high and piercing cry of a raptor, and they both plummeted from the sky.

I crawled out of the pit. La Reina had caught her descent on the arm of the cross and was lowering herself to the ground. Her slide left long, bloody streaks down the white marble. The lower half of one wing was shredded, dripping blood and pinfeathers. She sagged to one knee, using her copper-flamed sword to hold herself upright. "Where?" she searched the clearing behind me.

"He landed back in the trees." And very likely on his feet.

La Reina staggered to her feet and turned to scan the trees. "Is the node attuned?"

I shot a confirming glance over my shoulder. "Yes."

"Then go. You are of no more use here."

"But–"

"He doesn't want me. Go. I forgive you."

Which only made me feel worse. I sprinted down the hill at an only slightly out-of-control run, following the scarred furrow carved by my bike. I was under no illusion that it would still run, but the hill backed onto a residential street. Perhaps I could... what? Ask a friendly weekend warrior for his hog? Carjack someone? Assuming I could make it to street level before–

Lao Hu hit me at a full run, sending both of us into an uncontrolled tumble. My hat flew off. I ate dirt and fur in equal measure, but at least the rolling impact made it impossible for him to do much extra damage. We slammed into someone's back fence, Lao Hu taking the brunt of the impact. I kicked away and started running.

And then something caught me around the waist, and my pumping feet lifted from the ground, wheeling in midair. A hat slammed on my head – my fedora – cutting some of the glare and increasing my confusion.

"Thought you never went anywhere without that fedora of yours, Old Man," said my rescuer in a soft, Midwest drawl.

"Tom?"

"Yup. Figured I'd show you what a real rescue looks like." He looped around, and I caught sight of La Reina leaning against her blood-streaked cross. She gave us a feeble wave. Right. Backup. She'd called it. "Was that a tiger I saw you fighting?"

"Yes. And he took a rather good swipe at my shoulder, so if you wouldn't mind…?"

"Everyone's a critic," Tom grumbled goodnaturedly. He shifted his grip to lessen the strain on my shoulder. "Now, let's see about getting you to a hospital."

"No." I would have loved nothing better, but… "This isn't done yet. I need you to take me to Land's End."

FIFTEEN
Land's End

David Tsung wasn't waiting for me when Tom landed at the edge of Land's End. Sadly for me, Lao Hu was.

"Go." I pushed Tom behind me as though that would make him leave. As though anything could turn him from doing what he thought was right, even if it was suicidal.

"But–"

"You need to go back for La Reina. I have this." It was a lie, but if Tom had a weakness, it was believing everyone else was as honest as he was. I wondered if that was a flaw in his programming or intended design. "Go on."

"I better see you at HQ tomorrow, Old Man. I got a prisoner with your name on him and a passel of questions." With a final, stern look at Lao Hu, Skyrocket launched into the air.

"Your friend has no scent," Lao Hu said softly.

He lounged in the middle of the rock labyrinth. He must have been lying right on top of the bloody node, which meant it was almost certainly already attuned to Alam al-Jinn. All I had to do was attune it to Shadow.

"Yes, he takes clean-cut, all-American very seriously. How did you know we were headed here? How did you get here before us?" I kept my distance, assessing. The flat shelf of Land's End dropped off about ten feet beyond Lao Hu, a precipice much steeper than the slope we'd tumbled down at Mount Davidson. At the bottom would be rocks, if I was lucky and the tide was out. Rocks and the churning Pacific Ocean if the tide was in. Either way, I didn't want to test my luck by getting into a tussle up here.

Nor did I dare try my luck across the veil. Fog drifted past us like an army of ghost brides. We'd crossed over the fluctuating border of the Voidlands. I didn't know how well Lao Hu functioned there, but I knew I would collapse into helpless terror if I tried crossing over into that place.

Lao Hu lapped at his side. He'd cleaned away most of the dirt from our fall and the blood that had matted the fur at his shoulder. His eye was still swollen shut. "I have known where you would be at every step. Or did you think the djinni did not share your entire plan with me? I had hoped that your master would come to your aid somewhere along the way, but I did not credit how great a coward he would be." Lao Hu's tail lashed. Idly. He was done with our cat-and-mouse. "It was a good chase. I think Lung Di does not deserve a champion such as you."

"You and me both," I muttered. And here I thought I'd been playing Lao Hu all along. This is what I got for thinking I was smarter than a god. "So you always meant to attune the nodes? You were just toying with me with all that nonsense about letting the Voidlands expand?"

He shifted, and I caught a glimpse of the last node, burning with orange fire but not yet dampened by shadow. There was nothing for it. I'd have to go in. "Of course. I am a Guardian, after all."

Right. "What happened to David Tsung? Was he here when you arrived?"

"Lung Di's toady? He was. He fled. I let him."

I let out a shaky breath and hoped that Lao Hu would attribute any change in my scent or heart rate to fear. Well, he should. I was still very afraid. I searched the ankle-high rocks of the labyrinth, looking for something out of place. I spied it at the mouth of the labyrinth, a rock that was too small, too round, too pale to match the others.

Hesitantly, I approached the labyrinth. My hands hung loose at my sides. I did my best to keep my attention focused on Lao Hu and not my true target, lest I give it away. The curling tail tip proved to be a useful early warning system. It twitched. Lao Hu sprang. I snatched for the irregular stone and yanked it out of the ground.

An unholy crash sounded above me, followed by a deafening yowl and the screech of claws scraping metal. I scuttled back on my ass. Lao Hu remained within the confines of the labyrinth. A shining, translucent dome had risen around him on all sides. Sparks rose from his claws as he raked them down the inside curve of the dome over and over like a cat trapped on the wrong side of a door.

Which was, in effect, exactly what he was.

"What did you do? What is in your hand?" he snarled.

Slowly, I rose to my feet and held it up for him to see. "It's an egg. Goose, I think. Looks too large to be chicken. It also happens to be the key to your cage."

That got me more incoherent snarling. I waited it out. "I was wrong. You are exactly the filth Lung Di deserves as his champion. Let me out."

"So you can kill me? Explain to me the benefit of that?"

Lao Hu stopped clawing at the translucent shell and sat back on his haunches, tail lashing. "You will never attune the node if you do not. If I cannot leave, you cannot enter."

"If you cannot leave, I don't need to attune anything. With you as anchor for the other nodes, the Voidlands should be well contained." I was very aware of the irony of the current situation. I'd been infuriated by Lung Di's imprisonment of the other Guardians. I'd been horrified by what I'd helped do to Asha. I'd been disgusted by what the Conclave had done to Skyrocket. And yet here I was, considering doing the same thing to Lao Hu. I rolled the egg from one hand to the other, studying it instead of my prisoner, searching for some other way. "I am sorry," I said. "This wasn't how it was supposed to go."

"You mean you hadn't planned to trap me as your master did? And yet that key and these wards belie your claim."

"I mean I expected to arrive ahead of you and trap myself. Then, if you wanted me, you'd have to agree to attune the node to get to me. I didn't intend to leave things out of balance."

Lao Hu remained silent for several moments, his claws flexing into the ground. "So set me free and attune the node. I promise not to end you until you have done so."

"Yeah, that's not going to happen." I lowered the egg. "Back in Shanghai, I freed you from a trap you allowed yourself to be lured into. The other Guardians gave me a pass for releasing them, but you threatened me and my friends. This time, I'm going to free you. And you are going to abandon this vendetta against myself and Lung Di."

"If you think I will–"

"I think you will, and I think you'll be grateful I'm not demanding that you put yourself further in my debt," I said over whatever pointless threat he'd been about to make. I had a cat in a closed box. We both knew there was only one way this would end.

"Very well," he whispered, so low that I barely heard it over the crash of the ocean below.

"Your word." I said.

"You have my word, *Lung Bao Hu Zhe*. My vendetta against you – and Lung Di – is ended. Nor will I seek retribution against those who aided you this day."

"Good." I slammed the egg against the translucent dome. They both smashed and dripped to the ground in a slightly goopy mess. I watched, entire body tensed and ready to flee, as Lao Hu stood and gracefully padded out of the circle. His shoulder bumped my arm as he passed, which was threat enough to make my heart beat double time, but he didn't attack.

Right then. Egg dripping from my fingers, I strode up to the node and scraped my nails across one of my many wounds to bring up fresh blood. Holding the dripping gash over the titanium orb, I looked into across the veil into the Voidlands. I wanted to see this.

It started as a flicker of flame and smoke, meeting at the center of the node and collapsing in on itself. The orange flame grew brighter and brighter, the smoke darkness devoured that brightness, becoming so black it was impossible to focus on, even for me. The miniature star collapsed into a pinprick, throbbed, and then burst out beyond the confines of the node. The orange and black mottled sphere expanded to encompass me, Lao Hu, the shelf we stood on, and further and further out. Everywhere it touched, the Voidlands cringed and retreated. Across the bay, on the landside horizon, the leading edges of other novas expanded out to overlap with the one centered on Land's End. And then the furthest edge met the Land's End edge, crossing at the Golden Gate.

I tore my gaze from the Shadow Realms, raised my arms to shield my face from the wash of summer heat as the Golden Gate blazed with light on both sides of the veil. The heavy fog burned away under the onslaught, echoing the searing back of the Voidlands. By the time I dared to lower my arms, the lightshow was over, the sky was clear. The sun balanced on the horizon like a ball on a stick. The sky around it burned gold, the sea beneath black in comparison.

I took a step back from the node, glowing with a yin-yang swirl of darkness and light, and felt a little twinge of separation tingle down my spine. I concentrated on that frisson and realized I could feel other tingles, as though someone had implanted magnets beneath my skin. Nine connections snapped under my skin, through my blood. I didn't have much experience with this sort of thing, but I was going to take a wild guess and say that our ritual had worked.

"That's done, then," I murmured, swaying just a

bit as all the aches and cuts and bruises of my cross-city race caught up with me. I turned to face Lao Hu, sitting on the edge of the labyrinth circle with his tail curled primly around his feet as though he wasn't the cause of most of my injuries. "Now get the hell out of my city."

SIXTEEN
Argent Ace

Doris Han opened the banquet room of the Dragon's Pearl.

This was big. Huge. She only opened the banquet room for birthdays and New Year's. And, apparently, State visits from my son, but I wasn't going to let a little detail like that ruin my "you're awesome!" puppy glow. If I let piddly details muck up my glow, I'd be dim for eternity.

Details like the Lady's camp, which I'd found empty and abandoned when I went up to Muir Woods to see if I could find her. I couldn't call her army. I couldn't call my own. Not even Templeton.

My "you're awesome!" smile dimmed, and I had to struggle to stoke it back to brightness. Banquet room, dammit!

We'd gathered an eclectic group to celebrate: Doris and her extended family took up almost half of the five tables, with Johnny and his students filling another sizeable chunk. Shimizu and Jack sat together near Johnny – for mutual defense, I suspected. Abby had shown up, looking as subdued as I was trying not to look. No La Reina, Sadakat, or Skyrocket, of course. There was no way to explain why we were celebrating without revealing to them who I was.

Mian Zi sat on one side of the seat of honor with a passel of People's Heroes in suits matching his. Mei Shen and David Tsung counterbalanced him on the other side. And Jian Huo sat in the middle, patiently allowing Doris to ply him with all her best dishes. Every so often between all the toasting, I managed to catch his gaze from my place two tables away. Doris had put me in the cheap seats with Johnny's other students, which I suppose was what I got for not telling her who I was after my meeting with Mian Zi. As far as most of the guests at the celebration were concerned, the heroes of the day were the three dragons and Johnny. I was a guest at my own celebration, which was perfectly fine by me. Sitting with Johnny's students was a step up from the Han kids' table where Doris usually put me.

We'd eaten and toasted until we could *gan bei* no more and moved on to the musical chairs point of the meal. Mian Zi's people watched with blank faces – hiding horror, I was fairly certain – at all the American-born Chinese mixing and moving about. Mian Zi and Mei Shen eyed each other warily. Not talking, not with their father between them and David Tsung glued to Mei Shen's side, but at least they weren't fighting. Whatever had prompted them to bridge their differences at Twin Peaks, it seemed to be having a lasting effect.

I snuck another glance at Jian Huo, as I'd been doing throughout the eight-course meal. He'd ditched his usual hanfu in favor of a suit – I suspected Mian Zi had helped him there, since I'd never seen him in one. He was watching the twins as I had been, brow furrowed in a mix of concern and guarded hope. He caught me staring and gave me a nod and a slight smile that on anyone else would have been a wide grin and a thumbs up. Fuck etiquette. Doris could yell at me later. I shoved my chair back and headed his way.

"Masters. I need a moment," Abby said, catching my arm when I would have squeezed past her. I cast a helpless look at Jian Huo, hoping for a rescue, but Johnny had cornered him.

Awesome puppy, I reminded myself, and pasted a smile on my face to hide my disappointment. "Yes?" I perched in the empty chair next to hers. "I'm glad you came, by the way."

Abby's shoulders were hunched, her arms not quite crossed, but hugged close to her body. I might be glad for her presence. She didn't look glad to be there. She shrugged and answered with a closed-lip smile. "Yeah. Well. You know me and free food."

"I thought it was booze," I said, though there

had also been plenty of that.

"That too. Hey," Abby straightened, some of her moxy returning, "we found the leak. You know Fuller and Byrd?"

"The security heads I met at the Academy?" Shit. That was quite the leak.

Abby grimaced. "Also the missing Anglin brothers. We caught them when they tried to spring Morris. They've been slowly infiltrating Argent for years. Chillybritches is going to have them all moved to our own island facility."

"She must be furious."

Abby chuckled, the laugh of someone who hadn't been caught in the crossfire of Sylvia Dunbarton's fury, I suspected. "And not terribly quiet about it. Open office plans aren't known for being soundproof. Lots of people taking personal days this week."

The lull in our laughter carried on just a bit too long. Abby sighed and scraped her fingers through her hair. "About Asha…"

My own smile dimmed. I wasn't sure whether to congratulate her on her victory over her nemesis or comfort her on the loss of her sister. "Abby–"

"I got a delivery yesterday. My office. A carpet. *The* carpet. And I was just wondering if maybe she might have…"

"I don't know," I said, tugging her forearm before she ripped out any hair. "I went to the Lady's camp. The one in Muir Woods. It was abandoned.

Everything left behind. I can't call on her allies." Or mine. I'd spent hours trying to summon Templeton, to summon... Anne... and only gotten a migraine for my troubles. "I don't know what happened to either of them."

"Then who–?"

"Lao Hu pays his debts. And I suspect he'd see you as Asha's next of kin."

"Yeah. Right." She toyed with the ends of her chopsticks. She'd hardly touched her food. "I guess it's true that you can forgive anyone, even your own relations." She stood abruptly. "I need to go. Have a good party."

I watched her slip out the banquet room doors, taking the last vestiges of my urge to smile with her. I'd been trying not to think too deeply about what had happened to Asha or the Lady. Asha, because even though she'd sold me out, I still felt guilty for putting her in the position where she felt she had to. And the Lady because...

Because Abby had been right about family.

Mian Zi and Mei Shen had drifted close enough to each other that I was able to grab each of them before either one could raise a stink. I dragged them behind the rickety bamboo screen that Doris used to hide the folding chairs and tables when the banquet room wasn't in use.

"Shut up. Don't say anything," I told them and pulled them into a three-way hug. After a few moments of stiffness, they both relented. Mian Zi even hugged back.

"I'm sorry," I whispered into their hair, a blending of long and short. Mei Shen's sharp, lemongrass scent mixed with rich clove from Mian Zi. I breathed deeply, the way I used to when they were mooplings. It was the scent of contentment. Of home. "I'm so sorry I left. That I didn't say goodbye."

They didn't respond beyond squeezing harder. I didn't expect them to. Forgiveness wasn't the necessary response to an apology. It had to be earned. As did reconciliation. I released them and nudged them back.

"You." I poked Mian Zi in the chest. "David Tsung isn't so bad. And if it turns out I'm wrong on that, then wouldn't it be better if you were at your sister's side rather than standing in judgment? And you," Mei Shen got a similar poke. She rubbed her sternum, frowning. "You're the one making this a competition with your brother. You aren't loved less. You aren't trusted less. You aren't viewed as less than him. Not by me or your father or Mian Zi. So who are you trying to prove yourself to, other than yourself?"

I gave them both individual hugs and turned my back on their jaw-dropped shock. "I love you both. Work your shit out."

I left them behind the screen. Jian Huo wasn't in his seat of honor anymore. I slipped around the edge of the room, looking for where he'd run off to.

"He's outside," Johnny said, rocking onto his chair's back two legs so he could block my path. Despite stuffing himself through eight courses, Johnny had a plate of phoenix claws in front of him. He gnawed on a chicken foot and continued to block my path.

I sat. "That obvious I've been stalking him?"

Johnny shrugged and spat a nail into his palm. "I could say I've known you for a long time, but the real answer is yes."

I chuckled. "In that case, get out of my way before I kick those chair legs out from under you."

"Hold up a second. That lawyer friend of yours."

"Jack?" I scanned the room. He and Shimizu had latched on to Andrew Han, Doris' eldest, who seemed to be translating between them and one of the People's Heroes. "What about him?"

"How weirded out would you be if I asked him out?"

It was a good thing I wasn't balancing my chair on two legs, or I would have toppled over. How weirded out? Very. On every possible level. I couldn't think of a greater mismatch. Except possibly Jian Huo and myself. I smiled. "Go for it. I'll stock up on popcorn."

Johnny cleaned his hands on a napkin, strangling it as I suspected he wanted to strangle me. "The more you make fun now, the more teaching moments I'll be inclined to have during our next session."

"Mmhmm. Worth it. I'm gonna…" I gestured to the door. I had my own mismatch to pursue.

The front two legs of Johnny's chair hit the floor. He stood and twisted a few of his purple-red spikes. I don't think I'd ever seen him nervous. "Shit. I hate this part."

"Go get him, tig–" I broke off. I was never using that phrase again. "Er… you're a Giants fan, right?"

"Yes. Because I have a soul."

I patted him on the shoulder and used it to push him in Jack's direction. "Then you'll do fine. Good luck."

"You too."

As much as I wanted to watch, I slipped out of the banquet room and through the busy restaurant. I tracked Jian Huo through the kitchens to the alley behind the Pearl. It reeked of the usual trash and piss. It was the wrong place for him, for the conversation I wanted to have. Seemed I didn't have much of a choice, though.

"I was afraid you'd left," I said softly.

He turned, took a step toward me. His hair was looped over his arm so that it wouldn't drag in the alley muck. "I was making ready to. I have made my farewells to our hostess and the other guests. I only waited to say the same to you."

I touched the loop of hair hanging over his arm, letting my fingers trail through it. Little sparks of lightning kissed my fingers. Shit, I'd missed this. Missed him. "Will you come by the house later?"

I asked, wishing my pickup line didn't sound quite so much like a pickup line.

He lifted my hand, kissed my fingers, and then very deliberately pushed it away. "Missy, you know I cannot. It is as I said before. I cannot stay, or I will be tempted to meddle as my brother does. You must live your life."

Yeah. Right. Apparently I must live my life alone. I searched for some argument I hadn't already made when a voice from down the alley interrupted us.

"I can come by your house if my brother will not."

For fuck's sake. I glared at Lung Di, standing only a few feet away.

"Get out," Jian Huo told him, saving me the trouble.

Lung Di spread his hands, one gloved, I noticed. He wore his usual suit and an overcoat of black wool. He and Jian Huo looked like the brothers they were. Only Jian Huo's hair differentiated them. "But I must congratulate and reward my champion. It is only proper."

I placed a hand on Jian Huo's arm – the one not supporting his hair – to stop him from lunging at Lung Di. Not because I was Lung Di's champion. Because if anyone was going to kick his ass, it would be me. "It's fine. I'll handle him. Johnny won't thank you guys for leveling Chinatown, and if he kills me... well, that'll solve a lot of our problems."

Jian Huo's face showed nothing, but his arm

flexed under my hand for several tense moments before he turned his back on Lung Di. "I will wait inside until I am sure you are safe," he said, and strode back into the Pearl.

I studied Lung Di, wondering if it really was possible to beat the smirk off someone's face.

He tugged on his glove, paying my scrutiny no heed. "Once again, you neglect to invite me to your parties. Recall what happened the last time you failed to do so?"

"You kidnapped my kids. And I gave you that." I nodded at the glove pulled over his withered hand.

The gloved hand flexed into a fist. I'd been joking about the killing of me, but maybe I shouldn't be pressing my luck. He could still backhand me. Again. "So. Reward?" I said, hoping I could get rid of him quickly and painlessly. Like lancing a blister. "Oh, and I have your book."

Lung Di took a step closer. "Keep it. With these new wards of yours, it is safer here than anywhere else."

I sidestepped to maintain our distance. I wasn't letting him within backhanding range. "I don't want–"

"Keep it safe," he said, ominous as Gandalf pawning off the One Ring on a clueless hobbit.

Fuck. "Thanks," I muttered. "Always wanted my very own monkey's paw."

"Oh, I'm certain you're smart enough not to make any wishes in its presence." Lung Di held up his hands. "I am kidding, of course."

Right. Still, I was definitely going to be careful about anything I said in the vicinity of that book. "So, you've thanked me. You've rewarded me. You can mosey on now."

"Oh, the book wasn't your reward. Just another duty for my champion."

I was fairly certain I didn't want anything that Lung Di wanted to give me. "And duty is its own reward. So really, there's no need to–"

"Are you sure?" He reached inside his overcoat and pulled out a familiar-looking gauntlet with four stones embedded in it. Coral. Glass. Opal. And a blood-dark shimmer that flitted up and landed on my shoulder, wings snapping shut with a soft click.

I took the gauntlet. The leather creaked from the strength of my grip. "Where…?"

"Brought to me by those still loyal to me. I searched where they discovered it, but found no other traces of your rat or… anything else."

So it didn't mean anything. It didn't mean Templeton was gone. It didn't mean Anne was gone.

"So you see, I'm not such a bad guy," Lung Di murmured. Somehow he'd gotten close enough to touch the little scarab on my shoulder. Red Rover's carapace fluttered with a rapid *tick-tick*-ing, and he raised his back end like an angry stink bug threatening to let loose.

I was in complete agreement with the little guy.

I didn't want to be grateful to Lung Di. I definitely didn't want to see him in shades of grey. Even if he had been the one to keep the Voidlands in check for who knew how long. I retreated and transferred Red Rover to my other shoulder. "Doing good sometimes doesn't make you good."

"No. It doesn't, does it? I suspect the same could be said of many people. My brother. You. Your grandfather?"

I shivered at the way he lingered over that last taunt. Savoring it. "I'm going inside now. You're leaving," I said. I'd learned my lesson several times over. Listening to Lung Di's truths brought me nothing but misery. I'd find some other way to get the information I needed.

"Of course. Enjoy your victory celebration."

Victory celebration. Right. I trudged inside, Templeton's gauntlet hitting my thigh with every step.

Argent's China Basin headquarters were too new to have found their own identity. I'd wondered during our brainstorming sessions to find Asha why they didn't have an extensive campus somewhere on the Peninsula – that seemed more Argent's style. Sadakat had informed me quite primly that Argent didn't follow the pack, they led it. Abby had laughed and said that Argent's huge, quasi-military base near Gilroy might have something to do with it.

I parked my replacement Triumph at the edge of the entry plaza and strode past the obligatory public art, a towering amoeba of polished chrome. In some ways, Argent's struggle was my own writ large – how to maintain identity in a world that was quick to discard old for new.

Tom was waiting in ambush for me in the lobby. "Hey, Old Man. You got a minute?"

My steps slowed. I diverted off my path to the security desk but didn't quicken my pace. I'd been dreading this conversation. Possibly avoiding it, even.

"Tom," I said, softer than I usually was with him. "You're looking recovered."

He smiled sheepishly and rubbed the back of his neck. "Yeah. And I never properly thanked you for that."

I looked for the uncanny valley, but it was all straight road and smooth skies where Tom was concerned. Sweet lord, Argent's techs were geniuses. They hadn't just nailed basic human expressions. They'd nailed earnestness. Gratitude. Charisma. I was more frightened of that than just about anything else I'd been through these past few weeks.

"No need," I said. "As I recall, you also rescued me from a rather dire plight."

Tom led me to the elevators. "Don't think that makes us even. The medics told me I was pretty banged up inside. Took 'em days to sort me, and

I'm still not feeling..."

I set a hand on his arm when he fell silent, staring at the lift console. "Perhaps you shouldn't jump back into things so quickly."

"I don't remember much of what happened on that island. What they did to me. I guess they used some powerful sedatives to keep me out and get me talking. Who knows how much classified intel I gave up. At least nobody in our other facilities was hurt because I couldn't keep my trap shut." He pressed a hand over his face. He looked tired. He looked... sad.

The lift doors opened, and it was as though his passing hand had donned a mask. He perked up. We stepped off the lift, and he smiled brightly at a middle management type as he held the doors open for her. Gave her a jaunty wave through the closing doors. It was as though that moment in the lift had never happened.

What Argent was doing to him was cruel. He didn't know who he was or what had happened, and he had every right to.

"Tom." I planted my stance, refusing to follow when he would have led us further into the offices. I wanted to tell him the whole truth, but it would be a wasted effort. It might even cock up any chance I had to suss out a way to do it correctly in the future. Later. I had to bide my time. "Have you spoken to anyone? About what you're going through? If you ever need to talk–"

To his credit, Tom quickly stifled his laugh. "That's mighty kind of you, but I got all the talking people I need. Argent keeps the best mind docs in the field on their payroll, and they're used to dealing with a lot worse – and a lot stranger – than a bit of guilt. I don't need talk. I need action. But you went and tied this whole thing up neat as a Christmas present."

"How rude of me," I murmured, wondering if Tom's mind docs knew about Tom's special condition, or if they were as clueless as I had been. I wondered which was worse.

Tom shook himself. "Anyway. I don't want to keep you. All I really wanted was to say thanks."

I tipped my fedora. "Please don't mention it." We'd see if he still wished to thank me after I ripped his identity out from under him.

"You're here to see Lady Basingstoke, right?"

"I have an appointment and everything."

Tom smiled fondly and led me through an open floorplan of collaborative workspaces divided by thick cement columns and the occasional industrial printer. "First it's tigers, then it's lions. You should try living a less exciting life, Old Man."

I sighed and did my best to gird my proverbial loins. "Of that I am well aware."

"Mitchell. You are looking far better than reports would indicate." Sylvia Dunbarton rose from her desk to greet me. Tom, I noticed, made no delay in abandoning me to my fate, the coward. I let Sylvia take my hand, grimaced through the standard cheek kisses, and tried to put her desk between us at the first opportunity.

She was having none of it. "I've arranged tea. Come. Sit."

Sylvia's office was closed off from the rest of the floor, a huge room on the bay side of the building with both a desk and a sitting area. The floor-to-ceiling windows looked out onto the bay and Alameda across the way.

It was to the sitting area that she led me and motioned me to take one of the low, deep-cushioned couches. I perched on the edge so that it wouldn't swallow me. She sat across from me and poured for the both of us. Whatever my qualms about her, Sylvia was ever a joy to watch when she was serving tea.

She wore wide-legged grey trousers today, high-waisted, and a silvery blouse, and she sat like a lady, knees together, ankles crossed. She watched me over the rim of her cup, smiling like a cat and *dear lord* did I develop an immediate and abiding antipathy for that expression – both the words and the look on Sylvia's face.

"What?" I snapped, perhaps a bit too peevishly for the gracious welcome she'd offered. I didn't want to be here, didn't want to be doing this, but I'd weighed all my options and I didn't see any other choice.

Sylvia balanced her teacup and saucer on one knee. "You gave me a report. A real report. With details and explanations and useful information and everything." She beamed at me like I'd given her the moon.

"Yes. Well." I fidgeted. Stared into my tea. Someone who made tea this good couldn't be all bad, could they?

No. Best to stop there. That line of reasoning would lead to madness. "I am very grateful for all the assistance Argent gave to me. Both for the ritual and afterward."

"Yes. There was quite a bit of cleanup needed. Physical, social, and political. But we – I – am likewise grateful to you. For Tom. And for not saying anything about his condition."

My teacup hovered halfway to my lips. I lowered it without taking a sip. I hadn't said anything, but several pages of my report had been dedicated to a tirade regarding my feelings on the matter. Whatever secrets Argent needed to keep, it wasn't right that they be kept from Tom. The man – robot – whatever – had a right to know who he was and where he came from.

As did we all.

"Of course," I murmured. "I will leave it to you to decide how best to handle the matter. For now." Until I could come up with a way around Tom's programming. "That isn't why I asked to speak with you."

"Is it about Mr Morris? I instructed that you be given full access."

"No, he has been forthcoming enough. Only, he doesn't have what I need. Nor, would it seem, do the Brothers Anglin." I set my teacup aside and stood, moving to the windows. A cruise ship was docked, its white hull obscuring most of the view. Morris hadn't known much more than he'd said when we captured him – that he never thought Mr Mystic was dead. Of the Lady's accusation that the Conclave and Mitchell had stolen something from her, he claimed to know nothing.

Of the Lady herself, I'd still seen no sign. Her camp remained abandoned. None of her army came when I tried to call them. Nor did my scarabs. Nor did Templeton. All I had was the jeweled gauntlet that Lung Di had given me. And Red Rover.

"I understand Alcatraz has been closed until the full extent of the damage from the earthquakes can be assessed," I said, skimming a finger down the side of my reflected cheek. Or rather the shadow where my cheek should be reflected.

"Yes." Sylvia stood as well, puzzlement as clear in her reflection as it was in her voice.

"I would like access to do a thorough sweep of the island – the Shadow Realms side – so that I may ensure that all traces of the Conclave's influence have been removed."

"Of course. I'll see to the arrangements. Mitchell, you're acting oddly. Even for you."

I sighed. Snorted. If only she knew. "Sylvia, I need to speak with you privately."

She gestured at the empty room. "I don't believe it gets more private than this."

I turned to face her. "No. I mean privately."

Her bemused smile faded, revealing it to be a mask for the cool, hard face of the grande dame of Argent. "You mean–"

"I don't want any record of this conversation. And neither do you."

"Ah. I see. One moment." She swished over to the credenza behind her desk, opened a panel, and tapped several sequences into a small tablet. The windows darkened until the glass was smoke black and nearly opaque, the only indication that she'd shut down whatever surveillance she used in her office. She turned back to me, folding her hands before her. "Very well, Mitchell. It's just the two of us. What is this about?"

I removed my fedora and set it on her desk. Then I let the shadows fall from my face and dropped the illusion I'd been maintaining. My hair bled back to its natural color. I relaxed into a more comfortable posture and smiled in the face of Sylvia's slack-lipped astonishment. I did so enjoy rendering her silent.

"Lady Dunbarton. My name's Melissa Anne Masters. Missy. And I need Argent's help finding my grandfather."

ACKNOWLEDGMENTS

Everyone I know who has experience with second books told me they were challenging. They were right. I am so grateful to the people who held my hand, who gave me encouragement when I needed it and a whole lot of alone time when I needed that.

Special thanks go to Marie Brennan, who talked me down off many an authorial ledge and did the most lightning-fast beta read in history; to Adrienne Lipoma for doing the second-fastest beta read and for walking all over the city with me for "research"; to Wendy Shaffer (and Adrienne again!) for tromping around the California Academy of Sciences so I could work out fight blocking (and look at butterflies); and to Jason Pisano and Avery Liell-Kok for helping me brainstorm through story issues. Love, as always, goes to my CW2012 littermates for daily challenges and encouragement, and special love goes to my mom, Conna, and my brother Devon for all the ways they support me, big and small.

I suffered a lot of losses this past year – family, job, home – and the folks at Angry Robot were incredibly understanding about the delays this caused in my writing process. I am endlessly grateful to my editor, Phil Jourdan, for his patience and understanding, and to my agent, Lindsay Ribar, for stepping in and being the cooler head when the stress got to be a little too much for me.

Finally, huge thanks go to my cat, Thrace. He's mostly content to sit by my side – when he isn't trying to sit on my shoulders or my keyboard – and keep me company while I work. But he also dedicated endless hours to making sure I understood at a visceral level exactly what it feels like to be hunted through my apartment by a cunning and capricious feline. He is the best of cats.